John

J.A. Hoskins

Nom de Plume Publishing

JOHN

First published in Australia in 2026 by Nom de Plume Publishing

A catalogue record for this book is available from the National Library of Australia

Cataloguing-in-Publication Data
Creator: Hoskins, J.A., 1973-
Title: JOHN
ISBN:
9781923595071 (Paperback)
9781923595064 (eBook)

Book Cover by: InkWild Designs

Content Note
This novel contains depictions of domestic violence and emotional abuse, as well as themes of grief, death, and cancer diagnosis and treatment. Some scenes may be distressing to readers sensitive to these topics.

For Pa.
You were writing your final chapters while I was writing mine.
Forever loved, forever missed.

* * *

And as always, for Daryl.

Chapter 1

John

The girl kicked slush off her boots before stepping over the threshold at Jim's General Store and unravelling the woollen scarf from her head. I'd caught a glimpse of her through the window, and she had no idea I was there in the aisle, awkwardly craning my neck for a better look.

She smiled at Peter, the clerk, and they traded banal comments about the change in the strange late autumn weather. To my knowledge, the weather was always changing and often strange, but I had to admit it was rare to get snow this early in the Adelaide Hills.

She stopped at a display of new books and said something about maybe buying one for herself— a sort of birthday present. Peter's innocent inquiry saved me the guessing game. She'd just turned thirty-two.

Her hair was the same fiery red as mine, though I could tell hers was dyed, while mine was natural as anything. She moved around the shop like she was on a leisurely stroll, occasionally lifting something for a closer look. Then she turned, and I got my first real clear look at her.

Grey eyes that sparkled with her smile but held something else too. A kind of melancholy. She wasn't what you'd call classically beautiful, but boy, she was a magnet. Like a flame in darkness. I could spend all day looking into those eyes.

I shuffled a bit, hoping she'd glance my way so I could offer my most charming smile. I knew that if she'd just look in my direction, I'd be lost in those grey eyes forever, but I was willing to chance it.

She didn't turn towards me, not even a bit. I edged closer and waited, trying not to be too obvious about it. I didn't want to look needy or overly interested. I scrambled to think of something wittier to talk about than the weather, in case the opportunity arose.

She perused the magazines, then walked back the way she'd come. Before I knew it, she was gone.

I'd missed my chance.

* * *

The next morning dawned misty, and I was staked out in the town square, hoping for a glimpse of the girl. I vowed that the next time I saw her, I would say hello. Life's too short not to take the chances that matter.

In the still hush of the morning fog, I watched as the town stirred awake.

Mrs. Lynch was sweeping the porch of Jim's General Store when she spotted me by the bench. She hollered out an invitation to breakfast. Who could pass that up?

Faintly, I could hear the kookaburras laughing from the hills. The name of the place where I made my home echoed in my mind— Kookaburra Ridge, or just *The Ridge*, as we locals called it. It was a fitting name for the quaint town, nestled among the green mountains of the Adelaide Hills. A river wound through the valley, tracing six kilometres of bends and narrows. It was a place where most folks knew each other, and new faces were rare and easily noticed.

I dawdled over my breakfast, and a worrisome thought crept in, gnawing at the edge of my mind. Maybe the girl had just been passing through— a tourist taking a detour.

The thought twisted my insides. I held on to the memory of her— the way she'd stomped the slush from her boots, the sadness tucked deep inside her grey eyes, the sound of her polite laughter as she chatted with Peter, the idiot shop clerk.

And hey, look— don't think I'm being a jerk about Peter. He comes up from Adelaide maybe twice a year to cover for Jim at the store when he goes on holiday. The guy's a bit of a boob, to be honest, and I know he feels the same about me. He even locked me out the other night, so I didn't bother bringing in any firewood for him. Let him fend for himself.

I really couldn't wait for Jim to return from the UK, but in a way, it was a good thing he wasn't here. He knew me well enough to spot how on-edge I was, and I didn't feel like being teased for pining over a girl I'd literally seen once, for less than five minutes.

Each morning, sitting in Jim's storefront over breakfast, I found myself waiting, hoping that I'd see her again. I positioned myself at the window, my eyes scanning the empty streets of the Ridge, able to picture her dark red hair and silvery grey eyes with unsettling clarity.

Night after night, as the Adelaide Hills were draped in a blanket of stars, I found myself gazing at the moon, wondering if she was somewhere out there looking at the same sky. It felt like I missed her, even though I barely knew her. Loneliness washed over me— a longing for something I'd never really had.

Despite it all, I clung to a sliver of hope that one day I'd catch another glimpse of her. That maybe she'd walk through the door of Jim's General Store again.

* * *

It was a sunny morning a few weeks later, and Peter was reorganising Jim's coffee bean displays. The man wouldn't know a Brazilian roast from a bargain blend, but there he was, shifting everything around like he owned the place. This, after spending half the morning arranging all the books by colour instead of author, or even subject category. Wordsworth now sat between pruning guides and true crime, a poetic interlude amongst books with spines of blue. Very Martha Stewart, but hardly practical for a reader.

I watched Peter struggle with the ladder, wondering if I should warn him about the loose third rung, and decided against it. Some lessons should be learned firsthand. But then he wobbled, looking unsteady, and something in me couldn't just watch. I moved closer, tapping the third rung meaningfully.

"Oh, thanks mate," Peter said, noticing the loose rung at last. "Bit dodgy, that."

Not that my warning made any difference. A few minutes later I heard the crash, followed by Peter's yelp of surprise. The dodgy third rung had claimed a victim.

I wandered out to assess the damage, shaking my head in despair. Jim would have opinions about this when he got back. Peter sat in the middle of the mess, rubbing his elbow and looking bewildered. Staring at the chaos around him, I had to wonder if maybe arranging books by colour wasn't such a bad job for him after all.

I'd barely finished taking in the extent of the disaster when Mrs. Lynch appeared in the doorway. She took in the beans scattered across the floor, Peter still rubbing his elbow, and her lips disappeared into a thin line.

"What," she ventured cautiously, "happened to Jim's coffee display?"

"I'm reorganising!" Peter chirped.

Mrs. Lynch surveyed the damage with the kind of patience only retired teachers possess. Her lips, if possible, got even thinner.

"I'll fetch the broom," she declared, shooing Peter toward the register and me out to the back room— rather unfairly, I might add, considering I'd had nothing to do with creating the mess.

When she finished cleaning, she gave the store one last appraising look, shook her head, and headed out into the brisk autumn morning.

The door opened again shortly after, and I assumed Mrs. Lynch had forgotten something. But there stood the girl with the silvery eyes, pushing her sunglasses up onto her ruby hair, backlit by the glory of the day.

I was astounded. I'd resigned myself to the miserable fact that I'd likely never see her again. My feet tangled under me as I stood, shaking the dust from my coat. Did I even look presentable? I sauntered casually into the centre aisle, hoping once again that she'd look my way.

Peter— who seemed to make deliberate effort to annoy me something fierce— smiled at her, and again, they made polite conversation about the weather. It was painfully obvious that he would love to say something brilliant, something that might captivate her interest. But he missed his chance too.

* * *

I followed her at a distance as she left Jim's, feeling like a complete fool. She turned north up the main road, pausing to peer into shop windows. When she stopped to study the community notice board outside Pokey's Ice Cream, my heart nearly stopped— I had nowhere to hide.

Should I play it cool? Walk on by, pretending I hadn't been trailing her? It wasn't my finest moment.

Bugger me dead, I hoped to God that Mrs. Lynch wasn't about to step outside and find us both standing there, me frozen in place only a dozen paces from the girl and staring at her like a freak. But before I could summon the courage to approach casually, she moved on.

She walked with purpose in the late afternoon sun, like she knew exactly where she was going. I kept to the other side of the street as she continued to explore the town, confident I was far enough back to look harmless if anyone noticed me.

When she turned down the laneway into Sunnybrook's B&B, I peeled away and jogged back toward town.

Now that I knew where she was staying, I had time to plan my next move.

* * *

I caught a few glimpses of her over the next few days but didn't make contact. I was keeping my distance while I thought up plans for a casual hello— which happened the following Wednesday, by random chance.

I was barrelling down High Street to fetch some small logs and nearly crashed into her. It was truly no fault of my own— she literally walked straight into my path as she came out of McKeown's Realty.

I stepped back at once and hunched down a little, head bent, looking down at my feet. To be honest, I'm kind of huge, so having me come barrelling toward you at a fair clip can be somewhat, well, intimidating, I guess. That was the last kind of first impression I wanted to make!

She gave me a shy smile and a quick sorry as she side-stepped, and I shot an apologetic look at her in return before carrying on, trying not to trip over my own feet.

Once she was gone, I circled back to McKeown's as inconspicuously as possible. I leant against a fence post across the street and watched from the corner of my eye.

When I saw Pilar McKeown step to the window and remove the *For Lease* sign advertising the old stone cottage at Cooper's farm, I sighed with relief. The girl was going to stay!

Cooper's cottage was a bit rough, but the location was lovely—just far enough from town to feel private, close enough to walk in for anything. I could picture myself stretched out on the front porch, enjoying quiet evenings with the girl.

Not that I was expecting to be part of her life or anything. Geez.

My ears grew hot with embarrassment, even though nobody but I knew what I'd been thinking.

Chapter 2

John

Sunday night. The most uneventful night of the week. I'd tucked in early and was lying awake in my bed at the back of Jim's store when I heard the side door opening. The familiar tread in the hallway made me smile. Jim was finally home after six long weeks in the UK.

We settled into our usual spots by the fire, me in the worn armchair that had moulded itself to my shape over the years, Jim in the wooden rocker that had belonged to his father. We fell easily into the comfortable silence of old friends. The whiskey Jim had brought back with him caught the firelight as he poured himself a measure, the smell of peat smoke wafting from the glass.

"Christ, I'm knackered," Jim said, stretching back in his chair. "English rain's not like ours, John. Gets into everything— your clothes, your joints, your bloody soul. Not to mention that godawful never-ending flight."

He grumbled, but I knew the trip would have been worth every grey drizzly minute.

He pulled out his phone and motioned me closer. On the screen, Jim's eight-year-old granddaughter Alexandra stood awkwardly holding her new baby brother, Tommy— her expression caught somewhere between fierce protectiveness and abject panic. Beside her was Young Jim—Jim's son— beaming down at the both of them.

"You know, John," Jim leaned toward me like he was about to share a secret. I leaned in like I hadn't heard it before. "There've been five generations of Alexander Mackenzie Jameses in the family, and now, the new boy is called Thomas..." He trailed off, then shook his head, smiling as he sipped his whiskey. "They couldn't very well call him Alexander, I suppose. Not with a sister named Alexandra. But still..."

He launched into a story I'd heard at least a dozen times before.

"They never thought they'd be able to have another, you know. After Alexandra, the doctors told them... well." He swallowed, and I knew there were tears hidden there.

"But here we are. A baby boy. Thomas Alexander James will carry on the line. Even Great-Granddad would admit that's a fine legacy."

I was genuinely pleased for him. I was so darn glad to have him back— not just because it meant the idiot Peter would be heading back to Adelaide, but because Jim was my best mate in all the world, and things simply made more sense when he was around.

"I'm glad to be home," Jim admitted. "Missed this place. Missed you, you daft bugger."

The fire crackled, sending shadows dancing across the old timber walls. Jim's great-grandfather had hewn these boards himself— you could still see the marks from his adze if you looked closely. That was back when The Ridge was nothing but logging camps and desperate dreams of something more permanent. Now grapevines grew where timber once fell, and these walls remembered.

Jim reminisced about his son taking his first uncertain steps right there, between the counter and the coffee roaster. I heard again about the day he left, barely eighteen, with a backpack, a one-way ticket to London, and stars in his eyes.

Life marches on for all of us. We weave the new into our lives just as we weave out the old— through choices made by ourselves, or by others.

Poor Jim used to stand in that doorway every evening at closing time, staring down the empty road like his only son might change his mind and come home. Now he just scrolled through the photos Young Jim sent from overseas and planned the occasional visit.

The whiskey in Jim's glass had dropped by half when he spoke again. "Peter says you've been making the firewood disappear."

I studied the flames intently. Not my fault if the wood stacks found better homes on cold mornings. The man was a fool who didn't deserve good firewood. Or to work in this store. Or to lock the back door when he knew perfectly well I might be late getting in.

Jim's laugh filled the old room. "Told him he probably just forgot how much he'd used."

I had the grace to look ashamed, but I didn't look away from the fire.

The blaze settled into coals as we sat there— that perfect stage where the heat's still good but the light's simmered to a forgiving glow. Like two old friends who didn't need words to fill the spaces. Outside, The Ridge slept under stars that looked just like they had when the first Jim James opened these doors.

Some things change. Some things stay exactly as they should.

* * *

My walk the next morning took longer than usual— too many thoughts about Jim's return kept me from my typical brisk pace. By the time I made it back to the store, Mrs. Lynch had already arrived, perched neatly on her usual stool while Jim unpacked the gifts he had lugged back from England: a tin of proper Scottish shortbread, boxes of English chocolates, tea towels emblazoned with the Union Jack.

I waited in the back hallway, not wanting to interrupt their reunion.

"So, Young Jim's got a boy at last," Mrs. Lynch declared proudly, as if the baby were her own grandchild. In a way, I supposed he was— she'd been part of The Ridge's unofficial 'parental-figure' community since long before Young Jim was born, and that sort of thing didn't stop just because someone moved thousands of kilometres away.

"Yes, Anne, he has a boy at last." Jim beamed ear-to-ear. "Thomas Alexander. Nearly eight pounds. Came two weeks early, but healthy as anything."

The bell over the door chimed, and the flame-haired girl walked through the door. I retreated farther down the hall, leaning against the wall where I could watch without being seen.

"Morning," I heard her say with a cautious warmth.

"Morning," Jim replied, reaching for a cup. "Coffee?"

"Please. Flat white." She settled onto a stool.

Jim busied himself with the espresso machine, uncharacteristically wordless.

"Lovely morning for a walk," Mrs. Lynch offered.

"It is," the girl agreed. "I'm getting to know some of the trails around here. Everything's so lush and green."

"New to The Ridge, then?" Jim asked, sliding the coffee across to her.

The girl nodded. “Sort of. I’m staying out at Sunnybrook’s for now. Needed a change of scenery from Adelaide.”

They chatted a few minutes longer— the kind of pleasant small talk that fills a morning café. Jim asked politely about Sunnybrook’s, then drifted into his plans for the upcoming wine festival.

She wrapped her half-gloved fingers around the paper cup and, lifting it to her face, inhaled deeply. There was such loneliness in her eyes that it made it hard to look away. I sagged back against the wall.

“Well, I better push off before my morning walk turns into an afternoon stroll.” She gathered her things with a wry smile. “Thanks for the coffee.”

“Anytime.”

She left, and Jim stood there staring at the door, looking as though he were trying to untie a difficult knot.

“Christ,” he said finally. “But doesn’t she look familiar to you, Anne?”

Mrs. Lynch’s teacup paused halfway to her lips. She set it down warily, precisely, before she broke the news.

“Jim. That’s Simon’s daughter.”

The coffee beans Jim had been reaching for clattered across the counter. I wandered out from the hallway, wondering what the heck had gotten into him.

“Simon’s girl,” Jim breathed. “No wonder. No bloody wonder. Those grey eyes. And that red hair. Christ.” He shook his head. “I should have recognised her right off the bat. But there I went and served her coffee like she was any other tourist passing through.”

My gaze shifted from Mrs. Lynch to Jim and back again, waiting for someone to explain.

* * *

“That poor girl,” Mrs. Lynch was saying, stirring her tea absently as I listened in. “She was in town a couple of weeks ago too. I hear she’s going to be renting the Cooper place.”

Jim leaned against the counter. “Her Dad... that man was salt of the earth. Beautiful family, actually. I always thought for sure they’d move up here, but then— well. You know.”

I straightened, leaning hard against the bookshelves, suddenly alert. They knew her. More than that— they'd known her father? Her family?

"Terrible business, what happened," Jim stated. "Her turning up here of all places. You'd think it'd dredge up memories. Maybe it's fitting though. Like coming full circle."

Mrs. Lynch lowered her voice. "I've only had one conversation with her since she's been in town. Didn't say a word about Simon or... well— any of it. I didn't want to pry. Best to let her tell us in her own time."

I moved away from the shelves and sat rigid by the fire, my mind racing. All this time I'd been watching her, thinking she was just another city person seeking refuge in our peaceful town. But she had history here.

The Ridge had known her long before I did.

CHAPTER 3

John

A small moving van appeared at Cooper's farm the following week. The girl looked different— more determined somehow, but also deflated. Like she was sticking to a decision she wasn't quite sure about.

I watched from a shaded spot in the tree line as she directed the movers, noticing how little she'd brought with her. A small sofa and matching chair. An old rolltop desk. A new mattress. A few boxes, and that was all.

I shifted uncomfortably, watching her struggle with a heavy carton before a burly man lifted it easily from her hands. I probably should've offered to help, but what could I say? *Hi, I've been watching you from a distance like some kind of weirdo, and would you like some help?*

When the movers finally drove away, she stood in the doorway of her cottage and looked out across the paddocks. Something in her posture made my heart hurt for her— the way she wrapped her arms around herself, like she was trying to stop from coming apart at the seams.

A butcherbird swooped overhead, and she glanced up. For a heart-stopping moment, I thought she'd spotted me. But her eyes moved past my hiding place, sweeping across the trees and the distant hills. Taking in her new surroundings. I waited until she went inside before slinking away.

Tomorrow, I told myself. Tomorrow I'd find a proper way for an introduction. If only I could somehow position it without being too obvious. I wouldn't mention that I'd been watching her move in, of course.

Some things were better left unsaid.

* * *

I was looking out at the peaceful river when she approached and sat at the far end of the bench. She greeted me with a polite, friendly hello, and I nodded awkwardly in return.

L'esprit de l'escalier, they call it— when you think of a million witty remarks and appropriate things to say far too late to actually say them. Cascading thoughts barrelled into my mind, all the clever things that I could have done to capture her attention, but instead, a gawky sideways nod was all I could come up with, and then the moment was lost.

What a dork I was.

Thankfully, she was watching the smooth water flowing by and didn't see me blushing a brilliant red.

To top off my cringiness, Mrs. Lynch appeared on her daily river hike, zippered to the neck in a red rain jacket, the arms of her glasses tucked into the knitted grey beret perched atop her steely curls. A furled wooden hiking pole held firmly in each gloved hand, she stopped when she saw us sitting there. She smiled at me, then greeted the girl.

"Jude! How lovely to see you! I see you've met John!"

Oh God. I wanted to disappear. This was not the introduction scene I'd planned a thousand times over.

The girl—*Jude*— turned to me and winked playfully. I nearly died.

"Hi John," she said. "We've only just met now, haven't we?"

She turned back to Mrs. Lynch and I watched them talk, enthralled by the way the sun filtered through the leaves and caught Jude's unusual eyes, turning them a thousand shades of pale green in the light.

I shifted away from the bench and took up my usual leaning spot at the fence, staring out across the valley. I tried not to be obvious about overhearing, pretending to be engrossed in the river babbling lazily below. It was a fine winter day, and as the water cascaded past, it wore away the ice built up along the banks from an earlier storm.

Winter had only officially been in for a week, and I was already longing for a change— for the days to come when I'd be able to feel the warmth of a spring sun rising high in the sky, and hear the sound of insects buzzing around the reeds. I love all four seasons, but winter wears on me quickest of all.

Mrs. Lynch and Jude were still talking, and as I continued to tune in from a distance, I learned that Jude would be living alone at the old Cooper property, and that she had left her job back in Adelaide, aiming for a 'fresh start' here in The Ridge. I figured there were probably some stories behind that, but I could wait. I have the patience of Job.

She mentioned that she was getting a Starlink set up, whatever that was. Maybe she was one of those computer-people. So many folks spend their days tapping away at tiny screens, which I'll never understand. I prefer a simpler life— river vistas, long walks in the woods.

A tiny spark lit in my heart at the thought of maybe sharing some of those walks with Jude.

* * *

Okay, how to be cool right now? Seeming to be disinterested might be my best course of action. I wasn't prepared for any follow-on conversation. I felt completely blindsided, despite weeks of diligent preparation for this chance meeting.

My only clear option was to bolt while they were engaged in talking about the upcoming Winter Reds wine festival. Every July the Hills come alive with the sound of corks popping, crackling fires, and the merriment of visitors— some from as far away as overseas.

The wine festivals had become a big deal here, especially for the local vintners who relied on visiting tasters to appreciate their cool-climate wines, take boxes home, and spread the word about this young but important wine region.

I myself didn't drink wine, but I loved what the festival brought with it: fireplaces, strummy guitars, and delicious gourmet food. This year, Jim had decided to expand the wine section in the store, and to create a large outdoor area where he could host his events during the festivals. Renovations were due to start any day, and while Jim seemed excited about progress and growth, I was a bit more wary of change, and of letting strangers into our close-knit circle.

I pushed away from the fence rail and stretched, casually looking to the side as I feigned a yawn. Then I tipped my chin toward the ladies to indicate I was heading off. They both smiled and waved me on my way, and Jude's laughter, as cheerful as a summer breeze, rang out behind me. I was nearly out of earshot when Mrs. Lynch's clear voice cut through the crisp morning air.

"Oh Jude, I'm so glad you've met John. He's had some rough times, poor fellow. You know. You could do worse than to spend some time with him. He's an excellent listener— and very pleasant company. You can usually find him down here by the river in the mornings. He's forever walking somewhere."

Their voices began to fade as I inched down the trail. The temptation to stop and blatantly eavesdrop was tremendous, but I fought the urge and forced myself to pick up speed.

I wasn't ready to hear a rejection in real-time, before I'd settled on my plan.

Chapter 4

John

It was a further seven days before she joined me at the bench again. She wore a striped knit scarf tied in a knot at the collar of her puffy black jacket, reminding me of a little kid in a snowsuit. Her hair was pulled up in a high ponytail, tiny diamond earrings glittering as she moved. She sat down beside me and spoke with a cautious smile. "I've always kind of been a sucker for redheads."

Me too.

She took me up on my unspoken offer to take a walk around the river loop. It was our first walk, and I kept swallowing nervously, hoping she wouldn't notice. She admitted she hadn't been that deep into the woods before. I was happy to show her the bliss of the heavy green silence.

Jude had a tendency towards nervous chatter, so I let her talk. I was more than politely interested. She wasn't just unusual looking— with her freckly nose and deep grey eyes— but she also had a lot of interesting stuff to say, and I learned quite a lot from her idle chatter.

She marvelled at the tall trees. She laid her hand against the roughness of a towering brown stringybark and told me how much she loved these 'big sugar gums'.

I stared at the ground, a smile twitching at the corners of my mouth. Plenty of the townsfolk mixed the trees up too, but honestly— they're completely different trees. I didn't correct her though. Not on our first walk. I didn't want to appear arrogant.

Besides, I had a plan on how to show her the difference. When the weather warmed, creamy white flowers would bloom in clusters along these branches. It was only a couple of months away. I could bring her here again and surprise her with the glory of a grove of stringybarks in full bloom.

* * *

I could tell she was tiring. Her pace had slowed and so had her conversation. But to be fair, the trails could be demanding, especially for city folks not used to hiking in the hills. We walked back in comfortable silence until we reached the edge of town. Every now and then I stopped to point out a bird's nest, animal tracks in the spongy earth, or the way the light shifted as clouds drifted overhead.

The morning had warmed considerably, and Jude loosened her scarf, letting it hang around her neck. The sun caught her hair just right, making it glow like burnished copper. I led us back toward where we'd started.

"Thank you for showing me around, John," she said as we approached the bench. "I've wandered partway into these trails dozens of times, but I've never ventured quite that far. It's really so beautiful here."

I agreed. I always found the best way to collect your thoughts was simply to walk in nature, surrounded by ancient trees that had seen countless seasons pass. The Ridge had a way of putting life's troubles in perspective.

She adjusted her scarf, turning slightly toward town.

"Maybe we can do this again sometime?" There was a hint of uncertainty, like she wasn't sure if she was imposing.

I nodded, pleased that she'd enjoyed herself. I'd like nothing better. The trails could get lonely, and having someone to share them with... well, that would be real nice. I watched her walk away, her posture more relaxed than when we'd started. When she glanced back, I stood, and she waved.

The morning sun was high in the sky, warming the day. I felt lighter than I had in weeks as I trotted towards Jim's, suddenly ravenous for breakfast.

* * *

Life has a funny way of settling into patterns— the way morning dew collects on spider webs, or how leaves spiral down from trees in autumn.

Each day, I made my rounds through The Ridge, checking on folks, keeping an eye on things, taking note of what had changed, and always dropping off some firewood at the Peterson's. They seemed to go through it like it was going out of fashion, always needing a few more logs. Jim delivered it by the trailer load when he could, but I'd top them up in between— and sometimes stop for a spell to lie in the grass and watch the rabbits munch through the winter lettuce that Tom Peterson planted every year. The bunnies were bold as brass, yet unassuming and just plain cute.

The Ridge wasn't just a place to me— it was *home*, in the deepest sense of the word. Every tree, every worn fence post, every winding trail held memories. I knew where the first spring wildflowers would appear, which creeks would flood after heavy rain, and which corners of the woods held the best mushrooms— though I never ate them myself. Some things are best left to others.

Most afternoons, I found myself by the river, contemplating life's simpler truths. Like the way the water never stops moving, yet the river stays the same. Or how the smallest acts of kindness— a friendly greeting, a moment of shared silence— can matter more than any grand gesture.

Jim often observed that I was a philosopher at heart. I wasn't sure about that. I just knew what I knew— that loyalty matters more than cleverness, that actions speak louder than words, and that love, in all its forms, is worth waiting for.

This town had its share of troubles, like anywhere else. But we looked after our own. If someone needed help, word would get around, and somehow that help would appear— whether it was a hot meal, a load of firewood, or just a familiar face.

That's what made the Ridge special. Not the views, though they were spectacular. Not the weather, which was often peculiar. It was the way people watched out for each other. Even newcomers like Jude could feel it, I thought. The Ridge had a way of working its magic on troubled souls, if you gave it time.

I hoped she'd stay long enough to let it work on her.

* * *

My evening ritual seldom varied. As the day's warmth reduced into twilight, I'd make my way up to the zenith of the hills behind the Thompson place. Most folks in the Ridge didn't even know this spot existed— an old fence line marking where the logging track once cut across the hill.

That evening, sunset washed the old house in familiar shades of gold. Below, the neglected vines traced shadows across ground that might have produced some of the finest vintages in the Adelaide Hills, had Pat Thompson not died so young. I settled into my usual position, forearms resting on the weathered rail, and watched the light change.

The crunch of boots on the steep path startled me. In all my years up here, I'd never encountered another soul at sunset.

The surprise must have shown on my face when Jude appeared around the bend— equally startled to find anyone else in what she'd probably assumed was her private discovery. We stared at each other for a moment. We'd only shared that one walk, though I'd seen her exploring The Ridge's hidden corners over the past couple of weeks.

"Oh!" She took a half-step back. "I'm sorry— I didn't mean to intrude..."

I should have been more welcoming, but instead I simply nodded awkwardly and turned back to the view. Silence stretched between us— uncertain, but not exactly uncomfortable. She didn't retreat or carry on with her walk. She moved to the rail beside me, and we stood there together as the sun sank lower. The old stones caught the last light as though they were burning from within.

Finally, she whispered, almost to herself, "It's so peaceful up here."

I tilted my head to look at her, wondering if I'd been too abrupt, too caught off-guard by this interruption of my solitary ritual. Not that I minded her being there. There was something right about sharing this view. I'd just never had to share it before.

She left as quietly as she'd arrived, offering a whispered farewell, just as the first stars appeared. I watched her pick her way down the steep path with measured steps, suddenly guilty that I'd been so lost in my own thoughts that I hadn't even properly acknowledged her.

Before I could overthink it, I followed. Not to intrude—just to make sure she found her way safely in the growing dark. The path was treacherous enough in daylight.

She sensed my presence and turned, relief flickering across her face. "Oh! John! I thought... well, I didn't know if I had disturbed you."

We walked in companionable silence until we reached the fork in the road.

"Well." She stopped and turned toward me. "Thanks for seeing me back down safely. And for letting me barge in on your sunset."

With that, I turned away and started back toward town.

I had no earthly reason to tag along all the way to Cooper's cottage, but honestly, I just wanted to make sure she got home safely.

So, once she'd gotten a little way ahead, I doubled back, following behind her at a slight distance. I kept to the shadows, kicking myself in advance in case she caught me out.

* * *

As the lights of Cooper's cottage came into view, I sensed something wrong. Jude was walking at a decent clip, head down, eyes fixed on the road beneath her feet. She didn't see the flicker of movement behind the curtains. Or the front door, sitting slightly ajar.

I was over the rail fence and across her front yard before conscious thought could stop me. She looked up, startled as I sprinted past her, sharply warning her to stay back. She stopped dead in her tracks, staring wide-eyed at me.

I lunged onto the porch just as two figures burst from the door, scrambling over the railing and into the trees. I charged after them. Surprised yells faded into the forest as they ran.

When I returned, Jude stood frozen on the path.

"Did you..." Her voice shook. "Were you following me home, John?" She sounded annoyed. "I mean— thank you, but..."

I wanted to explain. To tell her I'd only been making sure she got home safely. Instead, I lowered my gaze and sheepishly walked down to the road, heading home.

My presence might do more harm than good right now.

She didn't call out to me. She didn't say another word.

Chapter 5

John

The next morning dawned rainy, so I skipped my walk. Lying on my bed at the back of the shop, I heard Jude asking Jim about me.

"John? Known him for years," Jim replied, rattling around with coffee beans. "Keeps to himself mostly, but he's got a way of being there when you need him. Looks out for folks, you might say."

"But I'm not sure if he was—" Jude hesitated. "I mean. He must have been following me."

"Probably just heading back towards town himself," Mrs. Lynch chimed in as she entered the shop, not yet knowing the full story. She had a habit of appearing as if summoned by gossip. "Or maybe he wanted to make sure you found your way safely. It's easy to lose your way up on those trails after dark. John knows every path in these hills."

Jude let out a breath. "Except he'd already walked me to the fork—we'd gone our separate ways. But then I think he hung back and followed me in the dark. And he chased off two men who were in my house."

"Men?" Mrs. Lynch enquired, sharp with worry. "What men?"

Mrs. Lynch was right to worry. I knew all the mischief-makers in town. Those men weren't from here, and they didn't seem like nice men with good intentions. I crept into the shop so I could better overhear.

"I don't know who they were." Jude's words came quicker now, like she was trying to get the whole story out before she lost her nerve. "I called the police. I'm supposed to go to the station this morning and give a statement. The whole thing really creeped me out."

I shifted behind the wood stove, my ears burning with shame.

"I'm not sure which bothered me more," Jude admitted, "the intruders, or John following me."

I kicked myself. I felt like such an idiot.

"I mean, he's so quiet," Jude continued, almost apologetic. "Barely makes a sound, but he's so easy to talk to. It's— well, it's just a bit unnerving, I guess." She gave a nervous laugh. "On our walk, I just filled all the space with talking. Afterwards, I felt so silly."

"Nonsense!" Mrs. Lynch scolded. "John is the purest of gentlemen. Nothing sinister about him at all— I can guarantee it."

I straightened my shoulders. Darn right.

"I'm sorry," Jude was saying. "I'm just spooked by what happened last night. And John showing up out of the blue like that—"

It hurt my heart that she'd had to ask, and I knew it was my own fault. I should have stayed with her and just walked her home properly. Now she thought I'd been lurking in the dark, hiding in the trees.

Which is exactly what I *had* been doing, but that was beside the point.

"Safest soul in The Ridge," Mrs. Lynch pronounced.

From the back room I watched Jude absorb that, saw something ease in her shoulders. Maybe that meant I'd be given another chance. And next time— if I ever had a next time— I'd make sure to do things properly.

No sneaking. No lurking. No trying to be clever.

* * *

"So, the police station— it's just down on River Road past the library, right?"

"You bet," Jim confirmed. "Take John with you, he'll show you the way."

Still hiding, I hung my head. How was I supposed to face her so soon when she thought I was a creep?

"JOHN!" Jim's deep voice echoed through the store. "Come on out here. Jude needs you to walk her to the cop shop! Chop chop!" He laughed at his own rhyming brilliance. You had to love the guy for trying.

I sighed and caught my reflection in the mirror. My hair was a bit shaggy. I tidied myself as best I could, then headed out to face Jude.

"Hi John," she exclaimed, and I felt certain the smile she'd slapped on was forced, matching her overly chipper tone. I wondered if she was wondering how much of her earlier conversation I'd overheard.

"You really don't need to walk with me," she dithered. "Honestly, I'll be fine now that I know where I'm going."

I knew for sure then that she was indeed wondering exactly how much I'd heard. I shrugged and started to retreat.

"John!" Jim's scolding stopped me in my tracks. "What is the matter with you? You take her. Walk with her there and wherever else she needs to go, and come on back afterwards."

I hung my head, resigned to my fate as the creepy companion.

"John, I'm so sorry. I was really freaked out last night. I didn't expect something like that to happen. Not here." She hesitated, gathering her words. "And you following me— well. I know now you were just being protective. Making sure I got home safe. But next time, don't follow me in the darkness, okay? Walk with me, or don't— but don't hang back, hiding in the trees."

I felt bad, because she was right. What I'd done wasn't fair. I was embarrassed too, knowing I could never admit to anyone that I'd followed her a handful of times and even sometimes checked on her house at night. Only from a distance of course— I'd never enter someone's property without an invitation.

But I was on a warning now, and I intended to stick to it— no matter how hard it was. Like a dutiful soldier, I walked with her in silence to the police station and delivered her straight to Constable Peacock.

* * *

I waited while Jude gave her statement. Constable Peacock seemed to think he knew exactly what he was dealing with.

"I'm thinking it'll be the Marshall boys," he muttered, scribbling notes, a well-chewed toothpick hanging from his bottom lip. "They bring all sorts of chaos to town with them whenever they come here. Trashed the last place they rented. Been causing trouble up and down the Hills since. Thought they were living down Adelaide way now, but I saw their old ute parked up at Shade's Pub yesterday afternoon. I'm betting dollars to doughnuts it was them."

I raised an eyebrow. *Dollars to doughnuts*? Where does he get his material?

In any case, Peacock was wrong. I hadn't seen any sign of the Marshall brothers, and normally I was right on top of that kind of thing. Besides, I'd recognise those derros in a heartbeat— and that's not who I'd chased off from Jude's place. I didn't speak up, though. I'd just keep my own eye out.

"I didn't see any ute. They ran off through the woods behind the carriage house. Well, *John* actually ran them off through the woods behind the carriage house." She gestured toward me with a half-smile. "But I don't recall any ute parked nearby. It seems like they only took my laptop. Everything important was backed up to the cloud anyway, thank goodness."

I looked at her approvingly, as though I understood. I did not.

"Well, we'll keep an eye out," Peacock assured her. "But you might want to think about getting some security installed."

"It's a rental. I'll have to talk to Pilar."

"G'luck with that," Constable Peacock acknowledged, readjusting the toothpick.

He assured Jude that a patrol car would drive by a few times over the weekend. It wasn't necessary, really.

Because while Peacock kept an eye out for the Marshalls and their jacked-up old ute, I already knew where I'd be. Camping out in the woods behind Jude's carriage house.

* * *

"I'm going to swing by Pilar's, John, if you want to head back to Jim's," Jude said.

I had nothing else on but my daily chores, and Jim was expecting me to keep an eye on her until the intruders were identified. I may as well tag along, so I walked with her towards McKeown's Realty office.

As we walked into McKeown's, two people I hadn't seen before were seated at Pilar's desk— an elegant woman with silver hair and a younger man in an expensive-looking cashmere coat. Something about their demeanour suggested mother and son.

"Just need a signature here," Pilar was saying to the woman. "Then we can start looking at the properties we discussed—"

She broke off as she noticed Jude, and then, quite deliberately, ignored her. She stood and turned toward the coat rack.

"I'll just gather my things and then we'll be on our way," she trilled to her new clients.

"Pilar?" Jude's approach was steady, though I could see she was nervous. "Sorry to barge in like this. Could I have a quick word about the Cooper cottage?"

Pilar didn't even look at her, although she did deign to reply.

"Uh, *hello*, I'm with clients." She rolled her eyes with exasperation while tightening the belt of her coat, showing off her trim waist.

Her lipstick was too vivid. Her perfume was too strong. I suppressed a shudder and edged closer to the door, my sensitive nostrils flaring in visible disgust.

"It'll just take a minute," Jude tried again, glancing at the clients apologetically.

"Jude, it'll have to wait, okay? Swing by tomorrow around eleven. I might be free then."

"Look, there was a break-in last night—"

That got Pilar's attention, though not in a good way.

"The house wasn't damaged, I trust?"

"No, no damage. I'd left the door unlocked."

"Oh right, so it's your fault," Pilar snapped. "I take no responsibility for that level of carelessness."

Distaste flickered across the young man's face as he watched the scene unfold.

Jude tried again. "I wanted to ask about installing some security cameras—"

"That would be at your own expense," Pilar cut in sharply. "And you'd need written permission from the owner, which I doubt they'll give. We can't have tenants making alterations. Now, if you'll excuse us."

She waved her hand dismissively at Jude as though shooing away a fly— then turned those icy eyes on me, a look that could have withered a stone angel.

The man's eyebrows lifted slightly at Pilar's tone. The older woman pressed her lips together in a way that reminded me of Mrs. Lynch when she disapproved of something. She shared a glance with the man.

"But surely—" Jude began.

"I *said*, I'm with clients," Pilar dismissed with finality. Then she turned to the clients, her whole manner transforming. "Now, are we ready to go? I have several lovely properties lined up for today."

The man shook his head, his anger barely contained beneath politeness.

Jude slipped out. I followed, noting how the man's eyes tracked her departure, and how he brushed Pilar off when she reached for his arm.

He stepped out after us, his stride confident, and touched Jude lightly on the elbow.

"Hey— sorry— Jude, is it? That was rough in there. Getting broken into— it's pretty scary. Are you okay?"

"I am, yes. Thanks for asking," Jude said. She gestured toward me. "John here chased the men off. I've just made the police report, and they suggested cameras. And, well..." She laughed and shrugged in a *what-can-you-do* sort of way.

"You know, there are some good wireless systems now. You wouldn't need owner's permission for those. I've got a mate in Adelaide who can get you something reputable, not too expensive."

He glanced back through the window, where Pilar was watching, lips puffed into a perfect pout. The silver-haired woman was easing into her coat.

"I could text him and get you some info, if you like?"

"Sure, okay. I'll be over at Jim's General Store later this afternoon, if you're back— I usually hang out by the fire."

"Great. It's a date." He grinned. "Andy Mitchell." He extended his hand.

"Jude."

By her flat response and brief handshake, I knew there was no way she thought it was 'a date'. I suppressed a chuckle.

* * *

Jude and I walked around by the river lookout, clouds rolling in and darkening the sky. She dropped onto the bench, propped her heels on the edge of the seat, and hugged her legs to her chest. Resting her chin on the torn denim over her knees, she stared out at the river.

"GAH!" The sound burst out of her, startling me.

She dropped her feet to the ground and pressed the heels of her hands against her eyes.

"I keep dwelling on what *didn't* happen! Isn't that stupid? Those men are gone. You chased them off. Nothing terrible happened. Yet my mind keeps playing these awful scenes that never even happened."

She trailed off, hands falling into her lap.

The last of the morning sun caught the river just right through the approaching clouds, turning the surface to diamonds. A few leaves drifted down from the old gum tree above us.

I settled beside her, watching a Superb Fairywren hop closer, then think better of it, flitting back to the fence rail.

I knew what she meant— the real moment was over, the danger past, but somehow the things that *didn't* happen felt more real than what did. Like shadows growing longer at sunset, the same object casting shapes bigger and darker than itself.

Strange how the mind works that way— turning one brief moment into endless what-ifs.

Chapter 6

John

A gust of wind tugged at Jude's jacket as we headed back toward Jim's. The drizzle thickened into proper rain, and we both picked up pace. Truth be told, I could've sprinted back and been toasty warm by the fire ages ago, but there was no way I was leaving her behind.

I still felt a little like I was under scrutiny, like she was watching me from the corner of her eye, weighing me up. But something had shifted too. Some of the fences had been mended. We weren't quite strangers anymore. And I reckoned we were finding our way back onto the track of whatever friendship this was becoming.

Inside, the wood stove radiated welcome heat. Jude waved to Jim as she stepped in, then hesitated when she noticed the customer at the counter.

It was Andy Mitchell— the man we'd met outside of McKeown's Realty.

Jim was sliding two cups across the counter. "One small flat white, one small tea. The other drink will be just a minute."

Thanking Jim as he tucked the two small cups into a carry tray, Andy spotted us and gave a friendly wave.

"Hey— hello again. I'm just grabbing coffees for the house-hunting adventure. Can I get you anything?"

"No, we're good thanks," Jude demurred, heading back towards the wood stove.

I rolled my eyes when Jim hollered— far too gleefully— what I knew would be Pilar's order.

"One extra-large half-skinny half-soy half-caf capp, double shot sugar-free vanilla and three raw sugars!"

Jim shot me a wink.

Andy waved to Jude as he fit the huge cup into the tray, and then hurried out into the rapidly darkening day. I could feel a deluge coming.

I didn't envy the poor bloke, having to spend a rainy afternoon with the odious Pilar McKeown.

* * *

The daily chores finished, I was snoozing by the fire when the door opened, bringing with it a rush of wintery air. I glanced at the old Regulator clock on the wall— it was just before five. Right on closing time.

The store was warm and inviting, a cosy haven from the driving rain and brisk wind outside. The smell of Jim's homemade beef stew drifted through the store, making my mouth water and my stomach growl. I could hardly wait to eat.

The elegant silver-haired woman stepped in first, followed by Andy, shaking the rain from his coat. Both looked weary from what I could only imagine was a long day with Pilar.

Jim glanced up from the counter, pleased to see them. "Well, well! Welcome in! How did the house hunting go? Can I get you folks anything?"

Andy rolled his eyes. "It was exhausting. And this rain! Relentless! We just got back. We're staying over at Sunnybrook's, but apparently they don't serve dinner on Wednesdays. So I thought we'd chase off the chill with a bottle of wine and maybe some takeaway, if you've got anything?"

Jim stuck his hand out across the counter. "I'm Jim. Sorry about the weather— it can be kind of unpredictable this time of year."

Andy clasped his hand with a warm smile. "Pleased to meet you, Jim. I'm Andy— Andy Mitchell, and this is my mother, Diana," he gestured toward the silver-haired woman as Jim stepped around the counter to greet her properly.

"Diana, the pleasure is all mine. Go warm yourself by the stove there. I'll show Andy our wine selection, then we'll sort out something for you two to eat. Only place open tonight'll be Shade's Pub. Food's not great. Might not be your kind of place," Jim added, glancing sidelong at Diana.

Jim led Andy back to the wood-panelled section where the wines were displayed. He prided himself on stocking some of the region's best bottles— even a few old and rare vintages.

"Apologies for the construction mess," I heard Jim say, then he described his vision to Andy: long, hand-hewn tasting tables over the rough stone floor underfoot, a future walk-in cooling room, comfortable armchairs arranged around a six-sided, glass-walled fireplace that would glow like a hearth.

Andy's face lit up as he ran his fingers along the labels in appreciation. "That sounds fabulous. And this is quite a collection you've got here. Oh wow. Is this the 2019 Shadow's Reserve Shiraz? That was a phenomenal year."

"You know your wines." Jim was pleased.

"I work with wine, actually. Sustainability consulting. I've been working with some of the vintners here in the Hills, helping them transition to more eco-friendly practices without compromising quality." He reverently lifted a bottle. "Hey, this one took gold at the Adelaide Show."

Mrs. Lynch bustled in, bringing with her the heavenly aroma of fresh-baked bread.

"Jim, that stew of yours has been driving me mad all afternoon— I swear I could smell it all the way over at Pokey's! Oh!" She stopped, surprised to see strangers in the shop past closing time.

Diana rose from where she was seated by the fire. "It sure does smell absolutely wonderful in here."

"That'll be Jim's beef stew," Mrs. Lynch noted proudly, setting the still-warm loaves on the counter. "And my sourdough with it is a match made in heaven."

"You're welcome to join us for dinner," Jim bellowed from the wine section.

"Well then!" Mrs. Lynch turned to Diana and reached out a friendly hand, "I'm Anne."

"I'm Diana," the woman replied. "And my son, Andy, is over there with Jim."

"They've spent the day traipsing all over the Hills with Pilar, looking at houses," Jim added, walking back toward the counter holding a bottle of wine.

"Oh God," Mrs. Lynch groaned. "An entire day with Pilar? Better get yourselves two of those bottles."

Andy held up a second wine bottle. "We'd love to join you for dinner, if that was a proper invitation. And we'd love to share this with you, if you'll join us?"

"Oh, twist my arm," Jim chuckled, already reaching for glasses.

I wandered out back to grab more logs for the fire as they arranged chairs and bowls. The rain drummed steadily on the roof, making the store feel even cosier.

These were the moments I loved best— when The Ridge wrapped its arms around people, turning strangers into friends over good food and warm conversation.

* * *

"So," Mrs. Lynch started, ushering Diana toward the armchairs, "did you see any nice houses?"

Diana sank into the chair between me and the fire with a sigh. "Oh, Anne. It was so *draining*. Pilar showed us everything except what we actually asked for."

"Huge modern monstrosities or complete renovator's nightmares. Even some large acreage properties," Andy added, shaking his head as he accepted a corkscrew from Jim and busied himself with the bottle. "We told her up-front we wanted something manageable, something with character. Something *in town*. But apparently she had other ideas."

"I've had quite enough of Pilar," Diana avowed. "It's quite clear she's more interested in her commission than finding what we actually want. One place was so far out in the bush I'd need a helicopter to get groceries."

Mrs. Lynch laughed heartily— the kind of laugh that always made me smile.

Over dinner, the conversation flowed easily: Mrs. Lynch and Diana discovered shared interests in gardening and local history, while Andy and Jim compared notes on local wines. I listened in silence to all of it, focused on enjoying my food.

As we finished our bowls of stew, sopping up the last of the sauce with sourdough, Mrs. Lynch went thoughtful.

"You know," she mused, "I might have just the right house." She glanced toward Diana. "A lovely character cottage next to Pokey's. Not officially on the market, but for the right buyer—"

Jim's eyebrows shot up. My head swung around toward her in surprise. We both peered closely at her as she rose nonchalantly and walked to the kitchen.

"Oh really? Maybe Pilar can connect us with the owner?" Andy wondered aloud.

"Pilar?!" Mrs. Lynch exclaimed, walking back toward the table with the second bottle of wine and a box of English chocolates. "Over my dead body! That self-righteous old moll won't be getting her hands on that listing, thank you very much."

I couldn't help smiling at the startled looks on Andy and Diana's faces as Jim broke in.

"It's actually Anne's cottage," he explained, amused. "I didn't realise you were thinking of selling, Anne?"

"I wasn't. So many family memories there." Then she straightened, as if making a decision on the spot. "But it's a shame it's sitting empty. So, like I said. For the right buyer. Give me a couple of weeks to tidy it up. It needs a good going-through."

The charming gingerbread-style house beside Pokey's was her family home. When Mr. Lynch died, she'd moved into the small apartment above Pokey's— her popular lunch café and ice cream parlour. The house had sat empty through the years ever since.

The door opened and Jude appeared, blown in by the wind and slightly damp from the rain.

Andy straightened immediately, pushing his chair back to stand even as she waved him back down.

"Hey, Jude, I'm glad you're here." He reached for his phone. "I got that security camera information— I can email it over to you. The whole setup would be under five hundred— and I'd be happy to help you install it next time I'm up."

I watched her hesitate— a familiar wariness flickering across her face— then she rattled off her email address.

CHAPTER 7

John

The bench by the river felt emptier than usual. I'd been there every morning for the past four days, watching the path where Jude usually appeared, but there was no sign of her flame-red hair or her cheerful greeting. Just me, the river, and the kookaburras cackling from somewhere in the hills.

I tried not to worry, but worry has a way of settling in your chest like a stone, heavy and cold. Had I done something wrong? Maybe insisting on walking around with her after the break-in had been too much. Maybe I'd seemed too eager, too interested. Maybe she'd decided I was creepy after all, despite what Mrs. Lynch had told her.

On the morning of the fourth day, I gave up waiting and took myself for a long walk instead. My route happened to take me past Cooper's cottage— not on purpose, of course, just the way the trails wound through the hills. Smoke curled from the chimney, a thin grey ribbon against the winter sky. So she was home.

My shoulders slumped as I made my way back toward town, taking the long way around so I wouldn't have to pass her place again.

* * *

Another full week passed, and I couldn't help myself. I found a reason to walk past Cooper's cottage in the late afternoon— checking on the Petersons— a legitimate errand that was almost in that direction.

The smoke was still curling from the chimney. Her old ute sat in the driveway, exactly where it had been the last time I'd loped past. Through the window, I could see the warm glow of a lamp.

She was fine.

I turned and headed back toward Jim's, trying to shake the feeling that something was wrong. Maybe this was just what it meant when someone needed space. Maybe this was what it looked like when someone was moving forward with their life, doing things on their own.

The thought made my chest tight.

I stayed up late by the wood stove that night, watching the flames dance. Outside, the wind picked up, rattling the old windows. We were well and truly into the thick of winter now, and somewhere out there at Cooper's cottage, Jude was sitting by her own fire, doing whatever it was people did when they needed time alone.

I just hoped she'd come back to the river bench soon. The mornings weren't the same without her.

* * *

It was afternoon on one of those perfect winter days where everything seems sharper somehow— the sky a deeper blue, the hills more vividly green. Sunsets come early this time of year, barely past four o'clock, and the light was already starting to shift toward that dusky hour.

I headed up to the ridge behind the Thompson place earlier than usual, wanting to catch the full sunset show. My feet found the familiar path without me having to think about it, muscles remembering every root and stone.

When I reached the fence line, I stopped and just breathed. *This.* This was all I needed. The valley spreading out below, the old house waiting patiently in its coat of weathered stone, the ordered rows of vines holding their silent vigil. Some feelings didn't need words or explanations— they just *were.*

From up here, I could see clear across the valley to where the sun melts into the horizon. The old house below catches the light differently every evening— sometimes blazing gold, sometimes muted amber, but always like it's remembering what it used to be. What it could be again. The vines stretch out in neat rows, stalwartly holding their shape after all these years—like dancers frozen mid-step, waiting for the music to restart. On evenings like this, when the light hits them just so, you can clearly see what Pat Thompson saw in this piece of land.

The rail under my forearms has been worn smooth by weather and time. And maybe, just a little, by me. Strange how a place can become part of you without you noticing. How many sunsets have I watched from this spot? A thousand? More? Each one different, each one the same.

Tonight the sky is putting on a magnificent show— streaks of purple and orange painting the clouds that drift like lost sheep across the hills. The last rays catch the old stone walls, and for a moment the Thompson place looks alive again.

"Room for one more sunset watcher?" Jude spoke quietly, careful not to break the evening's spell.

This time, I wasn't startled by her presence. Maybe I'd been half-expecting her, hoping she'd come back. Something seemed to have shifted between us— maybe we'd gone from acquaintances to friends. I stepped back in what I hoped was a friendly gesture of welcome, and she took a place at the rail.

"I never properly thanked you," she said. "Not just for helping me down that night, but for... well, for scaring off those men. For watching out for me in the evenings." She hugged herself slightly.

I must have looked as surprised as I felt. She chuckled. "Yes John, I know you check on me. Jim told me he'd asked you to, from time to time. Even if you were camping out there, it makes me feel better knowing you were around, okay?"

"I wanted to apologise too." She turned slightly toward me. "For being weird about you following me. It was just... but now I know you better! And I know you're just being you— kind, and protective."

She paused, and then shuddered. "If I'd gone inside while those men were there..."

I understood. I raised my eyebrows in agreement, my jaw set grimly. One couldn't be too cautious in an unfamiliar place, I knew that all too well.

"Listen, the old carriage house on the far side of the driveway is empty. Jim said he can hook us up with a bunk, some blankets. In case you want to stay there from time to time. Rather than being out in the cold." She hesitated, searching my non-committal face.

I wasn't sure how Jim would feel if I started spending nights elsewhere. I'd get his opinion on it before I decided.

We watched the stars appear, one by one, until the old house below became a darker shadow against the night. The almost-full moon provided enough light for the trek down, though she placed her feet gingerly on the steep parts.

This time I didn't pretend to peel off towards town. I walked her right to her gate, like a proper gentleman.

As she headed towards the house, she turned back suddenly. "Hey John," she called out in the moonlight. "Would you like to join me for a walk tomorrow morning? I'd like to try a new trail I found online. Meet at the bench where we first met?"

Delighted, I readily agreed.

* * *

I was there before dawn— we hadn't settled on a time but better to be early, and I rarely missed a sunrise anyway. I'd taken extra care with my morning grooming, but tried to look nonchalant as I waited.

The valley was still wrapped in pre-dawn shadows, and the eastern sky had begun to lighten, grey giving way to the first hints of apricot. Wisps of morning mist clung to the hollows, making The Ridge look like it was floating above clouds. A young galah landed nearby, tilting its head at me in greeting before hopping closer.

Jude appeared as the sun was cresting the horizon, looking slightly surprised to find me already there. The galah jumped and then flew away, alarmed by her arrival.

"Hi, John! I wasn't sure what time— I mean, good morning," she announced, flopping onto the bench beside me to watch the sun beams rise across the river. The rays caught the dew on the grass, turning every blade into a mesmerising prism. She suggested we walk, so off we went.

The air smelled like apples and crunchy leaves, and we fell into an easy rhythm along the trail, letting the morning settle around us. The trail she took us on was a section of the old logging track, a straightforward walk that many tourists took, convincing themselves they'd hiked in the Adelaide Hills. Our forests had so much more to offer, but I didn't mind seeing the track again.

After a while, Jude began to talk.

"My old boss called yesterday. They want me to come back to work. I work— well, *worked*, I should say— at a lab. Testing contaminated soil." She kicked at a loose stone. "I left pretty abruptly, when Dad died. Took an extended leave of absence."

I kept pace beside her, listening.

"I only came up here to get away for a bit, you know? Just to breathe, think about what I wanted to do next. Wasn't planning on more than a few months." She trailed off, looking out over the hills where the sun was just starting to touch the highest ridges.

A magpie warbled somewhere above us— one of my favourite sounds in all the world.

"But now," she gestured at the town below, sighing as though a difficult decision awaited. "I don't know. Something about this place feels, I don't know. I can't explain it. Like maybe I could start fresh here. Build something new— a future for myself."

I wasn't surprised. It was exactly what I had done. The trick to starting fresh is to carry only good memories with you into your new start and leave the heavy baggage far behind.

She fell silent for a while, the only sounds coming from the wind in the leaves, the cheerful song of the morning birds, and our footfalls on the forest floor.

She'd opened a small crack, but had chosen not to go any deeper, and that was okay. I'd be there to listen whenever she wanted to talk. Some things can't be pried open before they're ready. Push too soon, and you do more harm than good.

We kept moseying along the trail, the conversation drifting to easier things— the changing leaves, the ice on the river, whether Jim's renovations would be complete before the Winter Reds.

"Speaking of Jim's coffee," she declared with a sudden clap of her hands— which we hadn't been, but I let it go— "I could really use some breakfast. Want to head to Jim's?"

* * *

The morning regulars were milling about when we arrived. I'd already had my breakfast, so I stuck around long enough to be polite and let her know that I was thankful for the walk, then I made my way out back to take care of some business.

When I returned, Mrs. Lynch was there, and I could smell the fresh warm scones she carried over every morning. She chucked one in my direction. I caught it easily and then settled by the fire, half-dozing in the warmth.

I could hear Jude telling Mrs. Lynch about running into me at the Thompson place again last night.

"He's up there every night!" Mrs. Lynch exclaimed, setting down her mug. "Unless it's bucketing down rain, he's there, standing at that rail and watching the sun set over the old vineyard. Been doing it for years now."

"That place," she continued, "hasn't been the same since old Pat Thompson passed. Must be, oh, twelve or so years now. Maybe more. The nephew tried bringing in some caretakers to tend the vines, but that didn't work out. That's how John came to be here, actually."

Jim snorted from behind the counter. "If you can call them caretakers. Those people were nothing but trouble."

"Now Jim," Mrs. Lynch scolded, with no real heat in it. "Lord knows how they ever got approved to be foster carers for John. He was just a gangly young fella then— all legs and good intentions."

"Independent though," Jim added. "Used to see him walking for miles along those old logging tracks. Knew every trail in these hills."

"And when the caretakers left—" Mrs. Lynch's voice hardened. "Well. John was out somewhere in the hills when they were loading up. Maybe he didn't know they were leaving, or maybe he just wanted to stay. And would you believe— they just drove off without him! Never looked back. Never saw the likes of it."

"Found him up there that first autumn," Jim said, more to his coffee pot than to us. "Skinny as a rake, sleeping on the porch, keeping an eye on the place. Unofficial caretaker, he was." Jim smiled at the memory.

"Then we started finding neat piles of firewood on doorsteps all over town," Mrs. Lynch added. "Nobody ever saw who was leaving them, but we all knew. He made himself useful right from the get-go."

"Once the weather turned proper cold," Jim continued, "I offered him the back room here. Been part of the store ever since."

I studied the woodpile by the stove, remembering those first uncertain months. I licked my lips and swallowed hard, pushing down tears. The Thompson place had felt like home from the start, even if it wasn't meant to be. But Jim's back room— that had become home in a different way.

Chapter 8

John

Later that week, she found me in a pile of freshly raked leaves by the creek trail. I froze mid-jump, leaves stuck in my hair, trying to maintain some semblance of dignity. She pressed her lips together, clearly fighting laughter.

"Don't let me interrupt," she said, voice quivering with suppressed mirth. "Everyone needs a good leafy celebration now and then."

Her eyes crinkled at the corners and the edges of her lips twitched upward in a half-smile. Then, to my complete surprise, she set down her bag, took three running steps, and launched herself into the leaf pile beside me.

"I think I need to be more spontaneous," she explained to the sky, leaves in her hair.

I sent another cascade of leaves into the air, and her laugh echoed off the creek banks— a sound as welcome as spring rain.

* * *

Andy and Diana pulled up in a car outside Pokey's, and I happened to be hanging about. Well, maybe not exactly 'happened'—Jim may have mentioned they were coming by to see Mrs. Lynch's cottage, and I too was curious to see it.

The cottage sparkled. The porch had been swept clean, the windows shone, and Jim had even trimmed back the overgrown lavender and rosemary bushes by the front gate. Through the open door, I spotted fresh flowers on the hall table.

Mrs. Lynch came bustling out, looking pleased as punch, Jim following closely behind carrying a toolbox. He had that satisfied look he got when he'd actually fixed something rather than bungled it up worse.

"Anne's been baking," Jim greeted them effusively, holding the gate open for Andy and Diana to walk through, me following close behind. "Place smells like heaven and apple turnovers."

I waited just inside the gate, watching as they disappeared inside. Jim heaved the toolbox down and stood beside me. He was grinning like the Cheshire Cat, and I thought I knew why. There was something different about the way he and Mrs. Lynch moved around each other— a comfortable ease, like they'd been doing things like this together for years instead of just a few weeks.

Interesting.

I had a few chores to do up at Peterson's, so after a quick, approving look through the house, I headed that way, making a note to pay more attention to Jim and Mrs. Lynch in future.

* * *

Heading back, chores completed and lunch in my sights, I spotted Andy's car parked outside Cooper's cottage. He was up on a ladder by the front door, attaching a small black bracket while Jude held the ladder steady and passed him tools.

Right— the security cameras. Andy seemed to know what he was doing, explaining something about angles and motion sensors while Jude looked politely interested. I didn't want to intrude, but got close enough to see they were making good progress.

Jude invited Andy to lunch at Pokey's, as *the least she could do*. I hurried on my way, so I could circle back past Pokey's and eavesdrop.

* * *

Pokey's Ice Cream Shop did a brisk lunch trade in winter— hot soups, toasted sandwiches, and what everyone claimed was the best hot chocolate in the Hills. I hadn't been planning to go in, but I spotted Pilar

McKeown stomping down the sidewalk in her high-heeled boots— curiosity got the better of me. I sidled in and took a seat in the corner.

Jude and Andy were tucked into a booth, laughing and talking as they finished up their meals. Jude was gesturing animatedly, while Andy appeared overly interested in whatever she was saying.

Pilar swept in, her heels clicking sharply on the wooden floor. I watched her posture change when she spotted them— her shoulders flew back, her chin went up, her plumped-up lips pressed into what might have been a smile, if smiles were made of ice. She made a beeline for their table.

"I heard you were back in town," she oozed over Andy, one hand on his shoulder, not even acknowledging Jude. I could read body language well enough, observing Andy cringe at her touch— too familiar, too possessive. Jude's polite smile didn't quite reach her eyes. Andy looked plain uncomfortable.

"Andy, I have a new listing that I must show you—"

Andy cut her off mid-sentence. "No need, Pilar. I think Mum's found a place. A private sale. The cottage next door, actually."

Pilar's lip curled in annoyance, and her free hand clenched into a fist. I shuddered. I could only imagine how horrible it would be to have her harpy claw gripping onto my shoulder, feeling a pang of sympathy for Andy.

"It's not for her, you silly," Pilar shifted tack, flapping a hand at him. "It's for another client. He's interested in a vineyard, and I need someone who knows vines. When I saw your car out front, I knew you were just the man for the job."

She swivelled toward Jude. "You don't mind if I steal him away for a bit, do you, Jude?"

Jude sat back, looking at Andy, who put his hands up in a half-shrug. Then she said she had some other stuff to do anyhow, leaving a flabbergasted Andy in the lurch.

Poor Andy. Another afternoon stuck with Pilar McKeown.

Standing, Jude gathered her things and thanked Andy graciously for the camera help before going to pay the tab.

I snuck out of Pokey's and slid across into Mrs. Lynch's yard, but not before I spotted Pilar sliding into Jude's vacated seat, all smiles and batting eyelashes.

* * *

I heard about Diana's decision from Jim later that evening. She'd fallen in love with Mrs. Lynch's cottage— every charming nook and weathered floorboard of it. Said it just needed a few personal touches, but otherwise it was perfect. The sale would be handled privately, no real estate agent needed. Mrs. Lynch seemed relieved about that, and Jim— well, Jim looked happier than I'd seen him in years.

I also heard more about Pilar cornering Andy at Pokey's.

"Bloody nerve of that woman," Jim muttered as he stocked some new bottles in the wine section. "Jude told Anne all about it when she came in for afternoon tea. Pilar wanted Andy to look at some winery property for one of her clients. Needs his 'expert opinion', apparently."

Jim punctuated the words with exaggerated air quotes, his broad hands flexing like he was wrangling something invisible.

He snorted. "Winery client my eye. That woman's got her hooks out, mark my words."

I settled by the fire, watching the flames dance, an unfamiliar sense of something shifting lodged in my chest.

Chapter 9

John

The winter days rolled on. On nice days, she'd join me at the bench and we'd walk. The early morning frost made the trails sparkle, our breath clouding in the cold air. Sometimes she was pensive and quiet, and other times she'd be full of chatter.

Getting to know her better was a constant joy— she'd tell me stories about her former work, and the places she'd been. I hadn't travelled much, but I knew the area around The Ridge really well— I showed her all of my favourite places. We'd take long walks down by the river and watch the gentle undulations of the water. I'd have been content to stay there longer, but no sooner had we settled in than she'd want to be off again.

She accused me of being too easy to talk to, and sometimes, she'd ramble on for hours. I liked to listen, and I was particularly good at it, seldom interrupting. I had fewer stories to tell— I'd been raised to believe that we were given two ears and only one mouth for a reason. Plus, I didn't think nearly as fast as she did. Her mind was always racing in one direction or another— sometimes many directions, all at the same time.

To be honest, it was exhausting just to listen at those times, when her thoughts got away from her. I'd rather give thoughts and ideas the time they deserved, but there was no slowing her down. It seemed to me sometimes that she talked herself into problems that hadn't even happened. Then she'd either talk her way out of those fictitious problems, or get angry and down on herself. That was the hardest for me to take. I never knew what to say.

I came to learn her moods like I knew the river's— when to let the silence be, and when to listen.

The first time she stumbled, I was there before I could think twice, steadying her. She blamed it on an icy patch that I couldn't see from where I stood. After that, I began noticing that she was often unsteady on her feet.

We fell into patterns without meaning to. When it seemed like she was on a mission, that meant we'd take the shorter river loop so she could carry on with her day. When she dawdled, or seemed to have more on her mind, I knew she needed a longer walk, so I'd guide her around the forest loop.

We started to recognise the winter birds— a magpie couple that would swoop down to investigate, a curious wattlebird that liked to follow us. Maybe it was just my imagination, but even the sulky ravens seemed to accept us on their trails.

Some days she'd talk about the career she'd left behind— about soil chemistry and environmental impacts— and I realised that she was incredibly, but rather humbly, intelligent. I wondered if she was seriously contemplating the offer to go back to her old job in Adelaide, or whether she'd find a new path.

Some doors close quietly behind you, and by the time you think about turning back, the hinges have rusted. The room isn't yours anymore. Maybe you find it never was.

Other days she'd point out how the light caught the ice forming along the river's edge, or how the leaves leaked their colour into the morning mist. She had a way of seeing beauty in unexpected places— like how she'd stop to admire the patterns on fallen leaves, or pause at the lookout to watch storm clouds gather over distant hills.

Some mornings we'd find the river had frozen in patches overnight, thin sheets of ice stretching from the banks like reaching fingers. She was fascinated by the way it would crack and groan as the day warmed up.

"Shh, John, the river's talking," she observed one morning, and we paused to listen to the ice shifting. Her voice had that faraway quality it got sometimes, like she was remembering something— or maybe trying to forget.

Every now and then we'd run into other walkers— Barbara Tate with her yappy little terrier who barked at everyone like he was Little Big Man, Old Mr. Peterson taking his morning constitutional, sometimes

Mrs. Lynch, who always gave me a wink and advised that she'd see us later at Jim's. They'd all wish us good morning, but none tried to join us. The Ridge folks are good like that— they keep themselves to themselves, mostly.

The winter deepened. Frost painted delicate patterns on the store windows each morning. The birds' dawn chorus grew shorter as they huddled against the cold. But Jude kept coming to our bench most mornings, two gloved hands wrapped around her thermos, ready to walk whatever path the day required.

Everything was wonderful, yet something felt odd. I couldn't put my finger on exactly what, but I could feel it in my bones, the way you feel weather changing— that electric tension before a storm breaks.

I just didn't know what form the storm would take. I vowed to pay close attention.

* * *

I remember the day vividly, because it was a mid-winter Thursday in late July, and the renovations at the store were finally complete. It was a full week before the Winter Reds kicked off, and the whole town was buzzing with excitement, preparing for a flood of visitors.

Jim had been busily preparing for his outdoor movie nights that he hosted during the festival weekend— 'Jim's Spageddy Westerns'. He'd show old cowboy movies on the big screen outside, while he served up local wine and homemade spaghetti around the firepits. They were popular events, and often sold out long in advance of the festival.

Personally, I was more than happy to taste-test all the different versions of Jim's spaghetti, helping him choose his best homemade sauces before the event. I thought of it as part of my best-mate duties.

This year's festival agenda was supposed to be the biggest ever, for what was already the largest wine event in the Adelaide Hills. The anticipatory vibes seemed to make the air electric, even though it was still a week away.

Jude and I set off that Thursday morning on our river loop trail. Jude was talking way less than normal, and kept stopping to steady herself, shaking her head slightly as though she was clearing away cobwebs. I grew concerned when she'd done it three times in the span of five minutes, each time following with a quick smile that masked a slight wince. She probably thought I didn't notice, but that was the first real sign that she was unwell, and I had a gnawing feeling that something was very wrong.

"Mind if we cut it short today?" she asked. "I'm just not really feeling up to the full loop for some reason."

The walk back was calmer than usual. No rambling stories, no racing thoughts spoken aloud. Just the crunch of our feet on the path. When we reached the fork where I usually turned off, she surprised me.

"Fancy an ice cream?"

* * *

We strolled the rest of the way to Pokey's, and Mrs. Lynch's face lit up at the sight of us together.

"Well, look at the pair of you, bright-eyed and bushy-tailed as ever!" she exclaimed, reaching out for a hug from Jude.

I rolled my eyes as I settled into my usual spot by the window, but Jude just laughed. As she passed behind me, she laid her hand tenderly against the back of my neck— a casual touch that sent a thousand volts of electricity down my spine. It was the first time she'd ever reached out like that. Maybe even the first time she'd ever touched me at all, other than to occasionally steady herself.

I sat very still, trying to process this new development while she looked over the flavours in the cabinet. The touch had lasted less than a second, but I could still feel it— like a sunbeam had reached out and zapped me.

"I already know John's having a scoop of vanilla with a crunched up sugar cone, served in a bowl," Mrs. Lynch teased, casting a patronising yet loving gaze in my direction. I can't help it if I'm quirky yet predictable about my ice cream.

"What are you thinking of, Jude?"

"I think I might try the ginger. Just a small scoop in a cup, thanks. I'm feeling a bit out of sorts today," she explained, touching her forehead.

"Oh no, dear! I hope you're not coming down with something before next week!"

Jude promised she'd be alright, wouldn't miss it for the world, but something caused Mrs. Lynch's eyes to narrow as she reached for the scoop. I decided I'd keep a close watch on our Jude, make sure she was okay.

* * *

While Mrs. Lynch readied our ice creams, Jude wandered over to study the wall of photographs. They covered nearly every inch— more than twenty years of Ridge history captured in fading Polaroids and digital prints.

I watched her face as she scanned the images, noting how her expression changed when she reached the corner near the window. Her hand lifted, hesitated, then touched one particular photo.

Mrs. Lynch came up beside her, a cup of ginger ice cream in hand. "That was a good summer. Your mother loved the wildflowers that year. Said she'd never seen anything like them."

I nearly choked on my sugar cone. All this time looking at that wall of memories, and I'd never noticed her there? How many times had I stared at those photos, wondering about the stories behind each frozen moment?

"I'd forgotten about this," Jude whispered. "Dad brought us up here every summer until—" She broke off.

"We were all so sorry, dear. When we heard about your mother's accident. Losing your mother and brother— well. That must have been terrible for you. Your father stopped coming up after that. Until the year before last."

Jude's hand dropped from the photo. "Right. He brought that wine tour through. Before everything happened with Dylan. Dad was really keen to start something new up here— he just never told me what."

"Well," Mrs. Lynch handed her the ice cream, "I'm glad you've found your way back here. For whatever the reason."

Something passed between them then— understanding, maybe. Or recognition. One woman who'd weathered loss, seeing another still learning how.

I stayed in my spot by the window, watching the moment unfold.

* * *

Once Jude left, I casually beelined over to the corner. The photo was smaller than most, tucked between a shot of the '98 flood and the old post office before it burned. In the photo, a young Jude— maybe eight or nine— sat perched on her father's shoulders, red hair a wild halo around her face. Both of them were grinning. A woman with hair the same shade of red was pointing at something off-camera, while a small boy hung onto her sleeve.

My God, there she was— elfin face, missing her front teeth. Happy. Whole. Before loss had taught her to guard her smile.

"Different girl back then, John," Mrs. Lynch stated, appearing beside me. "She's lost the lot of them now. But she's still in there somewhere. Under all those carefully built walls."

I stayed there a long time, studying that captured moment of joy. Wondering if the girl on her father's shoulders ever imagined she'd find her way back here. Wondering if she knew she'd been here all along, watching over us from that wall of memories, waiting to come home.

I did a long, slow blink, trying to hold back tears. I felt an acute pain in my heart for the family my poor friend had lost.

Mrs. Lynch's comforting hand landed on my shoulder. "You're already helping her, John. Just being her trusted friend, that's what she needs most right now."

I looked at her, grateful for the reassurance. It's like that woman could read minds.

Chapter 10

John

It was later that evening, past sunset, that lovely gloaming where the sky is multi-hued just after the sun has dipped below the horizon. I was heading back toward Jude's carriage house when an old Holden Commodore blew past me and pulled right into the driveway, tyres crunching on the gravel.

I moved closer, keeping to the shadows, every sense suddenly alert. Something felt wrong. Very wrong.

Two men got out of the car and swaggered toward the porch, their postures subtly threatening. I recognised them, having chased them a few weeks back, and could confirm that these were definitely not the Marshall boys like Constable Peacock had thought. They were older men. Harder-looking.

I stepped into the centre of the driveway, my eyes fixed firmly on the two men. Jude's front door flew open. She came charging out onto the porch, brandishing her fireplace poker like Excalibur, her hair loose like flames around her face.

"What do you want?" she asked. "I've called the cops, by the way."

"Hey there, no need for the cops, or the poker," the taller one reproved, a false-friendly tone that made my hackles rise. "We're not here to do any harm. Just here for a little chat."

"Dylan asked us to swing by," the other added, eyeing me and putting a placating hand out. "Just to check on you, make sure you're settling in okay."

Dylan. That name again. Who the heck was Dylan?

The unspoken threat was clear as day. I moved closer, ready to step in, but Jude was holding her ground.

"Well then, you can tell Dylan it's no longer his concern. He and I are finished. And get off my property. Get out of this town, and don't come back," she ordered, shaky but firm.

The sound of an engine roaring into the driveway made everyone turn. Jim's old, restored Ram truck came barrelling in, Detroit iron rumbling like thunder. He pulled up beside the Commodore and stepped out to stand by the front bumper. He had his arms crossed, taking in everything— the men, the car, Jude with her poker, me standing in the middle of the drive.

The police car arrived seconds later, lights flashing.

"Okay, we get it. We're going," the tall one conceded, backing toward the car with his hands still visible. "We mean no harm. We're old friends of Jude's husband, just here to check in on her. No worries. We'll be leaving now."

Husband?

They climbed back into the Commodore, swung the car around behind Jim's truck, and drove away slowly. Not hurried, but not lingering either.

Constable Peacock got out of his patrol car, notebook in hand, jotting down the number plate as the Commodore drove away.

Jude lowered the poker, her shoulders sagging now that the adrenaline was fading. And I retreated into the shadows of the woods, my mind spinning with questions.

Dylan. Husband. Old friends who threatened women and broke into houses.

What exactly had Jude left behind in Adelaide?

* * *

The next morning, Jude didn't show up at the bench. I waited longer than usual, watching the sun climb higher, but the path stayed empty. A flutter of worry started in my chest— she hadn't seemed quite right the day before, that wobbly unsteadiness on the trail, the way she'd cut our walk short.

By mid-morning I was pacing the store, trying not to be obvious about watching the door every few minutes.

"John, you're wearing a track in my floorboards," Jim scolded. "Why don't you go look in on her?"

I didn't need to be told twice.

* * *

I found her on the porch at Cooper's cottage, wrapped in a blanket despite the winter sun doing its best to warm the day. She had that faraway look again, the one that meant she was somewhere else entirely.

"Hey John." She smiled when she noticed me, but her smile was tired. "Sorry I missed our walk. I'm just... I don't know. Feeling off."

I settled onto the porch steps, giving her space but making it clear I wasn't going anywhere. She waited for a long moment, staring out at the hills. Then, like she'd made some kind of decision, she started talking.

"There's a story I haven't told anyone. And it's weighing on me."

I waited, barely breathing. I should've known that her coming back to The Ridge wasn't just an escape. It was the beginning of a reckoning.

"It was a Sunday, late November year before last. I don't know why it matters that it was a Sunday. I'd called Dylan to see what was going on..."

Her voice changed then, took on a different quality— like she was watching it all happen again, right in front of her eyes.

Chapter 11

Jude

"Babe, I'm so sorry, I'm still at work. Ian's here with me and we're in a groove— hang on a sec... Yeah man, I'll be right there!" he shouted in the background.

The phone crackled as Dylan breathed sharply into it. "Sorry, babe. I gotta run. See ya when I get home."

The line went dead before I'd even had a chance to say one word. Sighing, I texted Dad.

Hey Dad, Dylan's working late tonight— some big proposal. He's been gone all weekend. Wondering what you're up to for dinner... maybe we can grab something and catch up?

His reply came almost immediately: *Sorry honey, I'll be working tonight too— covering a shift at L'Aubergine. Next week?*

I stared at the screen a moment, then tossed my phone onto the couch. There were a hundred things I could've done, but instead I reheated some pizza, flopped on the couch, and put Netflix on. When had life become so mundane?

It was well past nine when the garage roller door woke me. My empty pizza plate was still beside me, and the show had long since finished. I shook my head groggily, pushed my hair back, smoothed it into a low ponytail, and slipped the elastic from my wrist like I'd done a thousand times.

Carrying the plate into the kitchen, I was suddenly unsure I'd even heard the roller door at all. No sign of Dylan— and it had been at least five minutes since I'd heard the sound. I rinsed the plate, set it in the drying rack, and was about to head out to the garage when an engine revved— roared, really— and the whole house shuddered with a crash.

I ran for the garage and flung the side door open, only to see Dylan climbing out of the driver's side, his face twisted with rage.

"What the hell?" I cried, staring from him to the fridge he'd crashed into.

"What did you move that fridge for?" he yelled at me, stumbling around the back of the car.

"The fridge? Dylan— what are you talking about? I didn't move the fridge."

"You DID!" he roared, looming right up into my face.

"You put it right where I park so I'd HIT it— which is exactly what happened. You stupid, stupid, bitch." His eyes narrowed as he spat the words.

He shoved past me into the house. I followed, questions firing out faster than I could think.

"Dylan, are you drunk? What have you done to the car? Where are you going? Talk to me, goddamn it!"

He spun around, fury blazing. For a second it looked like he might cry— then he shouldered past me down the hall.

"You're not worth it. I'm leaving. I have to go."

He headed for the bedroom, grabbing a suitcase along the way. I stood in the hallway pinching the bridge of my nose, trying to stop my thoughts from skidding off the rails.

I was used to being told I wasn't worth it. Used to the yelling. The shoves. Even the occasional slap. What I wasn't used to was Dylan being this unhinged.

I followed him to the bedroom and caught a handful of t-shirts straight to the face.

"Get the fuck out of here, Jude! I don't want to see your smirky judgy face— whatever that... that face... that fucking face you make... just get the fuck out!"

He jabbed a finger at me, circling it in the air, his other hand clenched into a fist. He looked like he'd gone mad. I turned on my heel and walked out. Whatever this was— drink, drugs, some ugly cocktail of both— I wanted no part of it.

I went to the spare room, shut the door, and lay down, tears leaking sideways into the pillow. Through the wall, I could hear Dylan in the bedroom— not words, just animal roars, then something that sounded like sobbing. We'd had plenty of strange episodes over seven years, but this was new. I hoped he'd just pack and leave. Then the fear cut in— if he drove in this state, he could crash and kill himself— or someone else.

Should I call the police? Or Ian?

Ian felt safer. I scrolled until I found his number and hit dial.

"Hello?" Ian answered, groggy with sleep.

"Ian? It's Jude— I'm sorry to call so late. I figured you guys had just finished work so you might still be up."

"Work? It's Sunday, Jude. I don't work Sundays."

"Oh." My stomach dropped. "Dylan told me you guys..."

"Nope. No work on Sundays. What's going on?"

"I'm sorry— Dylan said he was with you tonight. I thought maybe you guys had gone for drinks after work. He's just..." I swallowed. "He's here, and he's going crazy."

"Jude, listen to me." Ian spoke sharply. "I haven't seen Dylan in over a month. Not since he was sacked. Haven't seen him since. Are you safe? Do you need me to call someone for you?"

The room tilted. "No... no, it's fine. I'm fine. I better go. Bye, Ian."

I sat on the edge of the bed, palms pressed to my face, dragging the skin of my cheeks upward like I could physically hold myself together.

Dylan had lost his job. And he hadn't told me. That explained the drinking. The late nights. The constant edge.

I stood, reaching for the doorknob— and the doorbell rang. I pulled the bedroom door open and saw Dylan sprinting down the hall, frantic.

He screamed into my face as he ran past me. "Don't answer that! If you answer that, I'll fucking kill you!"

He yanked the pullcord and the attic ladder dropped with a clatter. He shooed me back toward the spare room like I was a problem to be put away.

The doorbell rang again, followed by pounding.

"Dylan— tell me what is going on!"

"Fuck off!" he shrieked, and the attic hatch snapped shut after him.

"POLICE! Open the door, Mr. Craig!" boomed a voice from the front porch.

My heart lurched. Ian must have panicked and called them.

I opened the door, and froze. Two officers on the step— and more spread across the yard like it was a siege. Two were forcing their way through the hedge into the backyard.

"Whoa, whoa— wait," I began, hands out to either side.

"Mrs. Craig?"

"Yes, but it's fine. Ian was worried when I called him, but it's fine— we don't need the police."

The larger officer lifted an eyebrow. "Mrs. Craig, we're looking for Dylan Craig. Is Dylan Craig your husband?"

"He is," I admitted— and even to my own ears I sounded embarrassed. I tried again, firmer. "Yes. Dylan Craig is my husband. He's fine. I'm fine. It's all good."

I gave a small, ridiculous half-bow— then another— and I didn't even know why my body was doing it. I started to close the door.

The shorter officer put an arm out, stopping it. "Mrs. Craig, we need to speak to your husband. Right now."

"Right. Yes. Well. He's here." I heard myself babbling. "He just got home, actually. He's been at work. He's..."

I stepped back and let them in. The two from the porch followed me into the kitchen while others streamed through the house.

"Can I ask what's going on? I only called Ian because Dylan was acting weird, but—"

An officer walked past, calling out that Dylan wasn't in the bedrooms or bathrooms.

"Where is he, Mrs. Craig?"

A thunk came from the hallway. My eyes squeezed shut. "That'll be him," I advised.

"Dylan," I called, eager to make things normal. "The police are here. I think they just want to see that we're both okay."

He stumbled into the kitchen— hair wild, shirt torn, tears streaming.

"It was an accident," he blurted. "She didn't mean to do it. She didn't want me to drive, said I'd had too much to drink, so she picked me up. I'm sorry, Jude. I know you didn't mean to do it."

The two officers exchanged a look.

"I'm not sure what he's talking about," I said helplessly. "I didn't even move the fridge. I don't know who did."

"I think you both better come down to the station and answer some questions," the larger officer directed.

"Oh no— that's completely unnecessary. As you can see, we're both perfectly fine. And it was an old fridge anyway. We really should've just gotten rid of it."

"Lady, I don't know what kind of drugs you two are on, but go outside, get in the cars as directed, and we'll see you at the station once you've both sobered up. Unless you prefer to go in handcuffs?"

"Oh no." I sounded thin. "You have it wrong. I don't use drugs. And I wasn't drinking tonight. Not at all. I've just been home all night with my pizza."

I laughed— nervous and awful— and waved at the kitchen like it proved something. "As you can see."

Chapter 12

John

She paused in the telling, her fingers absently tracing patterns on a smooth river-stone she'd picked up on one of our walks. The winter sun caught the tears she was trying to hide, though her voice had remained calm and even. I'd noticed how she did that— held herself together through the telling of hard things, as if maintaining control of the story might somehow help her control the pain of it.

"If it wasn't so tragically true, it would almost be a funny series of misunderstandings." She forced a small laugh as she looked across at me, probably wondering why I hadn't interrupted. I had many questions, but it wasn't my place to judge, so I didn't ask a thing.

"John, I don't know if I'm ready to tell the rest of this story," she confessed as she turned to look at me. "I... well, nobody really knows the full story, although a lot of people know parts of it from the news and stuff."

Her hands trembled slightly as she tucked a strand of hair behind her ear, a gesture I'd come to recognise as one of her tells when emotion threatened to overwhelm her.

I stayed close, offering nothing but the peaceful companionship that had become our way. She'd carry on with the story in her own time.

* * *

It turned out to be the next morning when she was ready to tell the rest. I'd spent the night in the carriage house, listening to the sounds of her moving around the cottage, knowing she was rehearsing the harder parts in her mind. When she appeared at sunrise, thermos in hand, I knew she was ready.

She apologised for leaving me hanging, as if that was even necessary. Some stories can't be told all at once. Sometimes talking it through with a friend helps, and sometimes talking it through just dredges up icky stuff and leaves you feeling worse. I just walked beside her, and hoped that was a comfort to her.

We walked up the high ridge trail towards the grove of stringybarks that I knew were starting to come into early bloom. The morning was perfect— clear sky, faint breeze carrying the scent of eucalyptus and warm earth. A pair of rosellas flashed crimson feathers overhead, their peaceful calls a stark contrast to the memories Jude was sharing.

"I remember they put us into two separate police cars, and mine smelled so disgusting," she recalled, wrinkling her nose at the memory. "Like stale coffee and something worse."

"It sounds so stupid now, but I remember wondering if the car that Dylan was in smelled as bad as mine, and I actually made a mental note to ask him once the whole misunderstanding was cleared up."

She turned to face me. "You see, I still thought the police were there because Ian had called them, afraid for my safety! So there we went from separate cars into separate rooms, and there they left me. It felt like hours I was sitting there by myself..."

Chapter 13

Jude

The interview room was all hard edges and harsh fluorescent lighting that made my eyes ache. The metal chair seemed deliberately uncomfortable, its coldness seeping through my clothes. Every sound echoed— the tick of the wall clock, the distant slam of doors that made me jump each time, the protesting groan of the chair as Sergeant Rickey lowered himself into it.

Rickey sat across the table from me, pushing his glasses up onto his head as he flipped open a notebook.

"Mrs. Craig, I have a few questions."

"Fire away," I muttered, exhausted. "I'd love some water, if there's any chance of that?"

"Where were you from 4pm today?"

The question seemed innocent enough, but something in his tone made my stomach clench. Why did it matter where *I'd* been?

"I was home all day, all night. I called Dylan shortly after five, but he was still working— or at least he said he was working, but later when I called Ian, he insisted they *weren't* working, so I don't—"

"Mrs. Craig," Rickey interrupted. "Please continue detailing *your* whereabouts."

"Right. Sorry. Yes. Okay, so I called Dylan, but he wasn't going to be home for dinner. I microwaved some leftover pizza and watched a show on Netflix. I must have fallen asleep, because next thing I knew, the garage roller door opened, and that's what woke me up."

"And who was coming into the garage at that time?"

"Dylan. Wait. Well, I *thought* it was Dylan, but he didn't come inside right away. I went to the kitchen and rinsed off my pizza plate, and realised that he hadn't come in. Then I heard an engine roaring, and a big crash. I ran to the garage to see what was going on. Dylan was there, and he was yelling at me for moving the fridge..." I wondered the last part aloud, almost as though it were a question rather than a statement.

"But I hadn't moved the fridge," I hurriedly continued, "so I don't know what happened there, but what I did see was that Dylan had smashed his car into the fridge. But I swear I didn't move it."

"Okay, Mrs. Craig, thank you for those details. Now, can you tell me what happened after that?"

"Yes. I think so. Dylan was so angry. He was yelling at me about the fridge, and he ran to the bedroom and started packing, saying he was leaving me, and that I wasn't worth it. He said stuff like that all the time." I hesitated, tears springing unwelcome into my eyes as I waved the air around, trying to show that those kinds of comments came and went, meaning nothing.

Sergeant Rickey paused, pen poised over his notebook as he waited for me to continue.

Eventually, I started again. "Dylan was wild, out of control. He chucked a bunch of t-shirts in my face and— well. He said some pretty mean stuff. I don't think he meant any of it, he's just sometimes... deliberately cruel, I guess. I went and laid down in the spare bedroom, closed the door."

I took a second to gather my thoughts, and then continued.

"A little while later I called Ian, who Dylan had said he'd been working with that day. I wanted to know how much he'd had to drink. And whether there had been anything else— drugs maybe? Dylan used to have a bit of a thing with meth, some other drugs too, I'm not sure what. But that was a long time ago. Anyway, that's when Ian told me he hadn't seen Dylan in over a month. That Dylan had been fired! And he asked if I was safe. If I needed help, I think. Then you guys arrived, and the rest—"

I waved my hand around to indicate that Sergeant Rickey should be familiar with what happened next.

"Why did you send Dylan into the attic?" he asked.

"What? Why? I *didn't* send Dylan into the attic."

"Dylan says that you sent him into the attic and told him not to come back down until you'd left the house."

"Well. I don't know what to say about that. That's very odd. Can I talk to him?"

"No, you can't talk to him at this time. Mrs. Craig, do you maintain that you were home all evening, by yourself, and Dylan was out until shortly after 9PM?"

"Yes. Yes, I maintain exactly that."

"Thank you for being frank, Mrs. Craig. You are free to go, so I will arrange to have an officer drive you home. But I will tell you now that your husband Dylan has been charged with dangerous driving occasioning death, driving while impaired, and attempting to obfuscate a police investigation."

Stunned into silence, my mouth dropped open and then I quickly closed it again, shaking my head slowly from side to side in denial.

"But that's simply not possible—" my words broke off as I realised what must have happened. Dylan had hit someone, a pedestrian, or maybe another vehicle, while driving home drunk. He'd come into the garage, moved the fridge himself, and then run into it, perhaps to hide the evidence on the front of the car. Then tried to blame me.

I stared at Sergeant Rickey. "All of these questions... did. Umm. Did Dylan blame me for any of this?"

Sergeant Rickey closed his notebook and stood. "He did. He stated that he was too tipsy to drive after dinner with a colleague, and that you picked him up. You then struck a pedestrian while exiting the parking lot, and raced home. He claims that you told him to stage the fridge accident, and then to hide in the attic, while you made everything right."

"Oh my God," I reeled, gobsmacked. "None of that is true."

"I'll have Officer Short drive you home now. Is there someone you can call to be with you?"

"Yes. Yes, I'll call my Dad. He should be finished work by now."

Sergeant Rickey escorted me out to the front.

A young constable approached. "Sergeant, I have the details here for Simon Lattimer's next of kin."

The name hit me like a physical blow, the blood rushing in my ears. I heard it first without comprehending, then again as an echo in my mind. Simon Lattimer.

I whipped around, shock evident in every part of my body. "Simon Lattimer?" I sounded strange to my own ears. "Did you just say Simon Lattimer?"

The walls of the room contracted. I reached for the counter as the edges of my vision began to blur.

"Do you know Simon Lattimer, Mrs. Craig?"

"Simon Lattimer is my Dad." The words came out barely above a whisper. Then stronger, as if saying it again might somehow change what was coming. "He's my father."

The words hung in the air. A clock ticked somewhere down the hall. A phone rang in a distant office. Then Sergeant Rickey leaned forward, speaking more gently than he had all night.

"Mrs. Craig, come with me."

Sergeant Rickey took me by the arm and escorted me back to the interview room, this time leaving the door open, and settling me into a chair. He took the chair beside mine— not across the table like before. The change in position made my heart pound harder.

The fluorescent light buzzed overhead. A door slammed in the corridor. The ticking clock was impossibly loud.

"Mrs. Craig, I am sorry to have to tell you this," he hesitated, and his hands were tightly clasped. "Your father was struck and killed tonight in a hit and run accident outside L'Aubergine restaurant."

The words didn't make sense. My father was at work. I'd texted him. We were going to have dinner next week.

"There must be some mistake," I heard myself say from very far away. "He's working tonight. He's at..."

"L'Aubergine. Yes. It appeared he was following Dylan out when—"

"No." The word came out sharp, defensive. "No, that can't be, because Dylan was at work. He wasn't at L'Aubergine. He told me he was at work."

"Mrs. Craig—Jude," Rickey leaned forward slightly. "The driver left the scene. But we have witnesses. Security footage. And your husband's vehicle shows clear evidence of the impact."

My fingers had gone numb where they gripped the edge of the table. The room seemed to contract, then expand, the walls breathing in sync with my own ragged breaths. The room tilted sideways.

"Police have apprehended the driver— your husband, Dylan Craig. I'm so sorry, Mrs. Craig. We weren't aware of your connection to the victim until just now."

Connection. The word echoed in my mind. Connection. My father. The victim. Dylan. The fridge. The garage. The lies stretching back weeks, months, years. I could hear my own breathing, too fast, too shallow.

"He knew." The words came out in a whisper. "Dylan knew it was Dad when he... when he came home. He knew the whole time he was screaming at me about the fridge. Blaming me. He knew he'd killed my father."

The reality of my total isolation hit me then. No mother— gone years ago. No siblings. No close friends. Just my father, who'd been trying to protect me.

The lights suddenly seemed impossibly bright. The room seemed to spin on its axis. Dark spots danced at the edges of my vision. I heard Sergeant Rickey as if from underwater, saw his concerned face blur and fade as the darkness rushed in.

When I came to, I was lying on something firm but cushioned— probably the break room couch. Someone had placed a scratchy blanket over me. A paper cup of water sat on a low table nearby. The clock on the wall read 11:47. In less than three hours, my entire world had collapsed.

"Mrs. Craig?" Sergeant Rickey said from somewhere nearby. "Take your time. But when you're ready, we need to go through some formalities. Is there someone we can call for you?"

The question hung in the air. Who was there to call? No one. Dylan had made sure of that— years of subtle isolation, of making my friends uncomfortable until they stopped coming around. Even my work colleagues had gradually stopped asking me to lunch.

"No," I whispered the admission. "There's no one."

I pushed the blanket aside, struggling to sit up. The room swayed slightly, but I forced myself to focus on the institutional grey tiled floor, the hum of the lights, anything concrete and present. When I felt steady enough, I smoothed my hair back with trembling fingers.

"I need to see him." I sounded wrong, distant, like the words belonged to someone else.

Rickey started to speak, probably to tell me it wasn't possible yet, but my mind was already racing ahead, piecing things together with a clarity that felt almost cruel.

"The fridge," I realised, the words spilling out. "He moved it. When he got home. He must have... must have moved it first, then crashed into it. To hide the—" The words died in my throat as the full horror of Dylan's calculated actions hit me.

"We have officers at your house now. Forensics. I have to ask— did you notice any damage to the car? When you went into the garage?"

I closed my eyes, trying to remember. Everything was a blur of Dylan's rage and accusations.

"I... I don't know. I was looking at the fridge, at Dylan, I didn't—"

A horrible thought struck me. "Oh God. If I'd looked at the car instead of following him inside— if I'd seen— maybe I could have—"

"No. Jude, there was nothing you could have done. The evidence shows your father died on impact. And given your husband's state when he arrived home..."

He left the sentence hanging, but I understood. Dylan had been beyond reason. Beyond help. Beyond anything but his own desperate attempt to escape what he'd done.

Chapter 14

John

I'd intended to show her the stringybark grove, hoping its beauty might ease the weight of her memories. But as she spoke, laying bare the worst night of her life, I couldn't bring myself to interrupt for a scenic diversion.

The morning had crept up around us as we walked, neither of us really noticing where the trail was taking us until the familiar shape of the back of Jim's store emerged through the trees. Jude had fallen silent, spent from the telling. The sun had burned off the early morning coolness, but Jude seemed chilled, arms wrapped tight around herself as though demonstrating that she was holding it all together.

I could hear the old bell above Jim's front door chiming again and again as the morning regulars made their coffee pilgrimages. I guided us toward the side entrance— the less-used one that led straight to the chair by the wood stove. Jude followed without resistance, her usual independence temporarily surrendered to exhaustion.

Jim looked up as we entered, that keen gaze taking in Jude's pale face and trembling hands in a single glance. Some people talk with their eyes. Jim was one of them.

Without a word, he moved toward the kettle, his competent efficiency a balm in itself. The chair waited, worn velvet catching the morning light, offering the comfort of familiar things.

* * *

Jude's colour had returned to her cheeks by the time Jim arrived with a pot of tea for Jude, and some refreshing milk for me.

Jude blurted out in an almost-falsetto, "Oh thanks so much Jim! I've just been chewing John's ears off with the worst life stories ever!" She finished with a laugh that bordered on hysteria.

"Well, now," Jim rumbled with a kindly glance my way. "That tea will help, with whatever it is. And our John here has pretty big ears, but he knows how to keep a secret."

I gave Jim a side-eye glance, one eyebrow raised in mock-warning. Jim was lucky he'd known me long enough to get away with the crack about my ears.

A tear was rolling slowly down Jude's cheek as she cradled her warm mug of tea in both hands.

"Oh dear," Jim said, laying a comforting hand on her shoulder. "Some stories, once told, leave you hollow inside— but maybe that's nature's way of making room for new memories where there hadn't been space before. It may hurt now, but you'll feel better for the telling, I'm sure of it."

She smiled thinly at Jim, and then fell silent, pensive.

"I think I'm going to go home, John." Jude pushed herself up from the chair. She'd been sitting so still, so quiet, that I'd almost forgotten she was there. I'd been pretending not to be dozing off by the fire, as I did most mornings after a long walk.

When she spoke, I sort of snored myself awake and then shook my head in embarrassment.

I could tell she didn't want me to walk her home. Sometimes people need space after sharing their darkness, afraid you'll see them differently in the light.

I knew there'd be more to her story, and I was keen to find out the rest, but I wasn't going to pry. She'd tell me in her own time.

* * *

She didn't appear later that afternoon at the Thompson place to watch the sunset. I tried not to worry as I headed back towards Jim's for dinner.

As I approached, I could smell some sort of roast and hoped dinner was almost ready. Mrs. Lynch and Jim sat at the counter, a bottle of wine between them. I pushed through the screen door and settled myself near the table. I wasn't trying to be invisible, but nor was I obtrusive. Jim had the 'CLOSED' sign already up in the window, though it was early.

"So, she finally told someone the whole story," Mrs. Lynch was saying, making circles with her wine glass on the polished wood.

"And she told it to someone who keeps secrets tighter than Fort Knox." Jim glanced across at me standing by the table. "Would've loved to be a fly on the wall for that walk. Been wondering about what went down. Haven't wanted to ask her though. Figured she'd speak up if and when she was ready."

"When Simon was up here last year, he told me that Jude could only ever see the good in that boy— whatever good there was. Apparently Dylan was having affairs behind Jude's back, and Simon had started keeping tabs on Dylan. Getting evidence."

"Getting evidence, for what, in the end?" Jim leaned against the counter. "Newspaper reported that there'd been a confrontation, Simon chasing Dylan out to the parking lot."

"I think they had security footage to support that story," Mrs. Lynch interjected. "They showed Dylan fair and square turning the car, running down poor Simon and then driving off. Just left him to die." She set her glass down on the counter heavily, hard enough to spill some wine over the rim.

"Article I read said he tried to claim it was an accident. That Simon had run out in front of the car." Jim's voice held sadness. "Even tried pinning it on Jude, but they cleared that up pretty fast. So, is he in jail for good then? Or did they give him some lenient sentence?"

"Twenty-five years," Mrs. Lynch remarked. "And good riddance, if you ask me. Apparently there were additional charges for trying to obfuscate the police inquiry."

"Obfuscate, Anne? Have you been playing too much Wordle?" Jim ribbed her.

She flapped the dishtowel at him— somewhat flirtatiously, if I wasn't mistaken. I shifted awkwardly, wondering if I should sneakily exit stage left.

"It was in the newspaper. And Wordle doesn't have such big words as I know, Mr. James the Third."

Mrs. Lynch actually giggled. Definitely flirtatiously. Time to make myself scarce.

Jim smiled at her, refilling her wine glass. I slipped out the back door into the peace of a brisk starry night, thinking about Jude alone in her cottage, finally unburdened of part of her story, but still carrying so much.

Tomorrow, I'd be waiting when she came out for her morning walk. Painful stories take time to tell, and sometimes, healing needs to happen in the silence between chapters.

* * *

I waited at the bench, watching the morning sun climb over the ridge. The winter air had a dry, crisp edge that usually brought Jude out early, thermos in hand.

But the minutes ticked by, and no Jude appeared.

I tried not to fret— after all of the emotional revelations of the past few days, she might just need more rest. I moseyed past the Cooper cottage. The curtains were drawn tight. No smoke from the chimney despite the morning chill. And her ute—

Her little ute wasn't in the driveway. The kitchen window, where she usually left a small gap for fresh air, was firmly shut. Even the potted herbs she kept by the door looked lonely.

Jude was gone.

* * *

I sat there for a long moment, feeling the weight of her absence. Part of me had known this might happen.

The sound of Jim's truck approaching made me turn. He pulled up to the cottage, took one look at the drawn curtains and missing car, and sighed.

"Ah, hell," he muttered, climbing out. "Anne worried this might happen. Said Jude might need some time, having opened up old wounds. Come on, let's go cook up some breakfast."

He clapped me on the back as I lumbered up into the passenger seat, thinking a hot breakfast at Jim's might just cure most of my ills.

* * *

The next few days Jude stayed gone, and those days felt longer than all the weeks before she'd arrived.

I kept to my routines— morning walks to the bench, afternoon chores, evenings at my sunset spot on the ridge. But everything felt hollow without her there to share it. The trails seemed wider somehow, the silence heavier.

In my imagination, even the birds seemed to notice, their sweet songs carrying a questioning tone. I assured them she was coming back, just as Jim assured me.

"She'll be back," he declared on the second day, watching me stare out the window at the empty road. "Probably just has some things to take care of in the city."

I wanted to believe him, but doubt gnawed at me. What if opening up about Dylan and her father had been too much? What if she'd decided The Ridge held too many memories, even from long ago?

Mrs. Lynch was less concerned. "A few days is nothing." She busied herself with arranging fresh scones on the counter. "She's down there getting her affairs in order, mark my words."

"You sound awfully certain," Jim observed.

"I am certain. She isn't running away from anything anymore, she's running *toward* something. There's a difference, Jim James, and you'd know it if you paid better attention. She probably just has to tie off some loose ends."

Jim smiled into his coffee, wisely choosing not to argue.

CHAPTER 15

John

Each morning, I was back at the bench at dawn, same as always. The winter air had a characteristic bite that meant the season was finally starting to turn. Soon, we'd see signs of spring— new growth on the vines, wildflowers pushing through the frost-hardened earth. I wondered if Jude would be here to see it.

The sound of a car engine made my ears prick up, but it was just Old Tom Peterson heading into town for his morning paper. The sun climbed higher, warming the bench where I sat. A blue wren landed nearby, his vivid plumage a splash of colour against the grey of the winter landscape.

When I finally gave up and headed back to Jim's, Mrs. Lynch was already there, humming to herself as she arranged muffins under a glass dome.

One looked a bit misshapen. She peeled the paper wrap off and tossed it towards me, "Banana muffin, John?"

In moments like that, I wondered if she should be my best friend instead of Jim.

"Today," she announced with absolute certainty. "She'll be back today."

"How do you know?" Jim asked, looking up from the hissing espresso machine.

"Because it's been four days— that's how long these things take."

I wanted to believe her. But as the morning wore on with no sign of Jude, doubt crept back in.

And then, just past ten, the bell over the door chimed.

* * *

I'd been dozing by the wood stove, but that spring in those footsteps— I knew before I looked up.

Jude practically danced into the store, dark circles under her eyes that otherwise were lit from within by genuine excitement.

"Well, look who's back," Jim remarked with a wink, already reaching for a mug.

"I'm back," she announced, dropping her bag on the counter. "Where's John?"

I was sort of reluctant to approach, uncertain how Jude would feel after sharing the darkest parts of her life with me and then disappearing for four days. I didn't want her to think I was a threat, that I'd ever use her secrets against her. I didn't know what to expect, but I stood up and sauntered over anyway. All my silly doubts were extinguished when she greeted me with a big smile and threw her arms around my neck.

"John!" she exclaimed, looking me squarely in the eyes. "I have you to thank most of all for getting me through this past week."

She turned to look at Jim. "I think I really hit a turning point after our last walk— and my long talk—"

She broke off mid-sentence as Mrs. Lynch bustled in, a basket of fresh cinnamon scrolls steaming in her arms.

"I saw you drive past." Mrs. Lynch was trying to catch her breath and failing entirely to sound casual. "Thought you might need sustenance."

"Let's dig into these rolls, and I'll tell you all about it."

* * *

We settled around the counter. Jim poured fresh coffee and I positioned myself close enough to listen but not so close as to seem intrusive.

"First things first," Jude announced, pulling a stack of papers from her bag and setting them on the counter with a decisive thwack. "I'm filing for divorce."

Mrs. Lynch clapped her hands together. "Oh Jude, good for you!"

"Bloody time," Jim muttered approvingly.

"Should be straightforward— given everything." Jude said matter-of-factly, like she was discussing the weather rather than ending her marriage. "My solicitor said Dylan will have no legal claim on Dad's estate, which was the main thing I needed to sort out."

She pulled out another document, this one in an official-looking envelope. "I also met with the insurance company. Dad's policy is finally being processed. It took sixteen months, but..." She trailed off, her fingers tracing the edge of the paper.

"That's good news, dear," Mrs. Lynch observed. "Your father would want you looked after."

Jude blinked rapidly. Then she straightened her shoulders and her smile returned.

"And I did something else. Something I'm really excited about."

She pulled out a certificate with a gold seal. "Remember how Dad was a Master Sommelier? And how Mum loved plants? And I studied soil science?"

Jim leaned forward with interest while Mrs. Lynch nodded encouragingly.

"Well, I've decided on a career change. I enrolled in wine studies through WSET. I did the Level 1 certificate yesterday, and I'm starting Level 2 right away. It'll be intense study to catch up, but the Academic Director thinks I can handle it with my background." Jude's words tumbled out in a rush.

"If I can keep up, I might be ready for the Level 4 Diploma program next year— they only have one intake each year, so it'll be tight, but I'm keen to push forward quickly. And—"

"Now that makes perfect sense," Jim interrupted with genuine warmth, reaching across to cover Jude's hand with his. "Your dad would be over the moon about this."

"It's a beautiful way to honour both your parents," Mrs. Lynch added. "Combining your mother's passion for plants with your father's love of wine."

"That's exactly how it feels." She drew in a slow breath. "Like I'm bringing them both with me into this new chapter."

Jim was already moving toward his wine section. "You'll need to taste your way through my collection then. Can't learn about wine without drinking it. Well, you can, but where's the fun in that?"

"I'd love that. But maybe we should start tomorrow. I'm exhausted. Four days of running around Adelaide, dealing with solicitors and insurance companies and then the course— I barely slept."

"You do look a bit knackered, my girl," Jim agreed. "But happy-knackered, if there is such a thing."

* * *

I watched Jude as she chatted with Jim and Mrs. Lynch, noting the animated way she spoke. She did seem happy— lighter somehow, like she'd set down a burden she'd been carrying.

The dark circles under her eyes nagged at me— they spoke of more than just four days of busy activity. And the way she kept touching her forehead, smoothing the skin above her eyebrows for the briefest second, when she thought no one was looking. Maybe I was worrying over nothing. Maybe this was just what emotional healing looked like— messy and exhausting but moving forward anyway.

I wanted to believe that everything was as good as it seemed. That Jude had truly turned a corner, that the worst was behind her. But I still couldn't shake the feeling that something wasn't quite right.

I reached forward and gently touched her hand, trying to offer support without words. She smiled at me, and for a moment I thought maybe I was wrong.

Maybe everything really was going to be okay.

* * *

Andy walked in, shaking the chill from his shoulders.

"Morning all," he said easily, scanning the room. His gaze landed on Jude and lingered just long enough to register surprise. "Oh— hey. You're back."

"Just drove in this morning." Jude was smiling.

"Flat white, Andy?" Jim offered, already setting the coffee maker up to grind. "Jude here was just telling us about her new study plans."

Andy lifted an eyebrow. "Study plans?"

Jude hesitated for half a beat, then placed a protective hand on the papers still stacked on the counter. "I've enrolled in wine studies. WSET. Did Level 1 yesterday and starting into Level 2 right away. I'd like to start Level 4 early next year, so I have a lot of catch-up to do."

"That's fantastic," Andy enthused, a smile spreading across his face.

Jude laughed, a little self-conscious. "Why?"

"Because I can help you study. I do sustainable viticulture consulting, remember?"

Jude nodded slowly. "Right. Of course. I'm hoping to eventually focus on soil health and optimisation. You know, work from the ground up."

"Of course," Andy agreed. "Wine's made long before it gets anywhere near a barrel."

Something in that landed with her.

"Well," he added, "if you're diving into WSET, you'll get plenty of theory. But tasting in context helps too. Understanding why a wine tastes the way it does. I'd be happy to spin you around some of the local wineries."

She smiled, but didn't commit. "That sounds... helpful."

"If you want," Andy said casually, "Nothing formal. Just a drive through the hills."

Jude took a sip of her coffee, buying herself a moment. "We'll see. It's a busy time— Winter Reds this weekend and all that. I'll probably be at half the events just trying to keep up."

Andy was unfazed. "Fair enough. I'll be there too. We'll see each other somewhere along the track then."

"Probably."

There was no disappointment in his expression— just a subtle interest, parked neatly behind patience.

Chapter 16

John

The Winter Reds Festival was everything promised and more. Jim and I headed up in his truck after the morning rush, the old Ram rumbling contentedly as we wound through the hills toward the main festival grounds. The others— Jude, Mrs. Lynch, Diana, and Andy— had opted for the bus tour that would take them to multiple wineries throughout the day.

"You sure you don't want to join them on the bus?" Jim asked as we pulled into the parking area.

I was quite sure. The thought of being cooped up on a bus full of chattering wine enthusiasts for hours made me want to bolt for the nearest trail. Besides, I had my own plans— plans that involved sampling as much of the festival food as possible.

* * *

The festival grounds sprawled across a valley between two ridges, with marquees and wine stalls dotting the landscape like colourful mushrooms after the rain. Wood fires crackled in stone pits, sending up ribbons of fragrant smoke. Live music drifted from a stage at the far end, mixing with laughter and the clink of wine glasses.

A heavy-set woman shimmied her way out in front of the stage, bare arms raised high in the air as her bracelets jangled. Her eyes were slitted to half-mast, her mouth set like she was ready to fight anyone who dared to challenge her on the dance floor. Wine, I privately thought to myself, didn't always have everyone's best interests at heart. But she was having fun, dancing alone and looking tough.

As I moved past the stage, the smell of the food captured my attention.

Gourmet sausages sizzling on grills. Artisan cheese boards with honeycomb and quince paste. Slow-roasted lamb shanks that fell off the bone. Fresh sourdough bread— even better than Mrs. Lynch's, though I'd never tell her that. Local pâtés and terrines. And dessert—oh, the desserts. Mince tarts infused with shiraz. Berry pies with pastry so buttery it melted on your tongue. Cheese platters that could have fed a small army.

I worked my way methodically from stall to stall, sampling nearly everything. Jim laughed and shook his head but didn't try to stop me. "You're going to regret this later," he warned.

I didn't care. I was in heaven.

* * *

By early afternoon, I'd found a spot by one of the large stone fireplaces near the main marquee. The warmth, combined with my absolutely stuffed stomach, created the perfect conditions for a nap. I could hear the music in the distance, smell the woodsmoke and roasting meat, feel the heat radiating from the fire.

My eyes grew heavy. Then closed completely.

* * *

"John. John, mate, come on now."

Jim's voice filtered through the pleasant fog of sleep. I blinked groggily, trying to remember where I was.

"Time to go, buddy. We've got the first Spageddy Western tonight, and folks'll be stopping by the shop soon. We need to get back and open up."

I struggled to sit up, my stomach protesting the movement. Maybe Jim had been right about the regrets.

"Come on, you great lump," Jim prodded me with affection, practically hauling me to my feet. "Let's get you to the truck before you pass out again."

The drive back was a blur. I dozed in the front seat while Jim hummed along to the radio, occasionally chuckling at my food-induced coma.

* * *

Back at the shop, Jim had the fire roaring and several bottles of wine opened by the time the first festival bus pulled up outside. I'd positioned myself in my usual spot by the wood stove, still feeling heavy and sleepy but trying to look alert.

People spilled in— festival-goers flushed from wine and cold air, all talking over one another as they filed out to the side yard. The smell of garlic and tomato followed them through the door, clinging to coats and scarves.

Mrs. Lynch came in first, cheeks pink, eyes bright. Diana and Andy followed close behind.

Then Jude stepped inside. She looked spent.

Not a good kind of tired— not the glow of a long, happy day. Her face was pale beneath the flush of cold air, and she moved painstakingly slow, like someone trying very hard not to draw attention to how unwell they felt.

Andy hovered near her elbow, ready to steady her if needed. "You alright Jude? You look a bit peaky."

"Just tired." The words didn't quite ring true.

She made it as far as the chair beside mine and sank into it. Mrs. Lynch appeared almost immediately with a glass of water, which Jude accepted without comment.

"I barely drank any wine," Jude admitted to me, as if needing to explain her exhaustion. "Maybe half a glass at the second winery. I just... I don't know. I suddenly felt so wiped out."

She pressed her fingers briefly to her forehead, then dropped her hand as if she'd revealed too much.

Jim clapped his hands together from behind the counter.

"Right then! Out we go. Let's get the spaghetti served before the movie starts."

Outside, Jim had transformed the yard into something magical.

A wide canvas screen had been rigged against the old stone wall, lanterns hung from hooks and tree branches, and the firepits were crackling, throwing out warmth and the occasional spark. Adirondack chairs formed loose half-circles around the flames, people settling in with wine glasses and paper bowls full of homemade spaghetti. The smell of tomato and woodsmoke hung thick and comforting in the air.

Jim moved among the guests like a proud ringmaster, handing out fresh-baked sourdough garlic rolls. The first of Jim's Spageddy Westerns was queued up, the opening credits frozen on the screen as people claimed their seats.

Jude settled into the seat beside Andy's, a blanket pulled over her knees despite the warmth from the firepit. The flickering light tempered her features, but also highlighted the shadows under her eyes.

Andy leaned back in the chair, one arm resting on the wide wooden armrest, wine glass dangling loosely from his fingers. He was talking about something wine-related— I could tell by the hand gestures— and Jude seemed genuinely interested, though she didn't add much. Mostly she just listened. I settled nearby, close enough to keep an eye on her.

I suppressed a cringe when Pilar swept in.

"Oh, I was *heartbroken* to miss out on a ticket to this. You know how much I love old cowboy films," she announced to no one in particular, but loud enough to call as much attention to herself as possible.

She perched herself on the arm of Andy's chair, as if it were the most natural place in the world. Her gaze flicked to Jude's wine glass.

"Slow down, Jude," Pilar admonished lightly. "You look like you've had a few already."

Andy shifted. Jude didn't bristle. She didn't apologise either.

"I actually haven't." Then she stopped, listening inward. "But to be honest, I'm really not feeling well."

She stood slowly.

"I think I'm going to head home. I need to catch up on some rest," she told Andy. He tried to get up from his seat, but appeared to be pinned in place by Pilar.

Jude pulled her ticket out of her pocket and held it out to Pilar.

"You can have my ticket."

Pilar's smile came quickly. "Well. If you insist."

Jude turned to me.

"John, would you mind walking me home, please?"

Gladly.

Chapter 17

John

The week following the Winter Reds, Jude threw herself into Level 2 wine studies with an almost frantic energy. She'd offered to volunteer at Shadow's Reserve three mornings a week, spending the rest of her time buried in textbooks and tasting notes.

Mrs. Lynch said it was good to see her so focused. Jim said she was running herself ragged. But I suspected she was sick long before anyone else did. She didn't just have normal tiredness from being busy. This was something else— something that went deeper than too much schoolwork or exhausting festival days.

The headaches started small— or maybe they'd been there all along and she'd just gotten worse at hiding them. A wince and a pause when she stood up too quickly. Fingers pressed to her temples during our shortened morning walks. The way she'd pause mid-sentence, her eyes losing focus for a moment before she'd shake her head and carry on.

"I'm under a lot of pressure," she'd say when I looked at her with concern. "I feel like I'm falling behind, trying to absorb as much knowledge as I can."

By mid-August, she was popping headache pills like they were candy. I'd see her reach for the bottle multiple times a day, washing them down with water and pretending everything was fine. She was often a bit wobbly on her feet— I'd notice her grab the counter at Jim's, or lean heavily against a fence post during our walks.

One morning, a headache came on so suddenly that she crumpled to her knees right there on the trail, a hand pressed hard to her temple. I stayed close, helpless, until the worst of it passed and she could stand again.

"I'm fine," she insisted, her face pale and sweating. "Just came on fast, that's all."

She wasn't fine. And she was starting to snap at me— and others— without reason; sharp words that would fly out and then hang in the air. She'd always apologise later, sometimes in tears, but none of us wanted apologies. We just wanted her to be better.

* * *

Andy noticed too. He'd been coming up to The Ridge more frequently— ostensibly to help Diana get the gingerbread cottage ready for moving in, but he often stopped by Jim's when Jude was there, his eyes tracking her movements with the same concern I felt.

"She doesn't look well," he commented to Jim one afternoon when Jude had gone home to lie down. "Has she seen a doctor?"

Jim shook his head. "Stubborn as they come, that one. Says it's just stress from the studies."

"Those headaches aren't just from stress," Andy stated flatly. "I've seen enough people push through health problems to recognise when something's seriously wrong. I'll have a word to her."

But none of us could force her to seek help.

And Jude, for all her newfound determination to build a new life for herself, was equally determined to ignore what was happening to her body.

* * *

Sometimes she'd come home from Shadow's Reserve early, barely making it through the door before she had to lie down. The room would tilt on its axis, she'd tell me, and the only thing that helped was darkness and stillness. She'd hold down her left eyelid as it flickered and twitched uncontrollably, passing it off as 'just another headache' while I sat beside her, watching the waves of sickness pass.

I'd look into her grey-green eyes and beg her: *Please. Please see a doctor.*

But she'd just brush it off and say she was too busy. The pruning season at Shadow's Reserve was in full swing. The WSET Level 2 exam was coming up. There was always something more important than her own health.

* * *

When enough was enough— when I'd watched her suffer through one headache too many— I walked her straight to Dr. Morrison's office on Finch Street. She realised where I was taking her when we were almost there, and she stopped dead in her tracks.

"John, no."

I kept walking, not looking back.

"John, I'm serious. I don't have time for this."

I reached the doctor's office and stood by the door, looking at her expectantly.

She crossed her arms. "The deal was you could choose the trails we walked. So fine. We're here. But there's no expectation that I have to go in."

I didn't budge.

"Besides," she continued, her voice taking on that edge it got when she knew she was being unreasonable, "I'm too busy to wait around for a doctor."

I stayed planted by the door. She rolled her eyes and walked past me, heading back toward home.

* * *

The next morning, I walked her to Dr. Morrison's office again.

And the morning after that.

And the morning after that.

It became our new routine. Every day, our walk would begin at the bench and end at the doctor's office on Finch Street. I'd stop by the door and look at her expectantly. She knew what I wanted.

Sometimes she'd just keep walking, pretending she hadn't noticed that I'd stopped.

Sometimes she'd make jokes. "You're more persistent than the prize home lottery people, you know that?"

Sometimes she'd get angry. "Mind your own business, John!"

That was the most hurtful— because taking care of my friends WAS my business. Short of physically shoving her through the door, I couldn't force her to seek help. All I could do was show up, day after day, and hope she'd eventually listen.

* * *

Mrs. Lynch cornered me one morning at Jim's.

"I know what you're doing," she declared. "Walking her past Doc Morrison's every day."

I looked away, embarrassed to be caught in my campaign.

"Don't stop," she urged. "That girl needs someone stubborn enough to match her own stubbornness. Keep at it."

Jim agreed. "She'll come around. Just might take some time."

But time felt like something we didn't have much of.

CHAPTER 18

John

September arrived with crisp mornings and the first whispers of spring in the air. The vineyards were still dormant, their gnarled vines awaiting the warmth that would coax them back to life.

Jude was at Shadow's Reserve almost daily now, learning winter pruning techniques and soil management, despite the headaches that sometimes left her bent double among the sleeping vines. The real work— bud burst, flowering, and eventually harvest— was all still months away, but there was always something to learn, something to prepare for the vintage that would come in late summer.

Andy was around more often too. He'd hosted a wine tasting at Jim's, teaching folks to identify different varietals and regions. Jude had attended, and I watched them from my spot by the fire, noting how attentively he watched her, how quickly he'd take her elbow when she swayed.

I tried not to feel threatened by his presence. He was helping her pursue her dream, teaching her things I never could. But I also saw the way he looked at her sometimes— with something more than just friendly concern.

* * *

One morning in mid-September, as we approached Dr. Morrison's office for what must have been the fifteenth time, the door miraculously opened wide. Dr. Morrison himself stepped out, nearly colliding with us. I swiftly moved to hold the door, positioning myself between Jude and escape.

"Oh, Jude! Hello!" Dr. Morrison greeted her. "Lovely to see you. Everything alright?"

Before Jude could respond, he'd ushered her inside with a guiding hand on her shoulder, chatting about the beautiful spring weather. I followed hard on her heels, nudging her toward the reception desk before she could bolt.

She scowled at me and mouthed the words "You set me up, you rotten S.O.B."

But she was half-smiling as she shook her head and turned to the receptionist.

* * *

I let her do all the talking, relief flooding through me as the receptionist reviewed the schedule.

"We have an opening this Thursday at 2 pm. Would that work?"

Jude hesitated, probably thinking of a dozen reasons why Thursday wouldn't work.

"Yes," she meekly agreed. "Thursday at 2. I'll be here."

The receptionist made the note, gave her a reminder card, and we left.

* * *

Outside, I couldn't contain my relief. My whole body relaxed, the tension I'd been carrying for weeks now finally easing. She was going to see a doctor. She was going to get help.

Jude saw my reaction and laughed— her real laugh, the one I hadn't heard in weeks. "You're ridiculous, you know that? Marching me past here every single day like some kind of show pony."

We walked toward home, and for the first time in months, it felt like old times. She talked about the vines at Shadow's Reserve, about Shiraz grapes, about how she couldn't wait to learn to assess ripeness. She told me about Andy teaching her to blind taste, how she was getting better at identifying regional characteristics.

She talked and talked about her studies and her dreams and the funny things that had happened at the vineyard, and I listened with a shy smile, looking eagerly across at her so she knew I was keen.

When we got back to the cottage, she put her arms around me and held on tight.

"Thank you," she whispered into my neck. "For not giving up on me."

I rested my chin on her shoulder, grateful beyond words, and tried not to think about what the doctor might find.

Chapter 19

John

The shop was in a mid-morning lull— the kind that settled in after the coffee rush but before lunch. Jim was wiping down the counter, humming to himself, while Jude sat at the counter with her textbook open, brow furrowed in concentration. I was stretched out by the wood stove, half-dozing, half-watching.

Andy stepped in, pushing the door closed behind him and stretching his shoulders, the smell of sun and road dust following him inside. He nodded at Jim, then noticed Jude.

"Jude! Didn't expect to see you here."

She smiled. "I needed a change of scenery. Got my exam coming up soon."

"It's move-in day, isn't it, Andy? Need some coffee?" Jim offered, already grinding the beans.

"Please and thanks, Jim. Flat white for me and a tea for Mum. You're right, it's move-in day— the truck should be here within the hour."

Jim busied himself at the machine, then frowned. "Where the hell's the milk? I'll have to grab some from the back."

He disappeared through the swinging door, leaving the shop briefly hollowed out— just the three of us, and the tick of the espresso machine cooling down.

Andy shifted his weight. I felt it before I saw it— that restless energy people get when they're about to risk something.

"Jude." He lowered his voice. "Can I ask you something?"

She looked up, a cautious eyebrow raised.

"I know your plate's full," he began, "but I was wondering if you'd like to go to dinner sometime. Just dinner. No vineyards. No study talk."

She didn't answer straight away. Her gaze slid past him, out the front window, then back.

"I don't think I can," she declined. "Not right now."

Andy nodded. He didn't push. Didn't flinch. But something tightened and then was gone again.

"Fair enough," he yielded. "I've been meaning to ask."

"I appreciate that," she replied. And she meant it.

The silence that followed was brief, awkward, and slightly stinging.

Pilar stood partway down the aisle behind the preserves, as still as a hunting cat. I hadn't heard her come in, but she was very much there now, head tilted just enough to hear every word. Andy and Jude didn't see her, but I did.

Jim came back through the door, milk in hand. "Right— crisis averted."

The moment passed.

Andy thanked him, took his coffee, gave Jude a polite smile that didn't linger, and headed back out into the sunshine of the spring day.

Only then did Pilar step forward. She didn't look at Jude. Didn't look at me. She just smiled— small and private— and adjusted the strap of her bag as if something had gone exactly the way she'd hoped.

Jude turned back to her textbook. Jim washed the milk jug and tidied the counter. The shop settled again.

But I stayed alert. Because some things, once overheard, don't stay quiet for long.

* * *

It was Thursday. I'd been waiting outside Dr. Morrison's office for what felt like hours but was probably only forty-five minutes. The afternoon had turned warm, and I'd found a spot in the shade where I could watch the door.

When Jude finally emerged, I knew immediately that something was wrong. Not from her face— her expression was cautiously neutral— but from the way she moved, the paperwork clutched too tightly in her hand, the slight unsteadiness in her step. I stood up as she approached.

"It's fine," she said before I'd even asked. Her response was too quick. "He thinks it's just stress. Going to run some tests to be sure."

Stress. Right.

We started walking back toward the cottage, and I matched my pace to hers— close enough, but not hovering. The paperwork crinkled in her grip.

"He said it's probably nothing. Just ordered some blood work and an MRI to confirm. Nine times out of ten, it's nothing."

But if nine times out of ten it was nothing, that meant one time out of ten it was something.

I wanted to know what he'd said, exactly, word for word. Wanted to know when the tests were scheduled, what they were looking for, what 'probably nothing' actually meant. But Jude was already wound tight as a spring, and she wasn't forthcoming with any further info. So I just walked beside her, letting the familiar route to her cottage ground us both.

Birds trilled wildly somewhere overhead in a cacophony of spring song. Jude didn't seem to hear it. She was somewhere else entirely, trapped in her own head with whatever Dr. Morrison had told her.

We passed Peterson's garden, where the roses were just starting to bloom. Passed the bench by the river where Jude and I had first met, all those months ago. Passed all the familiar landmarks of The Ridge that usually brought me comfort. None of it helped today.

By the time we reached the cottage, Jude's shoulders had hunched forward slightly, like she was carrying something heavy. She hesitated at the porch steps, one hand on the railing, her fingers trembling against the weathered wood.

"Stop looking at me like that, John. It's fine. I'm going to wait for the test results before I worry about anything." She looked brave, but the waver in her voice betrayed her.

I wanted to let her know it would be okay. Wanted to promise her that the tests would come back clear, that this was nothing, that she would be fine. But I'd never lied to her before, and I wasn't about to start now. Instead, I just stayed close as she climbed the porch steps, watching her place each foot, there to steady her if she stumbled.

Inside, she dropped the paperwork on the kitchen table like it might burn her fingers, then moved to the window, staring out at the hills. The afternoon light caught in her red hair, but her face in profile looked pale and drawn.

I settled near the door, giving her space but not wanting to leave. Because whatever this was— stress or something worse— I didn't want her to face it alone.

She shooed me out anyway, saying she needed a nap. I knew some battles weren't worth the fight, so I headed home to Jim's.

Chapter 20

John

I was at my usual spot by the fire when Jude came through the door. Something about the way she moved made me get up and go to her immediately— she had the measured, deliberate pace of someone who'd been put through the wringer. Her exhaustion went deeper than just lack of sleep. She held herself protectively, like any sudden movement might break something.

"Hey John," she whispered, her hand reaching out briefly to touch me before she moved toward the counter.

Her touch was feather-light. Uncertain.

Jim was already reaching for the kettle, and he was cataloguing the same things I was seeing. The pallor of her skin. The pinched look around her mouth. The way she sank onto the stool like her legs had given out.

"Tea?" Jim asked casually, but I heard the concern underneath.

"Please."

I settled back near the fire, but not in my usual relaxed sprawl. Watching. Every instinct I had was telling me to stay alert.

"So," Jim fussed, keeping his hands busy with the tea. "How'd the appointment go yesterday?"

"Dr. Morrison sent me for some tests so I drove down to Mount Barker this morning— blood work and an MRI. Results'll take a few days. But I had a killer headache last night, didn't get much sleep. Feel pretty low, to be honest."

The words hung in the air like smoke.

"You know I'd have driven you down, Jude," Jim reproached as he slid the mug across to her.

She wrapped both hands around it, staring down into the tea. I'd seen her do this before— use the mug as something to focus on, something to do with her hands when her mind was racing somewhere she didn't want it to go.

Diana swept gracefully through the door with Andy trailing behind.

"Oh perfect!" Diana exclaimed. "Jude, I was hoping you'd be here. And John, lovely! Saves me tracking everyone down."

Andy was trying not to look at Jude too obviously, and Jude's shoulders tensed slightly when she heard his voice. She gave him a small smile that looked like it took effort.

"How are you settling in?" Jim asked, and I could hear him trying to shift the mood, make everything feel normal.

"Wonderfully! The cottage is perfect, everyone's been so helpful." Diana beamed at Jim. "Which is actually why I'm here. I want to properly invite you all to dinner tonight— Anne, you, Jude, and of course John. Would you all come? Nothing fancy, just a proper English roast in my new kitchen."

"That sounds lovely," Jim accepted.

"Oh, I don't know—" Jude started, still staring into her tea.

I watched her face intently. She didn't want to go. Wanted to go home, crawl into bed, hide from Andy and whatever was happening to her. But Diana's warm expectation was pulling at her, the same way Mrs. Lynch's kindness always did— making it difficult to say no.

"Please do come, Jude," Diana pressed, and she sounded so kind, so genuine, that Jude's resistance crumbled. "It would mean so much."

Andy shoved his hands in his pockets, still not quite looking at Jude. The awkwardness between them was thick enough to taste.

"Sure," Jude finally agreed. "I'm a bit tired so I'll have a nap first, but dinner would be nice. Thank you."

"Wonderful! Six o'clock then?" Diana was already heading for the door, mission accomplished. "Come on, Andy. We need to stop at the butcher's."

Andy followed, throwing one last glance at Jude that she didn't see because she was still staring into her tea.

The bell chimed as they left, and the silence they left behind felt heavier than before.

Jim moved around the counter, and I suspected he was deciding whether to push or let it be. He was pretending to be casual while worry carved lines around his eyes, and Jude was pretending to be fine while exhaustion and fear pulled at her from every direction.

The afternoon light slanted through the windows, and I thought about dinner at Diana's. Thought about Jude having to smile and make conversation and pretend everything was normal when nothing felt normal anymore. Thought about Andy's new awkwardness and Diana's warm kindness and how sometimes the hardest thing was accepting help when you were drowning.

Jude finally stood, leaving most of her tea untouched.

"I should go. Rest before tonight."

"Good idea," Jim said. "Take it easy. John'll walk you home."

I followed her to the door, propping it with my shoulder for her to pass through. Outside, the spring afternoon was perfect— warm sun, cool breeze, birds singing. The kind of day that usually made everything feel better. But today it just felt like a lie.

Jude paused on the porch, looking down at me with tired eyes.

"I'm okay, John," she muttered. "Really."

I didn't believe her. But I nodded anyway, because sometimes that's all you could do. Let people keep their dignity intact while everything else was falling apart. She walked down the steps and turned toward home, moving with that same cautious deliberation. I walked slightly behind her— far enough that she maintained her independence, close enough that I'd be there if she stumbled.

Once she was safely inside, I headed back to Jim's. He was still standing at the window where we'd left him.

"She's not okay," he said mildly. Not a question.

I didn't disagree. I settled by the fire, staring at the flames and thinking about MRIs and stress and the way Jude's hands had trembled around her tea.

Probably nothing, according to Dr. Morrison.

Probably.

I'd never hated a word more in my life.

* * *

I took up residence in the corner of Diana's kitchen as Andy expertly decanted a bottle of red. The evening had started formally enough— welcoming Diana to the neighbourhood— but Jude became more animated when Andy mentioned the '98 Penfolds he'd brought.

"Ninety-eight was the year Dad won his first international recognition," Jude realised, and for once, mentioning her father brought a smile instead of shadows. "He always told me that year was magical for South Australian reds."

Andy's eyes lit up. "He was right. The climate that year was perfect— just the right balance of rain and sun."

And suddenly they were deep in conversation, the former awkwardness washed away by their mutual interests. I watched as Jude leaned forward in her chair, describing the upcoming exam, telling Andy her theories about soil chemistry, both of them talking over each other in their enthusiasm.

"My background's in environmental science too," Andy was saying. "But I went down the track of sustainable agriculture. These past few years consulting with vineyards, watching how climate change is affecting growing seasons—"

"That fascinates me too," Jude broke in. "How everything connects— the soil, the weather, the vines. I don't know what I'll do with my studies yet, but—"

"You'll find your path," Andy professed with such certainty that Jude blushed slightly.

"Speaking of paths..." He glanced at his mother, widening the scope of the conversation. "I haven't even told Mum yet— I've been interviewing for a new position. With an international consortium – The Reed Group."

Mrs. Lynch was serving up a tray of roast potatoes. "Oh? Reed wines are very well known."

"It's my dream job, really. Been working toward it my whole career." He tried to sound casual, but I could hear the excitement underneath. "A director role. Coordinating sustainable practices across their holdings— California, France, here in Australia. Some other responsibilities too, not sure what all it entails. Won't hear back for a while yet, though."

"That sounds incredible," Jude said, sounding impressed.

Jim raised his glass. "Well then! To new beginnings," he proclaimed. "Diana's move, Andy's interviews, Jude's studies..."

"To new beginnings," everyone echoed.

Chapter 21

John

Every morning the sky exploded in a chorus of raucous laughter as the kookaburras called in the dawn, their wild cackling echoing off the hills. Most of the townsfolk slept right through it— Lord knows how— but for both Jim and me, it was an alarm clock that couldn't be ignored.

Just as I knew the sun would rise about half an hour from that call, I knew Jim would amble down to the shop around the same time and get the fire stoked up before opening. In winter, I'd have wandered out and piled up some firewood ready for the day, but in spring and autumn, I'd always complete my chores the night before so that I could swim the river as the sun was rising.

The river, having only just shed the worst of its winter chill, felt like liquid ice as I dove in from the bank below the town bridge. Momentarily stunned by the freshness, I came up gasping for breath. It would be a short swim, but I had no regrets.

Pulling myself upstream through the silky water with long, smooth strokes, I thrilled to see the sun peeking up over the horizon, beaming down through the tree branches where it could find its way, and casting glinting gems of shimmering light on the surface of the water.

Having covered some distance upstream, I gracefully stretched deep into the water, diving under and rising back to the surface on my back. The sun hit my face and chest as the current lazily drifted me back toward town.

The river had its own moods— I'd learned them all over the years. Today it was playful, the current tugging at my legs like eager hands, but I knew how quickly that could change come the summer storms.

The water was still a bit too chilly to fully enjoy the float, so I turned back over and swam my hardest downstream, streaking through the water like a speeding bullet as my strong shoulders and legs supplemented the pull of the current.

With a splitting grin befitting the beautiful morning, I arrived at Jim's as he came out to sweep the porch.

"Jesus, John— don't tell me you've been swimming this morning."

I actually *had* been swimming, so I couldn't tell him otherwise.

"Go sit by the fire, you'll catch your death of cold if you don't warm up," he grumbled. I could see his breath in the cold morning air.

I never understood why people made ridiculous prophecies that have only the smallest percentage of ever happening. I was healthy and strong, and maybe not so young as I used to be, but hey— none of us were. I'd heard of people swimming in places where the water gets much colder than the Adelaide Hills, and I'm quite sure if they all 'caught their death of cold', people simply wouldn't do it anymore.

As for me, it made my day to dive under that glorious fresh water and swim until my muscles screamed and then float my way back to the bridge.

I burned with annoyance that Jim had tried to tarnish the joy from my first spring swim. Maybe he should try a morning swim sometime. Work off a bit of that winter belly he was lugging around.

I shook off my cattiness as I dried myself in front of the fire— I'll admit it thawed me out and felt pretty damn good. Jim meant well. He just didn't understand that some of us need these subtle moments of challenge, these private victories that remind us we're alive.

Chapter 22

Jude

The text came through just before noon the following Monday: *Can you come in to see Doc Morrison at 2 pm today? – Maree*

I stared at it for a long time, sitting at my little desk with my viticulture notes spread out in front of me, all of them suddenly meaningless.

I'd just had the scans on Friday. Results should have taken *a few* days. Surely they don't count weekends? This was too fast. Or maybe I was catastrophising— reading danger into a perfectly routine message.

My fingers hovered. *Yes, I'll be there.* Send.

Two hours. Two hours to sit here and spiral, or two hours to do something useful. I tried to return to the assignment in front of me but the words swam together. I closed the laptop.

Through the window, I spotted John loping past with his long, lazy stride. I stepped outside and waved, knowing he'd be interested to hear the results were in. When he got to the porch, he looked at my face, a question already in his eyes.

"Doctor's appointment at two," I told him. "I think the results are in."

He turned immediately, ready to go. I laughed.

"It's two hours away!" My protest sounded stronger than I felt. "And John— I'm sorry, but I need to do this one alone. But let's have tea before I go?"

An expression I couldn't read crossed his face— hurt, maybe, or fear. He settled against the post on the top step of the porch while I went to put the kettle on. Understanding, even if it sat wrong with him.

We had tea, the comfort of closeness surrounding us, and then I sent John on his way with a promise to catch up with him later at Jim's.

An hour left to kill, I turned my attention to cleaning the already-clean house. I reorganised the kitchen before I admitted I was doing laps around my own anxiety. Changed my clothes twice before settling on jeans and a t-shirt. As if it mattered what you wore to hear news that was probably nothing.

At quarter to two, I walked to town.

Dr. Morrison's waiting room was empty. Maree, the receptionist, gave me a smile that seemed overly chipper. "Go right in, Jude. He's expecting you."

The walk down that short hallway felt endless.

Dr. Morrison stood when I entered, which seemed odd. Formal. "Thanks for coming in so quickly."

He gestured to the chair opposite him as he settled back into his own. A folder was open on his desk— images I couldn't quite see beneath a scatter of papers.

"The MRI's back," he noted, like he was choosing each word with care. "Jude... it isn't stress."

The air thinned.

"The scan shows a mass," he continued. "A tumour. It's positioned deep in the brain— at the pineal region— extending slightly toward the left frontal midline. That location explains the headaches, the dizziness, the eye symptoms."

He turned the monitor toward me, pointing to a grey swirl, a darker shape that meant nothing and everything all at once. Nothing made sense and yet everything did.

"It's about four centimetres," he confirmed. "Significant enough that we should move quickly."

A tumour. In my brain.

The words existed separately from reality, floating somewhere above my head.

"Is it..." I couldn't finish the question.

"We can't know for sure yet. The scan is suggestive of a glioma, but this MRI can't confirm that. We'll need more detailed tests."

He waited, the uncertainty sitting between us.

"I've already spoken to a colleague of mine in Adelaide. Dr. Sarah Chen. She's a fantastic neurosurgeon. I'd like to send a formal referral to her now, if you agree."

I nodded vaguely, and he continued as though my agreement was a moot point.

"Her team will contact you in the next day or two to schedule a consult and discuss options."

He kept talking— treatment options, timelines. About how catching it now was 'good, actually' because it could be addressed before it grew larger. I heard maybe half of it.

"What happens if I don't treat it?"

"Jude—"

"What happens?"

He was pensive for a moment, then folded his hands, choosing honesty.

"It will continue to grow. The symptoms will worsen. You could develop severe neurological issues— seizures, pressure on the brain that becomes life-threatening. Tumours in the pineal region can block cerebrospinal fluid flow. This isn't something that waits. Eventually..."

He didn't need to finish.

Eventually, it would kill me. The thought hit me like a physical blow.

"So this just happened? No reason?"

"There's rarely a reason. Most brain tumours aren't caused by anything you did or didn't do. They're biologically random. A terrible kind of luck."

Terrible luck. A lightning strike inside my skull.

He watched me thoughtfully. "Jude, are you alright?"

Was I alright? No.

"How long do I have? To decide about treatment, I mean?"

"Well, from my discussion with Dr. Chen, we're talking days, not weeks. The location makes timely intervention important."

"I need to go." I stood abruptly, the chair legs scraping on the hardwood floor.

"Jude, I know this is a shock, but—"

"I need to go."

He handed me a folder filled with brochures and printouts and words I couldn't yet face.

"Call me if you have questions. Anytime." He followed me to the door.

"And Jude— this is treatable. We've caught it early enough to make a real difference. You're young, you're otherwise healthy. There's every reason to be optimistic."

I nodded again as I walked quickly away, and then I was in the endless hallway and then the waiting room and then out into the glary afternoon where everything looked the same except nothing was or ever would be again.

I stood on the corner for a long time, staring at the folder in my hands.

Tumour.

Four centimetres.

Neurosurgeon.

Random.

Random.

Terrible luck.

I walked at a fair clip, taking no notice of my surroundings— not home, not to Jim's, where both Jim and John would be waiting for an update, but to the river trail. I needed to be somewhere I could think without anyone watching.

I needed to walk.

To think.

To figure out what the hell had happened to the life I woke up with this morning.

And I needed to do it alone.

Chapter 23

Jude

Thankfully, the river trail was quiet, as I suspected it would be in the mid-late afternoon— too late for the morning walkers, too early for the after-work ones. Just me, the hush of water over stones, the creak of old gums, and a breeze threading through the undergrowth.

I walked without any real plan, letting my feet follow the paths John had shown me over the past few months. The bend where the river carved out deep, cold pools. The track that climbed toward the ridge.

Brain tumour.

The words echoed, no matter how many steps I put between myself and the doctor's office.

The past year had been the slow rebuilding of a life I barely recognised anymore. Losing Dad. Starting over after Dylan. Moving here. Starting school. Making friends. Letting myself believe that maybe—just maybe—I could plant something new and watch it grow.

And then this.

My phone buzzed. I didn't look. Probably Jim checking on me, or maybe Anne. I couldn't handle their concern. Couldn't handle saying *anything* out loud yet. Silence was easier. Distance was easier.

The trail steepened. My legs burned. My lungs worked harder. That was a pain I understood— honest, predictable, physical. Nothing like the chaos inside my head.

The unfairness of it all hit in waves. I was finally starting to live again, and now a four-centimetre accident of biology was lodged in my brain, threatening to take everything I'd only just reclaimed.

A random mutation. A cosmic roll of the dice.

By the time I reached the high ridge, my vision pulsed at the edges. I stopped, hands braced on my knees, waiting out the rising tide of fear.

I wasn't dying today. That was something.

But the road ahead— surgery, treatment, uncertainty— loomed like a cliff edge.

I straightened, wiped my face, and kept walking until the trees thinned and the overlook opened up. The Thompson place lay below, its ruined stone walls glowing in the afternoon light. I loved this view, and was grateful that John shared it with me— rows of vines, a ramshackle old house, the long-abandoned garden. I'd planned to ask Jim more about the place— I had an idea for a school project that I was keen to explore.

Now that idea felt like it belonged to someone else. Who plans projects with a tumour in their brain? Who plans anything?

I leant hard against the log railing, the folder from Dr. Morrison still dangling from my hand. I should read it. I should look at the printouts. I should do a lot of things.

Instead, I stared at the shifting light over the valley.

My phone buzzed again. I almost ignored it— until I saw the number.

An Adelaide number. Dr. Chen's rooms.

The voicemail icon lit up. A second later, a text arrived:

This is Dr. Chen's office. We'd like to schedule a telehealth consultation for tomorrow morning. Please call us back when you can.

There it was. The next step. The part where everything became real.

I locked my phone and tucked it into my back pocket.

For a long time, I felt nothing but numbness. Then— slow, rising heat under the ribs— anger.

Not panic. Not grief.

Anger.

At my body for ambushing me. At chance for choosing me. At the years I'd spent afraid to want anything, only to be punished the moment I started wanting again. At wishing I could stick my head in the sand and pretend this wasn't happening. That I didn't have to deal with this invasion.

And beneath the anger, equally present— determination.

I'd rebuilt a life from nothing once. I could do it again, even with this looming over me. Even with a tumour in my brain.

I stood, legs stiff, and called Dr. Chen's office back, accepting an appointment over Zoom for 8:30 the following morning. They weren't mucking around with long wait times.

I started back down the trail. The sun was starting to sink— I'd been up here longer than I realised.

By the time I reached my cottage, I'd made a decision. I wouldn't think about any of it until tomorrow. Tonight, I wanted one more evening of being simply Jude— the woman studying wine, walking ridgelines at sunset, imagining a future she might still claim.

And tomorrow morning, I'd talk to Dr. Chen. Tomorrow, the real fight would begin.

I mounted the porch steps, determination settling into my bones with weight and clarity.

* * *

I'd spent the night rehearsing how I'd tell them. Practised the words in my head until they lost all meaning. Brain tumour. Surgery. Adelaide. Simple facts, cleanly delivered.

But when morning came, I couldn't do it.

I couldn't walk into Jim's store and watch their faces change. Couldn't bear the way John would stare at me with his big, concerned eyes. Anne would immediately start problem-solving, and Jim would start offering help with everything, and Andy would look at me like I was broken.

So I stayed home. Didn't meet John for our morning walk. Didn't show up at the store for coffee.

Just me and my laptop and Dr. Chen's face on the screen, talking about surgical approaches and recovery timelines and statistics I couldn't quite process.

By midday the following day, I knew I couldn't hide forever. The walls of the cottage were closing in, and I needed to see faces that didn't know. Needed to be normal before the news made that impossible.

I walked to Jim's slowly, trying to arrange my expression into something neutral. Something that wouldn't give me away.

John was on the porch before I'd even reached the steps. Of course he was. He'd probably been watching for me for two days, worry written into every line of his body. His eyes searched my face with an intensity that made me want to turn around and run back home.

Not yet, I thought. I'm not ready yet. But before I could figure out what to say, I heard Andy's whoop of joy burst through the open door.

"Guess what? I just got a call— The Reed Group wants me in Adelaide next week to discuss an offer!"

I paused in the doorway, John beside me, and took in the scene. Andy practically vibrating with excitement. Diana beaming at her son. Anne clapping her hands together like this was the best news she'd heard all year.

"Three months minimum in Napa Valley, then straight to France. Can you believe it?"

"Oh Andy, that's wonderful!" Anne congratulated him with genuine happiness. "We were all hoping you'd hear good news for your dream job!"

The contrast was so stark it was almost funny. Andy's world expanding. Mine contracting to the size of a four-centimetre mass.

I felt John shift beside me, his attention split between the celebration inside and whatever he was reading on my face. I shook my head slightly— not now, please, not now— and stepped through the door.

"I really wasn't sure," Andy was saying. "They have very specific ideas about implementing their sustainability program. They need someone who understands both the agriculture and the business side—"

"Which you do," Diana interjected proudly.

I stood there watching them, and something twisted in my chest. Not jealousy exactly. More like grief for the version of myself who could have been purely happy for him. Who wasn't carrying news that made everything else feel impossibly small.

"The timing though," Andy ran a hand through his hair, finally noticing me in the doorway. "I hate leaving just as you're getting settled, Mum."

Jim's eyes met mine, trying to read me the same way John had. Trying to figure out if this was the moment to ask about my appointment, about my results.

"Well, if they want you in Adelaide next week, we'd better celebrate properly," Anne announced. "Jim, we'll fire up the outdoor oven this weekend. And Jude! Perfect timing— you can help us plan a proper send-off for Andy."

I pulled my expression into something that resembled a smile. "That's wonderful news, Andy. Really wonderful." I opened my arms to give him a hug.

Secretly, I was proud that I sounded normal. A small victory.

"Congratulations," I added, and meant it. Whatever was happening in my life, Andy deserved this. Deserved his excitement and his dream job.

"Coffee?" Jim asked me, already reaching for a cup.

"Tea, actually." My hands trembled slightly as I moved toward the counter. "Just tea."

I could feel John's eyes boring into me, concerned. Could feel Jim's watchful attention as he put the kettle on. Could feel the weight of their worry pressing against the mask I was trying to hold in place.

Andy was still talking— something about vineyard visits in Burgundy— but the words washed over me, unheard. I focused on breathing. On keeping my hands from trembling. On not letting anything show.

Just a little longer, I told myself. Just get through this conversation, drink your tea, go home. You don't have to tell anyone today. Tomorrow, maybe. Or the next day. When you've had time to process. When you know exactly what you're facing.

The kettle whistled, and I wrapped my hands around the mug Jim placed in front of me, grateful for something to hold onto.

Chapter 24

Jude

My cottage had become a war room of sorts— papers spread across every surface, colour-coded folders, lists upon lists. My laptop sat open to three different tabs: the WSET exam guidelines, Dr. Chen's surgical instructions, and a spreadsheet I'd made tracking everything I needed to accomplish in the next forty-eight hours.

Two more days to hold my life together before it all fell apart. I'd started on a course of steroids to reduce swelling before the surgery, and somehow, they made the headaches recede. In some small way, I was feeling confident that I could do this.

Through the window, I saw John making his way up the drive. Right on schedule— he'd been stopping by more frequently since I'd seen the doctor, but not disclosed the results. Guilt twisted in my stomach, but I pushed it down.

"Hey." I opened the door. "Sorry I've been scarce. Exam prep is killing me."

He looked at me with those knowing eyes, and for a moment I thought he could see right through me. But he just stood there, patient as always.

"Feel like a quick walk before I get back into studying?" I asked, even though the last thing I needed was time away from my textbooks.

We walked for an hour, then stretched out on the porch swing while I pretended to focus on my viticulture notes. In truth, I was running through the mental checklist again:

Thursday afternoon: more scans. Friday morning: Level 2 exam. Friday afternoon: Hospital admission and blood work. Saturday morning: Surgery.

Then recovery. However long that takes.

Tell no one.

Except— could I really tell no one?

The thought had been nagging at me. What if something went wrong? What if I didn't wake up from the surgery? Would they just wonder where I'd gone? Would John sit at that bench every morning, waiting for me to show up?

My stomach churned. I looked up to find John watching me with concern. I'd been staring at the same page for ten minutes.

"Sorry. Just tired. This pinot noir section is dense." I forced a smile. "I should probably get back to it though. Exam's coming up and I'm nowhere near ready."

He stood reluctantly, giving me one last searching look before heading down the drive. I watched him go, my throat tight.

When he disappeared from view, I pulled out my phone and stared at it. I had to tell someone.

Not John— it'd break his heart, and I didn't want him to worry. Not Andy— he had his own stuff going on. Not Anne— she'd tell everyone, organise a support brigade, make a whole production of it.

Jim.

The thought settled with a kind of inevitability. Jim, who'd become something like a father figure. Jim, who could keep a secret. Jim, who'd cover for me while I disappeared for a couple of weeks.

I looked at the clock. Quarter past five.

John would be heading up to the Thompson place for sunset any minute now and Anne usually dropped in after Pokey's closed up, bringing dinner to share with Jim. That gave me maybe forty-five minutes.

Now. It had to be now.

Before I could talk myself out of it, I headed for town, walking fast.

The decision crystallised with each step— I couldn't do this completely alone. Not because I needed emotional support— I could handle that part. But because someone needed to know. Someone needed to be able to tell people I was okay, that I'd be back, that they shouldn't worry.

Someone needed to lie for me.

By the time I reached Jim's, the sun was sinking lower.

Perfect timing.

This was it. I was about to share the secret I'd been guarding.

And once I did, there was no taking it back.

* * *

I stood outside for a minute, watching through the window as Jim wiped down the counter. The "CLOSED" sign was already up, the evening settling into that golden hour before dusk.

I could still turn around. Go home. Keep this to myself a little longer.

Dr. Chen's words kept circling: Surgery scheduled for Saturday. We need to move quickly. She hadn't specifically used the word 'urgent', but everything about it seemed to be.

My hand was on the door handle before I'd consciously decided to move. I entered and Jim looked up, surprised. Then he saw my face, and the cloth in his hand stilled.

"Hey, love. Everything alright?"

I closed the door behind me. Locked it. My hands were shaking.

"Jude?"

"Jim, I need to tell you something. And I need you to promise you won't tell anyone. Not Anne, not John. No one."

He came around the counter slowly, trying to read what was coming. Trying to prepare himself.

"Jude—"

"Promise first." I wrapped my arms around myself, holding everything in. "Please."

"Alright. I promise. Whatever it is—"

"I have a brain tumour."

The words left my mouth and hung there between us, solid and terrible. Saying them out loud made them real in a way they hadn't been when it was just me and Dr. Morrison, or me and Dr. Chen's face on a screen.

Jim's face paled. He sat down heavily on the nearest stool, one hand gripping the counter like he needed something solid to hold onto.

"The MRI showed a mass. Four centimetres." I was talking too fast, words tumbling over each other, but I couldn't stop. "I've been referred to a neurosurgeon in Adelaide— Dr. Chen. I had a consultation yesterday. They want to move pretty fast. The surgery is scheduled for Saturday morning."

"Jude—"

"I'm writing my Level 2 exam Friday, then booking into the hospital that afternoon." I took a breath, tried to slow down. "Recovery will be a week, maybe two in hospital, then I'll probably need some treatments depending on what they find. But you're the only one I'm telling, and I want you to stick to my story, okay? I'm just going to Adelaide for my exam and to take care of some other business. Maybe getting a jump start on Level 3. Okay, Jim?"

"You can't—" Jim stood, moved toward me. "You can't go through this alone—"

"I'm not asking for permission, Jim." My voice cracked, and I felt the tears threatening. "I'm telling you because someone needs to know. Just in case. In case something goes wrong. In case I don't wake up. Someone needs to be able to tell people where I went. What happened."

The look on his face nearly undid me. Horror and love and helplessness all mixed together.

"Christ, Jude."

"I hate asking you to lie for me." The tears were coming now, hot and fast, but I pushed through. "But when people ask where I am, you tell them Adelaide. Wine exam. Some vineyard visits, maybe. Extra coursework. Whatever sounds believable."

"Why?" he asked roughly. "Why do this alone? Why not let us help you?"

"Please." I was begging, tears streaming down my face, all my composure gone. "Please, Jim. I know what I'm asking. I know it's not fair on you. But I need this. I need to do this my way. Just... please just promise you'll cover for me. That's all I'm asking."

"What about John?"

The question hit like a physical blow.

"Especially not John." I tucked my chin down onto my chest, looking at the floor instead of Jim. "He already worries too much. I can't— I won't burden him with this."

"Jude, love, it's not a burden—"

"Jim, I can't—" And there it was, the truth I'd been trying not to look at. "I can't handle everyone's worry and their questions and their pity. I can't be that person, Jim. The sick one. The one everyone tiptoes around."

I was crying in earnest now, all the control I'd been maintaining for two days dissolving. "I just got my life back. I just started feeling like myself again, like maybe I could have a future, and now—"

The silence stretched between us. I watched him wrestling with it— the urge to argue, to tell me I was being foolish, to insist that people who loved me had a right to be there. But something in my face must have convinced him. Or maybe he just understood that this was the only way I could face it— on my terms, with my control intact, even if that control was an illusion.

"What about Andy?" he tried.

I shook my head. "He's leaving for California next week. There's no point in—" I couldn't finish. "This is my fight, Jim. Mine."

"Alright." He sounded defeated. "I'll cover for you. Adelaide, wine exam, extra coursework."

"Thank you." The words came out as a sob.

And then Jim was there, closing the distance between us, pulling me into a hug. I let myself collapse against him, this man who'd become something like a father, and cried into his shoulder.

"You listen to me. You're coming back better than ever. You hear me? You're going to beat this thing, and you're coming back healthy, okay, my girl?"

I nodded against his chest, unable to speak.

"And when you do come back," he continued, "you're going to let us help you through whatever comes next. No more doing everything alone. Deal?"

"Deal," I whispered.

We stood there for a long time. Through the window, I watched the daylight fade, making everything look backlit by the glow. I could hear normal evening sounds. Everything was normal, but everything would be different now.

"When do you leave?" Jim asked finally.

"Thursday midday. I'll drive down, get some pre-surgery scans, get settled, try to sleep before the exam."

"Call me. Keep me posted on everything. Anytime, Jude. Even just to hear a friendly voice. And Jude?" He held me at arm's length, looking me in the eyes. "You're not doing this alone. Even if you think you are. I'll be there in spirit, every minute. Understood?"

"Understood."

I pulled away, wiping my eyes, trying to compose myself. My face felt hot and swollen.

"I should go. Before John gets back from sunset."

"Right." Jim walked me to the door, unlocked it.

"Jude—"

I turned back.

"You're one of the bravest, strongest people I've ever known. Your dad would be so proud of you."

The words hit something deep inside me. My Dad. Who'd died trying to protect me. Who'd never know about this, never know what happened next.

I didn't trust my voice, so I said nothing more and slipped out into the twilight.

The walk home felt longer than it should have. My legs were weak, my whole body wrung out from finally letting someone in. But underneath the exhaustion was something else.

Relief.

I wasn't completely alone anymore. Jim knew. Jim would cover for me. Jim would be there if something went wrong.

It wasn't the same as telling everyone. Wasn't the same as accepting help on their terms. But it was something.

I made it home just as full dark fell, and sank onto my porch swing, watching the stars appear one by one. I closed my eyes and let the night settle around me, holding onto Jim's words like a lifeline.

You're coming back.

I had to believe that.

Chapter 25

John

Jude was gone and something was wrong with Jim.

I'd known him long enough to read the signs— he was keeping himself way too busy, measuring coffee beans with unnecessary precision, and whistling while he worked. Not to mention, he wouldn't quite look at me.

That was the real tell. Jim always looked me in the eye. Always.

But not today. And, I realised in retrospect, not yesterday.

I'd been watching him since I got back from my morning walk, and he'd found a dozen reasons to be anywhere in the store except near me. Now he was fussing with the wine display, moving bottles from one shelf to another for no apparent reason.

Instead of settling into my usual spot out back, I took up a space at the counter and just waited.

Minutes ticked by. Customers came and went. I didn't move. Just watched him with what I hoped was a pointed stare.

Finally, he glanced my way, caught my eye, and immediately looked away again. "What?" he asked, too casually. "Why are you looking at me like that?"

I didn't say a word.

"I'm not doing anything," he protested, turning back to the wines. "Just tidying up. Place gets messy, you know how it is."

The place was immaculate. We both knew it. I shifted slightly, cocking my head to the side, making sure he could see me in his peripheral vision. Unblinking. Patient.

"John, honestly." He moved to the counter, started wiping it down even though he'd already done that twice. "You're being weird."

Was I though? Or was *he*?

He glanced at me again. I widened my eyes and tilted my head back. The universal sign for 'I know you're hiding something.'

"I'm not hiding anything!"

The protestation was too quick, too loud. I raised one eyebrow— a skill I'd perfected over the years specifically for moments like this.

Jim threw down the cloth with a frustrated sigh. "Fine. Fine! You want to know? Jude's gone to Adelaide."

I waited. There was clearly more.

"She... had her wine exam this morning."

That made sense. She'd been studying hard. But it didn't explain why Jim was acting so strange. I kept mum, watching him with patient eyes.

"And she has some other business. Maybe extra coursework. Could be gone a couple weeks."

A couple of weeks seemed a long time, but that still didn't explain Jim's behaviour.

"That's it. That's all I know." He turned back to his unnecessary tidying.

I didn't buy it for a second. I got up from my chair and moved closer, positioning myself directly in his line of sight.

"Oh, for Christ's sake." Jim ran a hand through his hair. "You're relentless, you know that?"

I knew. It was one of my better qualities.

"John, I can't—" He stopped himself, looked at me properly for the first time since I'd gotten back. Something in his face made my chest tight. "She made me promise not to say anything."

There it was. The truth trying to claw its way out.

"It's not my secret to tell," he protested. "I made her a promise."

I understood promises. I understood loyalty. But I also understood when something was seriously wrong, and every instinct I had was screaming that this was wrong.

I kept looking at him. Steady. Unrelenting.

"God, you're good at this," Jim muttered. "How do you do that? Just sit there and make a person feel like they've committed war crimes?"

Practice.

The silence stretched out. I knew he was wavering, the weight of whatever secret he was carrying pressing down on him. He wanted to tell me. Needed to tell someone. I just had to wait him out.

"She's going to kill me," he lamented, slumping into the chair opposite me. "Actually kill me. You can't tell her I told you anything."

I stared at him solemnly. Whatever this was, Jude wouldn't hear from me that Jim'd spilled the beans.

Jim looked at me for a long moment, then sighed— a deep, exhausted sound that seemed to come from his bones.

"The wine exam is real," he acknowledged. "She really did take it this morning. But that's not the only reason she's in Adelaide."

I leaned forward, every muscle tense.

"The rest—" He was clearly wrestling with how much to say. "No. The rest isn't my story to tell, John. I gave her my word. But I will say, when she comes back, she's going to need all of our support. So be ready."

I made a frustrated sound— the closest I could come to expressing that this was ridiculous, that if something was wrong with Jude I had a right to know.

"I know you're worried. I'm worried too. But she needs to do this her way. And part of that is trust." He stopped, choosing his words. "She needs you to trust that she'll be okay. That she'll come back."

Be okay? Come back? As if there were a question of whether she would? The fear must have shown on my face because Jim leaned forward, put his hand on my shoulder.

"She's coming back, John. I promise you that. She's just got some things to take care of, and she needs to do it alone. It's killing me too, mate. But we have to respect her wishes."

I wanted to argue. Wanted to demand the full truth. Wanted Jim to take me to Adelaide right now to make sure she was alright.

But something in Jim's eyes stopped me. This wasn't just about keeping a promise. This was about giving Jude something she desperately needed— space to handle whatever she was facing on her own terms.

Even if it was torture for the rest of us.

I sat back, the tension draining out of me. Not satisfaction— I still didn't know what was really happening— but acceptance. Jim had told me as much as he could. As much as he would.

"Thank you," Jim said. "For understanding. Even if neither of us understand at all."

That about summed it up.

"She'll be back in two weeks. Maybe less." He trailed off. "And then we'll see."

I turned away slowly and headed out to the back room. My mind was racing, and I needed to arrange my thoughts. Two weeks in Adelaide. For a wine exam and whatever else.

Jim's face when he was telling me, like he was trying to convince himself as much as me. The way Jude had been lately— I couldn't help but think something had gone very wrong with those medical tests.

But if she needed to face it alone, then all I could do was wait. And trust that Jim would tell me if things got bad enough that I needed to know.

Chapter 26

John

It was late on Saturday afternoon, and both the store and the town had been abuzz with visitors all day. Jim had just started to wind down and sat down at the counter with a cuppa when Mrs. Lynch bustled in, and I knew she meant business.

"Jim James," she said pointedly, hands on hips. "We need to talk."

"Afternoon, Anne." Jim was too casual, not even looking up from his phone. "Coffee?"

"Don't you 'afternoon Anne' me." She marched up to the counter. "What is wrong with John?"

I raised my head, looking at her in surprise. I'd been hanging around Pokey's more than usual, trying to assess whether she knew anything about Jude, but otherwise, I didn't think there was anything wrong with me.

"What do you mean, what's wrong with *John*?"

"He's been acting strange. Coming into Pokey's, just standing there staring at me, then leaving without a word."

Jim glanced at me, and I held his gaze. Tell us.

"He's worried about Jude," Jim stated flatly. "Aren't we all? She's down in Adelaide for her exam—"

"Which was yesterday," Mrs. Lynch interrupted. "I've tried calling her twice this morning to see how it went. No answer."

Jim's hand moved toward his phone, then stopped. I saw it. Saw the way his fingers twitched, the way he had to force himself not to check it again.

"She's probably just busy—"

"Jim." Mrs. Lynch leaned across the counter. "What do you know?"

"I don't—"

"Don't lie to me. I've known you for forty years. You're terrible at it." She glanced at me, then back at Jim. I moved around the counter to stand beside Mrs. Lynch— a united front, to which Jim was going to have to answer.

"This is ridiculous," Jim tried. "I already told John I wasn't hiding anything—"

Mrs. Lynch started listing facts, cutting through Jim's denials. "Her exam was yesterday at nine in the morning. Even if she celebrated after, even if she stayed up all night drinking every wine that appeared on her exam, she'd have answered my calls by now. Unless something else is going on."

She studied Jim's face closely.

"What do you know, Jim?"

I watched Jim look between us— Mrs. Lynch with her no-nonsense glare, me with my unwavering, unblinking gaze.

Please be okay. Please be okay.

The thought wasn't mine— it was Jim's— but it was written all over his face.

"Jim," Mrs. Lynch insisted. "You have to tell us."

I moved even closer, and now we were both right there. Jim's defences were crumbling. I could see it happening, see him realise he couldn't keep lying to us.

"Promise me. Promise me this doesn't leave this room. Not until she's ready to tell you herself."

Mrs. Lynch's face went pale. "Jim, what is it? What happened?"

"Promise first."

"Promise," Mrs. Lynch agreed.

Whatever it was, I promised too.

"The exam was real. She did take it." He hesitated, and I felt my whole body tense, bracing for whatever was coming. "But that isn't the only reason she went to Adelaide."

The silence stretched. Mrs. Lynch gripped the counter.

"She has a brain tumour."

The words hit me like a physical blow.

"Four centimetres. They found it on the MRI." Jim sounded far away. "She's in surgery right now. Started at seven this morning. At the Royal Adelaide Hospital."

Brain tumour. Surgery. Right now?

Mrs. Lynch's hand went to her throat. "In surgery? Right now? And she went alone?"

"She made me promise not to tell anyone. Needed to do it her way." Jim was looking at me now, and guilt was written all over his face. "I'm sorry. I wanted to tell you. Both of you. But I gave her my word."

I couldn't move. Couldn't breathe. Jude was in surgery. Someone was cutting into her brain. Right now. While I'd been standing here in Jim's store, running errands, worrying about Jim's silence, she'd been on an operating table.

"How long—" Mrs. Lynch couldn't finish.

"The surgery could take anywhere from ten to twelve hours. Apparently it's deep in the brain, delicate. They have to go slow." Jim looked at his watch. "Could be a few more hours before we hear."

The sound that came out of me was small, wounded. I couldn't stop it. It turned into a low moan as Mrs. Lynch put her arms around me and pulled me into a hug.

"She promised she'd call me as soon as she could. Might be this afternoon. Could be tonight. I don't know."

Mrs. Lynch sank onto a stool. "Ten to twelve hours. Oh God, Jim."

I stayed standing, but barely. My legs felt wrong. Everything felt wrong.

Jude had known. Had known for days— maybe longer. Had still studied, taken her exam yesterday, then went to the hospital and let them cut into her brain. And she hadn't told me. Hadn't let me be there. Hadn't let any of us be there.

"Dr. Chen is supposed to be very good," Jim was still talking, but the words washed over me. "Oh, God, I can't believe I gave away her secret." He dropped his face into his hands.

Mrs. Lynch snaked a hand across the counter and held tightly onto Jim's wrist, a solitary tear rolling down her cheek.

I moved to the cold wood stove and sat in my usual chair, statue-still. If I moved, something would break. If I let myself think about Jude on an operating table, about what could go wrong, about how I should have known, how I should have made her tell me—

No. Just sit. Just wait.

The rest of the afternoon crawled by like something dying.

Mrs. Lynch made tea. Nobody drank it. Jim checked his phone, and checked again. I stared at nothing and thought about Jude.

Thought about the morning walks we'd taken. How the corners of her eyes crinkled when she smiled. How the melancholy she brought with her to The Ridge had thawed through camaraderie and stunning mountain vistas. I thought about the sunset spot where she'd found me that first evening and I'd been so awkwardly rude, following her home. The way her eyes had looked when she'd stumbled on the trail, when she'd pressed her fingers to her temples and thought nobody was watching.

The clock on the wall ticked, each second feeling like an hour.

At six-fifteen, Jim's phone rang.

He nearly dropped it, hands fumbling. "Jude?"

"Mr. James?" A woman's voice, professional. Not Jude.

My whole body went rigid.

"This is Nurse Avery from the Royal Adelaide Hospital. I'm calling on behalf of Judith Lattimer."

Jim's face had gone white. "Is she—"

"The surgery is complete. It took just over ten hours, but Dr. Chen was very pleased with how it went. Judith is in recovery now— still very groggy from the anaesthesia, but her vitals are stable."

Jim sagged against the counter. Mrs. Lynch grabbed his arm. I stood up, moving closer. Mrs. Lynch pulled me closer, roughly rubbing my arm. "It's good news, John. That's good news."

"Can we speak to her?" Jim asked.

"Not tonight, I'm afraid. She's being monitored closely in the ICU. She's sedated and comfortable. But she did ask me to let you know as soon as the surgery was over. She's in good hands here, no need to worry."

Mrs. Lynch was crying now, tears streaming down her face. I felt something loosen in my chest— not relief exactly, but the absence of crushing fear.

"When can we visit?" Mrs. Lynch demanded.

"Tomorrow morning at the earliest, but only once she's moved to a regular ward. Family only for the first forty-eight hours. You can call in the morning. Are you family?"

I watched Jim look at Mrs. Lynch, then at me.

"Yes," he answered firmly. "We're family."

Chapter 27

John

I didn't sleep.

Couldn't sleep.

By the time the first rays of sun peeked over the horizon, I was already at Jim's truck, standing by the passenger door.

Waiting.

It was a beautiful morning. I didn't care.

Jim appeared on the porch with his broom, saw me, and sighed.

"Mate," he said. "Visiting hours don't start until ten."

I didn't move.

"Tell you what," Jim bargained, unlocking the truck. "Make yourself useful and deliver this bag to the Tates' place. Then we'll go. Deal?"

Every fibre of my being wanted to refuse. Wanted to climb in that truck and not move until we were driving to Adelaide.

But Jim's face said he needed me to do this. Needed the routine, the normalcy, the sense that life was still continuing even though everything had changed.

So I carried the bag to Mrs. Tate's place, dropping it off neat and quick. Mrs. Tate commented on the weather, about how nice the day looked. I barely heard her. By the time I got back, Jim was tucking a thermos of tea and some of Mrs. Lynch's scones into the truck. Her handbag was on the floor.

I scrambled into the middle seat before Jim had even finished loading, sitting tall, my head nearly touching the ceiling, staring straight through the windscreen.

Adelaide. We were going to Adelaide.

To Jude.

Mrs. Lynch hurried over, and then we were three across in the bench seat— Mrs. Lynch by the window, me buckled snug in the middle, Jim driving.

"Traffic shouldn't be too bad on a Sunday." Mrs. Lynch started talking as we pulled onto the highway. "Though the roadworks near Stirling might slow us down."

I didn't respond. Couldn't. All my attention was focused forward. Adelaide. Hospital. Jude.

"I brought some toiletries for her," Mrs. Lynch continued. "And a change of clothes. Hospital gowns are so dreadful, and once she's feeling better—"

She trailed off. Jim said nothing. I said nothing.

The silence felt right. Words would have been wrong.

"Jim, you'll need to watch the speed limit through Crafers. They're always sitting there with the radar guns—"

"Anne," Jim chided gently.

"I'm just saying—"

"I know." His hands were tight on the steering wheel. "I know what you're doing. And I appreciate it. But I can't. I can't do small talk right now."

Mrs. Lynch's hand reached across me to touch Jim's arm briefly. Then silence again.

The kilometres rolled past. I watched the landscape change from hills to suburbs to city. Every kilometre taking too long, but also too fast because what if she wasn't okay? What if the nurse had been wrong? What if—

No. Don't think. Just watch the road. Count the kilometres.

Jim pushed the speed limit where he could. I appreciated that.

"She's going to be alright, you know," Mrs. Lynch tried as we hit Adelaide. "I Googled Dr. Chen. She's supposed to be the best—"

"Supposed to be," Jim agreed. "But we won't know for sure until we see her."

Until we saw her breathing. Moving. Alive. My chest felt like it was going to burst.

The Royal Adelaide Hospital appeared ahead— glass and steel and fluorescent lights.

Jim parked. Killed the engine. None of us moved for a brief second.

"Righty-O," Mrs. Lynch announced. "Let's go see our girl."

I was out of the truck almost before she finished speaking, legging it to the front door while Jim hurried to catch up.

Our girl.

We made a quick stop at reception, then Jim led us through automatic doors, down corridors that smelled like antiseptic and something else— something basic and human— maybe fear. A nurse led us toward the neurology ward.

"Room 247. Just through here. But please— she's very sensitive to light right now, so we're keeping it dark. And she'll tire easily. Don't overwhelm her."

Mrs. Lynch clutched her bag tighter. I wanted to push past everyone, wanted to bolt down the corridor and burst through the door. But I forced myself to walk. To take care.

The nurse opened the door to a room so dark I had to pause, let my eyes adjust. Heavy curtains blocking the windows. A single small lamp in the corner.

And there, in the bed—

Jude. Smaller and paler than usual against white sheets. Red hair stark against the pillow. A bandage on the back of her head where they'd shaved and cut.

"Hey, John," she sighed. The break in her voice broke something in me.

I was across the room before I could think, before Jim could tell me to be careful. But I was gentle— gentler than I'd ever been. I just needed to hug her, needed to know she was real and alive and here.

She opened her arms and I leaned in ever so carefully, and she hugged me. Her arms were weak, but they were there, holding me, and she was alive.

I pulled back. She was looking past me to Jim with an expression that would have been funny if everything wasn't so terrible.

"Jim," she said scathingly. "I can't believe you can't keep a secret. Who else did you tell?"

"Just Anne and John." Jim sounded defensive yet amused. "And only because they cornered me! Anne was calling you, and John was acting strange, and they both—"

"Ganged up on you?" A tiny smile. "Yeah, I can see that happening."

I took up a position near her bed, as close as I could get without being in the way. I just needed to be nearby.

Mrs. Lynch settled into the only chair, crying. "Oh, sweetheart. How are you feeling?"

"Like someone drilled into my skull. Which, to be fair, they did." Jude shifted and winced. "Everything's blurry. Double vision. And the light." She gestured at the dark room. "Looking at my phone is like staring into the sun. I can't focus."

"Is that normal?" Mrs. Lynch asked.

"Apparently. Something about the location of the tumour, near the eye movement pathways." Jude squinted at us. "I'm seeing about one and a half of each of you right now, which is disconcerting. Vaguely nauseating."

A knock, and a woman in a white coat entered. Dr. Chen. The surgeon. The one who'd cut into Jude's brain and somehow, miraculously, made her okay.

Jim stepped forward, introduced himself as Jude's uncle. The lie came easily, and I was grateful for it. Family only, the nurse had advised. We were family.

Dr. Chen talked about the surgery. Grade 2 glioma. Ninety-five percent removed. Six to ten days in hospital, then radiation.

I listened to every word, cataloguing the information. Grade 2 was better than Grade 3. Ninety-five percent was good. Radiation meant more treatment, but treatment meant fighting it.

"You'll need to stay in Adelaide for the duration of your recovery and treatment," Dr. Chen said sternly. "Do you have someone here you can stay with?"

"Yes," Jude confirmed. "Absolutely. No trouble at all."

No trouble at all?

I looked at Jim. He looked at Mrs. Lynch. We all knew she had no one in Adelaide. No plan. No place to stay. But she'd agreed anyway, because Jude never wanted to ask for help. Never wanted to be a burden.

Dr. Chen left. Mrs. Lynch swivelled toward Jude with her school-teacher gaze.

"What do you mean 'no trouble'? Who in Adelaide are you going to stay with?"

Jude protested that she'd figure something out, find a hotel nearby. I just sat there beside Jude's bed, watching her try to fend off Mrs. Lynch.

She looked at all of us— exhausted and overwhelmed and trying so hard. Her eyes filled with tears.

Mrs. Lynch settled into the chair, talking about one day at a time. Jim promised we'd sort everything. And I just sat there beside her bed, watching her chest rise and fall in a steady rhythm.

She closed her eyes, exhaustion pulling her under. "I'm so tired."

"Then sleep," Jim told her. "We'll be right here."

And we were. She was asleep, but alive.

All day, we stayed in that dim room. Rotating between the chair, the window, and keeping vigil by the door.

Making sure she wasn't alone.

Not anymore.

Chapter 28

John

The hospital waiting room was a study in uncomfortable silence. I sat beside Jim, staring at the clock on the wall. Afternoon visiting hours didn't start for another forty minutes, but I'd been ready since we left Jude's room that morning.

Jim had a newspaper he wasn't reading. His eyes hadn't moved across the page once.

The automatic doors whooshed open and Mrs. Lynch came in, phone in hand, wearing that look—the one that meant she'd been *Solving Problems and Making Arrangements.*

"Right," she announced, settling into the chair across from us. "I've sorted the accommodation."

My head snapped toward her.

"You what?" Jim asked.

"Diana's house. The one she's selling in Adelaide— it's still mostly furnished. I called and asked if I could rent it for a couple of months."

I swivelled back to Jim to see his reaction.

"Anne, you can't—"

"Diana said yes. Wouldn't hear of charging rent, but I insisted on at least covering utilities." She pulled out a small notebook. "It's in Burnside. Ten, fifteen minutes from the hospital. Three bedrooms."

"Did you tell her why?" Jim asked.

"No. Just that I needed temporary accommodation." She flipped a page. "Now. I've been thinking about schedules."

Jim sighed. "Schedules?"

"Week about caring for Jude. You take the first week down here with her. I'll manage both the store and Pokey's until Peter arrives. Then we swap. He can mind the store while you take care of Pokey's during my week here."

My head moved back and forth between them like I was watching one of those tennis matches on Jim's little TV.

They were making plans. Good plans. Plans that meant Jude wouldn't be alone.

But there was someone they'd forgotten. I waited until they both paused, then cleared my throat— firm and definitive. They looked at me.

Wherever Jude is, that's where I'll be.

"John, mate," Jim began carefully. "You can't stay in Adelaide for two months—"

I just stared at him.

Mrs. Lynch laughed. "Oh, give it up, Jim. You know how stubborn he is. If Jude's there, he's there. End of discussion."

Exactly.

Jim looked between us— Anne with her practical notebook, me with my fixed glare— and relented.

"Right then," he said. "We'll just have to run the plan by Jude."

A nurse appeared in the doorway. "Jude's awake now, if you'd like to see her."

We all stood at once.

Mrs. Lynch tucked away her notebook. Jim folded his newspaper. I was already moving.

"Let's go tell her," Mrs. Lynch said briskly.

"She's going to hate it," Jim muttered.

"Probably," Anne replied. "But she'll get over it."

I looked at Jim.

Tell her. Don't ask her.

They could debate her reaction all they liked. I knew one thing for certain: She was stuck with us now. All of us. For as long as it took.

And there wasn't a thing she could do about it.

Chapter 29

Jude

Jim's solo visit on Wednesday was unexpected but welcome. I was sitting up in my hospital bed when he knocked, feeling stronger than I had in days. I could stay awake for more than an hour at a time without feeling like I was drowning in exhaustion.

"Jim!" I smiled as he came through the door. "I wasn't expecting you today."

"Thought I'd come down, see how you're doing. Make sure you're settling into the idea of us camping out at Diana's place." He eased into the visitor's chair with a small groan. "You're looking better."

"I feel better. The double vision's almost gone— just occasional blurriness now. Still can't tolerate light for more than ten minutes without a headache, and no chance of seeing anything on my phone, but it's progress."

"That's good. Really good."

I took a breath, preparing myself for what I needed to say. "Jim, about the arrangements—"

"We're not going to argue again—"

"I was going to say thank you." The words came out quieter than I'd intended. "I know I fought you guys on it. But I've had a lot of time to think, lying here. And I... I'm grateful. Truly."

The relief that washed over Jim's face was almost comical. "You mean that? You're okay with it?"

"I'm terrified of being a burden. But after the past couple of days, I'm more terrified of trying to do this alone." I picked at the edge of the blanket, finding it easier to look at my hands than at him. "So yes. I'm really thankful."

A knock at the door interrupted us. Dr. Chen entered, tablet in hand, a professional smile on her face.

"Mr. James, good to see you. Jude, how are you feeling today?"

"Better. Stronger."

"Excellent. Your recovery has been remarkable, actually. Better than we typically see at this stage." She pulled up a chair, settling in. "Which is why I wanted to discuss next steps. If you continue progressing at this rate, we're looking at discharge on Friday."

"Friday?" I sat up straighter, ignoring the way the movement made my head swim slightly. "Really?"

"Provided you continue to improve, yes. You'd need full-time care though— someone with you at all times."

Jim leaned forward. "I'll be here for her. And can you tell us a bit about what's next?"

Dr. Chen settled back, shifting into explanation mode.

"Jude'll need to recover for a couple more weeks before we start radiation. Five days a week for five to six weeks. An hour to two for each appointment."

Five to six weeks. Daily. Twenty-five to thirty treatments. The number felt enormous.

"Before the first treatment, we'll make what's called an immobilisation mask. It's a thermoplastic mesh that we mould to fit Jude's face and head."

Dr. Chen was still speaking directly to Jim, and I wondered if she thought she'd need his support— if she thought I'd be stubborn about radiation. I hadn't planned to be, but the idea of the immobilisation mask made something cold settle in my stomach.

Thankfully, Jim asked the question for me. "A mask?"

"It sounds more intimidating than it is."

I could hear a slight wariness in Dr. Chen's tone, which probably meant that it *was* as intimidating as it sounded.

"We take a perfect mould, creating a mask that clips right into the table and keeps your head completely still. It ensures you're in exactly the same position for every treatment."

A mask. Fitted to my face. Clipping into a table.

"That sounds kind of horrible."

"I won't lie to you— some patients find it claustrophobic. You can't move, can't touch your face if you have an itch. It can feel restrictive."

Claustrophobic. Restrictive. Can't move. The room felt suddenly smaller. I'd never been good with enclosed spaces, with being trapped. Even elevators made me uncomfortable if they were too crowded. And now I was supposed to lie there, face covered, bolted to a table, unable to move?

"How long?" I knew I sounded strained. "How long do I have to wear it each time?"

"Ten to fifteen minutes of actual radiation. But you'll be in the mask for the setup as well— probably twenty to thirty minutes total per session."

Twenty to thirty minutes. That didn't sound long. But multiplied by twenty-five or thirty treatments—

I realised I'd stopped breathing properly. Forced myself to inhale.

"Side effects?" Jim asked, and I was grateful for the redirect, for giving me a moment to compose myself.

"Cumulative. The first week or two, she'll feel relatively normal, but still very weak. Weeks three and four, it gets harder. Severe fatigue, nausea, increased sensitivity to light, possible hair loss at the radiation site, difficulty concentrating."

She looked at me directly. "This is why you need support, Jude. By week five, most patients can barely manage daily tasks on their own."

The room fell into a hush. I could feel them both looking at me, waiting for me to say something. But my mind was stuck on the image of that mask, of being strapped down, unable to escape.

"Look." Dr. Chen's voice filled the silence. "We're very optimistic. The combination of surgery and radiation gives us the best chance of preventing recurrence. Your age, your overall health— these are all in your favour."

Best chance. That's what mattered. *Survival.* Not the mask, not the claustrophobia, not the fear crawling up my spine.

I forced myself to speak. "Okay. When do we make the mask?"

"Just before your first treatment. You'll come in, meet the technicians, and familiarise yourself with the radiotherapy room at the same time. Then when you're comfortable, we'll start your first actual session."

"Okay. We'll cross that bridge in a few weeks then." I tried to sound confident, capable. "And I can leave on Friday?"

The hope in my voice was embarrassing, but I didn't care. I wanted out of the hospital.

"If you continue improving at this rate, yes." Dr. Chen stood. "But Jude— I need to confirm that reliable full-time care here in Adelaide has been arranged? Someone who can be within reach at all times, help you with daily tasks? The first few weeks of healing are critical."

I looked at Jim. "Jim's staying with me. In Burnside. And John, of course. And Anne. They've arranged everything."

"Perfect." Dr. Chen made a note. "Then we'll plan for Friday discharge, pending reassessment that morning. If anything changes— if you have any setbacks, hydrocephalus or seizures— we'll have to push that date out. But I'm optimistic."

I waited until she left before I turned as excitedly as I could manage and said, "Jim! I could be out of here Friday."

"If you keep improving," Jim cautioned.

"I will. Friday is my goal." I needed to change the subject, needed to think about something other than masks and radiation and being trapped. "Can you do me a favour?"

"Of course. Anything."

I held out my phone. "Can you please scroll through my email for my WSET login info? I want to know the results of my exam, but I can't focus on the bloody thing."

"Jude, that's not important now—"

"It is. To me. Thanks Jim."

He took the phone, and I watched him navigate my email, find the link, log into the WSET portal.

"You passed, dear. Flying colours. 94%."

The relief was physical, warming me from the inside out. Something I'd done right. Something I'd accomplished before everything fell apart.

"What does it say about Level 3?"

"The next intake starts Monday. You're enrolled, but you can defer—"

I laughed— my first in a long time. "I know I can, Jim, but I don't want to. Don't worry. I'll be ready to start."

"Are you sure? I mean—"

"I'm sure. And I know you and Anne will help me if I need it."

Jim squeezed my hand. "We're in this together, love. All of us. You just focus on being strong enough to get out of here Friday. And I'll arrange to pick up the books on this reading list for you. Let's not tell Anne yet, shall we?"

"Deal."

Jim left, and I lay back against the pillows and stared at the ceiling. Discharge on Friday. A few days to rest. WSET Level 3 starting Monday.

And in three weeks, *the mask*. I pushed that thought away. Three weeks was forever away. I'd deal with it when I had to.

For now, I'd focus on Friday. On getting out.

Chapter 30

John

The Friday morning they let Jude out of hospital arrived with a flurry of activity. We'd driven down at dawn— Jim and I riding down in the Ram, Mrs. Lynch driving solo in her little vee-dub, packed to the hilt with stuff.

Diana's house was everything Anne had promised— a neat brick bungalow with a small, well-tended garden and enough space for all of us. Three bedrooms, two bathrooms, a little courtyard off the main bedroom. The courtyard would be nice on sunny days— Jude could sit outside without being overwhelmed.

I wandered through the rest of the house, making sure everything was suitable. The place smelled like old wood and lemon polish— clean and safe. A daybed was pushed up against the wall in the little sitting room. I stood in the doorway, measuring the distance with my eyes. Close enough to Jude's bedroom that I'd hear if she needed anything. Far enough to give her privacy. I claimed this room as my own.

Walking back outside, I suppressed a chuckle watching Jim unload what looked like enough supplies to survive a month in the wilderness.

"They do have grocery stores in Adelaide, Anne," Jim commented, wrestling the third esky from the truck bed.

"I just want to make sure she eats properly," Mrs. Lynch shot back, not slowing down for a second. "She needs nutrition to heal."

She took over the kitchen with the efficiency of a general planning a campaign. I watched her stack containers in the fridge, arranging things just so, chattering too loudly to Jim the whole time.

"Pumpkin kitchari," she announced. "Easy on the stomach, full of nutrients. She can have it anytime— breakfast, lunch, dinner, midnight if she needs something."

"What the hell's 'kitchari'?" Jim asked.

"And I've made bone broth, and there's fresh fruit—"

"Anne—"

"And these protein smoothies, and—"

"Anne." Jim caught her hand. "Breathe. It's going to be alright."

Mrs. Lynch stopped, looked at me, avoided looking at Jim. I could see the worry she'd been hiding behind all the bustling efficiency.

"Let's go get her, hey?" Jim said, holding the door open and escorting us out.

We didn't need to be asked twice.

* * *

By the time we collected Jude from the hospital— paperwork signed, discharge instructions reviewed twice by a very thorough nurse— it was just past noon. Jude looked wrecked from the effort of getting dressed and into the wheelchair that hospital policy required, but a glimmer shone in her eyes that hadn't been there a week ago.

"Freedom," she sang quietly as we wheeled her out into the spring sunshine, wearing dark sunglasses that almost obscured her entire face. She squinted and covered her eyes. "Ow. Okay. Sunglasses not yet sufficient."

The drive to Burnside was easy. Jude slumped in the passenger seat of Mrs. Lynch's little car while I travelled with Jim.

"Right then. Jude, you're in the master with the ensuite. No arguments." Drill Sergeant Lynch barked orders as Jim helped Jude from the car.

Jude didn't argue. I led her to the master bed and she gratefully lay down, one hand covering her eyes.

"She looks so fragile," Mrs. Lynch whispered to Jim.

"She's stronger than she looks. You know that."

"I know. I just..." She trailed off, then squared her shoulders. "Let's get her settled properly."

I wandered back out to the sunroom and settled on the day bed, listening to them fuss and worry in the kitchen.

I could see Jude from where I sat. That was enough for now.

* * *

We found Jude sitting on the edge of the bed looking like she might fall over.

"Okay there?" Jim asked.

"Just weak. It's ridiculous— I haven't done anything, and I'm exhausted. I'd like to use the loo."

"You just had brain surgery a week ago. You're allowed to be exhausted." He helped her up and guided her to the ensuite.

Mrs. Lynch was busily unpacking yet another box of supplies. "Small speaker for audiobooks or music— easier than trying to read with the vision issues. Water jug for the nightstand. Bell here if she needs anything and we're not in earshot—"

I looked at Mrs. Lynch, amused. A bell?

We heard the toilet flush behind the closed door.

"You right, Jude?" Jim called out.

"Fine," came the muted reply.

Mrs. Lynch was arranging things just so, tucking an extra blanket at the foot of the bed.

"Anne," Jude murmured faintly as she came back into the bedroom. "Thank you. Really. For all of this."

Mrs. Lynch's eyes filled with tears. "Oh, sweetheart. Of course." She pulled Jude into a restrained hug, and then leaned forward to tuck her in.

"You just focus on healing. Everything else, we've got covered. Now, there's kitchari in the blue containers in the fridge. Just heat and eat. There's—"

"Anne. She's asleep," Jim rumbled, reaching out a hand to touch Mrs. Lynch's arm.

"Right, sorry," Mrs. Lynch whispered, backing out of Jude's room and pulling the door partway closed.

* * *

Mrs. Lynch and her relentless fussing finally left to head back to The Ridge. The house exhaled.

Jude slept that week. A lot. She'd wake to eat a little, and then sleep again. Jim said her body was catching up on everything it had been through.

I found my own rhythm. I'd take long solo walks through the Adelaide suburbs when Jude was sleeping, and sit patiently in the sunroom when she was awake— close enough if she needed me, far enough to give her space.

On Thursday, she asked Jim about her laptop.

"I'd like to check out my course materials," she mumbled groggily, propped up against pillows in bed.

"Jude, are you sure you're ready—"

"Jim. Please. I don't want to put my life on hold." She sounded firm despite the exhaustion. "I have to at least see if anything is due this first week. Can you help me get set up, please?"

I moved closer to the doorway, watching as Jim positioned her laptop on a bed tray, turned the brightness down, made the text bigger to compensate for the lingering vision issues.

"Maybe you can still defer," he wondered, watching her squint at the screen.

"I probably can, but I don't want to." She looked up at him, something fierce in her expression. "All I have is healing, and this. This will be what keeps me going, Jim. Having something to work toward that isn't all brain cancer and treatment and whatnot."

I understood that. She needed something that wasn't *illness*.

"Alright then. But you take breaks. And if it gets to be too much—"

"I'll tell you. Promise."

Chapter 31

John

Over the next couple of weeks, the mornings were hardest—Jude was groggy from the medications, moving slowly, everything a struggle. By afternoon she'd rally, spending an hour or two on her coursework, squinting at the screen, writing slowly in her notebook.

Evenings, when the light faded and her eyes could handle it better, she'd sit in the courtyard with us. Just a few minutes at first, feeling the fresh air, the last of the day's sunshine that didn't stab through her skull. Then, longer.

"Doing nothing really takes it out of me," she admitted one evening, wrapped in a blanket despite the mild Adelaide temperature.

Jim looked up from his book. "You're healing. That's hard work, even if it doesn't look like it."

Strength returned in small ways. Sitting in the courtyard, laptop balanced on her knees, She'd study wine regions and instruct me about grape varietals and soil composition, and I listened, rapt. I knew that it pleased her to teach me things, so I sat with her, paying fierce attention while she recovered, bit by bit.

* * *

Jim's phone rang on our third Sunday evening there, just as we were settling in for the night. I could hear Mrs. Lynch's voice even from where I sat.

"How'd the drive go?" Jim asked.

"Fine. Seemed long. I'm beat."

She sounded flat with fatigue. Her entire week here had been filled with activity— pots clattered, curtains opened and closed, questions arrived in steady succession— was Jude warm enough, cool enough, hungry, comfortable, tired— Mrs. Lynch's care came with constant motion.

"But that's not why I'm calling," she continued. "Diana's acting very strange."

"Strange how?"

"She practically ambushed me with a casserole before I was even out of the car— and this look she was giving me. Like I was made of glass. She kept asking if I'm okay. Offered to help half a dozen times. Asked if I needed her to take over the lunch shifts at Pokey's."

"Maybe she's just being nice?"

"Jim, she asked if I needed help getting my groceries in from the car. I had one bag. And she was speaking in this weird, probing voice like I'm about to have a breakdown."

"That is strange."

"Something's going on. She knows something, or thinks she knows something. I just can't figure out what."

They talked for a few more minutes before hanging up. I looked back through the window at Jude, already asleep in her chair, exhausted from healing and studying, no doubt worrying about radiation.

Whatever was going on with Diana, it would have to wait.

* * *

The following Sunday, Jim drove back to The Ridge while Mrs. Lynch came back down for another week 'on-duty'.

Jude had made it through her first week of radiation— five treatments down. She was holding up well, all things considered. Tired, yes, but no major side effects.

"Apparently week three is when it really hits," she'd told Jim that morning before he left. "So I'm going to try to get ahead on my coursework if I can."

I'd overheard Jim on the phone with Mrs. Lynch later that night, telling her about Diana cornering him outside the store.

"She asked about you," Jim rumbled, his deep voice carrying through the open courtyard door. "Poor Diana. She's wondering what's going on."

Mrs. Lynch replied, firm and clear. "Well, she'll have to keep wondering. We can't be telling her Jude's business."

I settled back onto the daybed, thinking about the irony of Mrs. Lynch and me bullying Jim into giving up Jude's secret.

I felt bad for Diana. She clearly cared, and it's hard being the one kept in the dark.

Chapter 32

Jude

It was Tuesday afternoon, my second week of radiation.

I could still smell the radiotherapy room. Even though we'd been back at Diana's for over an hour, the smell stuck— warm plastic and disinfectant— and I realised that I was getting used to the treatments. Once I was clipped into the mask, there was nothing to do but stare at the ceiling and listen to the machine hum to life— a low, mechanical sound that felt much louder inside my own head.

The weight of the mask pressed against my face, holding me perfectly still. For those minutes, I learned to ride out panic and trust in stillness, even when every instinct told me to move.

I was in the lounge room studying while Anne busied herself in the kitchen, and John was out for a walk. All things considered, I wasn't feeling too bad except my eyes tired quickly, and the words on the screen kept blurring together.

The doorbell rang.

"I'll get it," Anne called from the kitchen.

I heard the door open, then Anne's surprised voice. "Diana! What are you doing here?"

"I brought some flowers. And a casserole— that chicken I told you about. Thought you might need some proper food."

"That's very kind, but you didn't have to drive all the way to Adelaide—"

"Of course I did. I wanted to see how you're managing."

There was something odd in Diana's tone. Something enquiring that made me sit up straighter and listen.

"I'm fine," Anne was saying. "Really, there's no need—"

"Anne, you don't have to be brave with me. I think I know what you're going through."

I heard Anne's sharp intake of breath. "Diana, I don't think—"

"When you asked about the house, and with all the trips back and forth, how tired you've been looking... I understand. You don't have to pretend."

Oh God. She thought Anne was sick.

I should have stayed on the couch. Should have let Anne handle this. But something made me stand up, made me move toward the door even though every muscle protested.

"Diana?" I said, stepping into view.

Diana turned, flowers still in her hands, and froze.

I saw the moment it registered— the slow way I was moving. The shaved surgical site still visible through my hair. I knew how I looked—thin, hollowed out. Exhaustion showing in my face.

"Jude?" Diana barely whispered.

"Surprise?" I tried for a smile.

"I thought..." Diana looked between me and Anne. "I thought Anne was—"

"Having cancer treatment?" I finished awkwardly. "No. That would be me."

Diana sank into the nearest chair, her face pale. "Oh my God. Jude, I had no idea."

"It's okay." I eased myself back onto the couch. "Really. You couldn't have known."

"I'm so sorry." Anne's words were tight with guilt. "Diana, I couldn't tell you. It wasn't my story to share—"

"No, no, I understand." Diana wiped her eyes. "Oh, Anne, no wonder you've looked so exhausted. You've been taking care of her, and I've been pestering you with casseroles."

Despite everything, I laughed. It came out weaker than I intended. "Poor Anne's been dealing with a lot."

"Brain tumour?" Diana asked, her eyes on the surgical site.

"Yes. A glioma. Had surgery nearly a month ago now. Started radiation last Monday." I gestured vaguely. "Hence the need for the Adelaide accommodation. Daily treatments for the next five weeks."

"And Jim and Anne have been taking care of you?"

"Week about. They've been amazing. John too." I glanced at John, who'd snuck in through the open door behind Diana and was waiting patiently in the hall.

I looked at Anne and felt a rush of gratitude. I could feel tears threatening to spill down my cheeks. "I couldn't do this without them."

Diana spent a long moment processing. Then she stood decisively. "Right. Well. I'm able to help too. Anne, I'm covering lunch shifts at Pokey's. And any others you need covered. No arguments."

"Diana, you don't have to—"

"I absolutely do. You can't run yourself into the ground." Diana looked at me. "And Jude, is there anything you need?"

"Oh, Diana, the house. It's been perfect. Close to the hospital, comfortable. I'm so grateful."

"Of course. Stay as long as you need. I'll get out of your hair," she fidgeted with her handbag, looking embarrassed. "Anne, I'll call you later about those shifts."

"Diana," I called to her. "It's okay. Would you like to sit for a while? Have some tea? I'm really grateful for the visit." I was only half-surprised to find that I truly meant it.

She gave me a shy smile as she joined me and John in the living room, and Anne arranged tea. Sitting there with this small group who loved me enough to help me through this, I could feel another chain loosening in my chest. I wondered why I had insisted on keeping everything so cloak-and-dagger. Now someone else knew, and the world hadn't ended.

Eventually, I excused myself for a rest. I could hear their muted murmurs for a little while longer, and then Anne came in to check on me. I was sitting propped up in bed, laptop open.

"That's one mystery solved," she announced.

"She thought you had cancer."

"Apparently." Anne shook her head. "The casseroles make sense now."

I closed my laptop and set it aside, too tired to focus any longer. "I honestly couldn't stomach a casserole. Anne, I'm sorry. This is all so complicated."

"It's life. Life is complicated." Anne moved to sit on the edge of the bed. "Now stop apologising and get some rest. You've got another treatment tomorrow."

* * *

Anne left early the following Sunday morning, and I was looking forward to seeing Jim when he headed back down to look after me for my third week of radiation. Not that I didn't enjoy the weeks with Anne, but it's a different dynamic when it's just Jim and John here. Less fussing. More unobtrusive companionship.

I looked at John, flopped on the daybed in the morning sunshine.

The radiation was taking its toll— my eyes burned, and I was plagued with a bone-deep fatigue. I was determined to stay on track with my coursework before the side effects worsened, so I fit in some study every chance I could. I'd just set my laptop to the side and closed my eyes when the doorbell rang, startling both of us.

"I've got it, John." I pushed myself up. "I need to stretch my legs anyway."

I swung open the front door and froze. There stood Andy, leather duffel at his feet, briefcase in one hand, looking like he'd been travelling for days. His shirt was wrinkled, his hair messed up. And his eyes took in everything in one fell swoop, cataloguing the situation.

"Andy! Why aren't you in California?" The words came out strangled.

"Are you okay?" he asked, and I watched his face change as he really looked at me. Saw what the illness had done— the weight loss, the exhaustion, the way I held myself like every movement hurt.

Heat flooded my face. Shame first, then anger.

"Did Diana tell you?" I kept my control, but I could hear the annoyance underneath. Of course, Diana would have told him.

"Yes, she called and told me you'd had brain surgery. That you've been undergoing radiation. Why didn't you say anything? I've been in California thinking everything was fine, that you've just been busy. Happy."

Because I didn't want this. Didn't want him seeing me like this. Didn't want to be the reason he gave up his dream job. Didn't want to owe him anything.

"How's the new job?" I asked, deflecting.

"The new job is fine, but that's hardly important, is it?" His reply was tight with anger— not at me, I realised. At the situation. At not knowing. "I told my boss we had a family emergency. Grabbed a flight back as soon as I could."

Oh God. "Andy, that's ridiculous, you really—"

"I don't care." He reached out, touched my arm so lightly it made my throat tight. Like I was made of porcelain. Like I might shatter. "Some things are more important than any job, Jude. You're one of them."

The tears came before I could stop them. I felt something crack open inside me.

"Andy, you can't throw away your dream job—"

"I'm not throwing it away. I told them I need to work remotely for a while. If they say no to that, then it could never be the right fit anyway." He took my hand, and that undid me completely.

I was crying now, really crying, and I hated it— hated that he'd flown halfway around the world because I was so breakable.

"I don't want to be a burden—" I tried and failed to wrench my hand away.

"You're not. You never could be." He squeezed my hand, gathering me closer, holding me steady. "Now, what's the plan? What can I do? What do you need?"

"I don't need—"

"Jude."

I stared at Andy, feeling my defences crumbling. The walls I'd so wilfully maintained— with him especially— starting to fall. Because he was *here*. And he wasn't looking at me with pity or fear, just with this fierce determination to help.

I glanced at John, where he was watching from the hallway. "I do need tea," I admitted with a small smile.

"Tea I can do," Andy declared, already heading toward the kitchen like he'd been here a hundred times before— which, I realised with a start, he probably had been, considering it was his mother's house.

"I'm sorry," I admitted. "I hate needing help." I flopped my head back onto the cushion.

"I know," Andy replied from the counter. I heard him fill the kettle, pull down some mugs. "But that's what friends do. We help."

Friends.

The word settled around me. No romance. No pressure. No obligation. Just friends.

I relaxed slightly. "I can't believe you flew back from California for this."

"Nowhere else I'd rather be." He smiled at me, warm and genuine, as he came back with two steaming mugs of tea. "Now, when did you last eat? Mum warned me you've lost a lot of weight."

"Diana's been reporting on me?"

"She's very concerned, Jude. And apparently very proud of herself for figuring out the mystery, even though she got it completely wrong."

I heard the screen door swing closed and knew that John had gone out for a walk, giving us privacy once he was sure I'd be okay.

Andy had called us *friends*. Had flown back from his dream job without hesitation. Had looked at me— thin and exhausted and broken— and made me tea.

Maybe, just maybe, I could let him help. The others had already proven that I didn't have to do this alone.

* * *

The weeks after Andy arrived blurred together in a rhythm of treatments and recovery.

By week five, the radiation had hollowed me out. By the final week, Andy was half-carrying me to the car. I still pretended I wasn't leaning on him.

The final week truly sucked. The days merged into one another— the calendar kept moving forward.

Twenty-eight treatments. And then, finally, I was done.

Chapter 33

John

Packing up Diana's house felt like dismantling a field hospital after a long campaign. Eight weeks of our lives compressed back into boxes and bags.

Andy moved between the kitchen and his makeshift office, laptop open on the dining table, phone pressed to his ear. "Yes, I'll be on that call at three... the report's already sent... I'll put together the revised blend notes before Monday."

He'd made it work somehow— working internationally and being here. Video calls at odd hours to accommodate different time zones, working late into the night after helping with Jude's evening routine. He hadn't complained once.

Jim, directing the packing operation, offered a reprieve. "Andy, we've got this. You've done more than enough."

"No worries, Jim, happy to help." Andy stacked another box by the door.

Jude appeared in the doorway, Mrs. Lynch hovering protectively behind her. Nearly six weeks of radiation had left their mark— she was impossibly thin, still squinted against light even with the dark glasses. Dr. Chen had been firm— the radiation might be finished, but the recovery wasn't. Weekly check-ups were mandatory, and rest was paramount.

"Are the books already packed?" I heard her ask.

"In that box there," Andy pointed. "Your laptop's in your bag, charger too."

"Thanks."

She was polite but distant. Wary. While she'd gotten better at accepting help from the rest of us, she'd still kept poor Andy a little bit at arm's length. Like she was afraid of owing him something. Or maybe afraid of something else entirely.

"Jude, you'll ride with Anne," Jim directed. "John will ride with me. Andy, we'll see you up in The Ridge later this week?"

"Yeah. I'll be up Thursday, spend the weekend." He looked at Jude and something crossed his face. Hope, maybe. Or resignation.

Jude was already turning toward Anne's car.

I looked at Andy, still on his phone, still working, still juggling everything to be here. He'd been good to Jude these past weeks. Good to all of us. I had to give him that.

* * *

The drive back to The Ridge felt long. I could feel the anticipation radiating off me. *Home.* Finally going home. I knew my vibes were making Jim feel jumpy.

When we pulled into The Ridge ninety minutes later, everything looked exactly the same as it had two months ago. Jim's store with its faded sign hanging over the porch. Pokey's Ice Cream on the corner. The bench by the river where this whole thing had started, where Jude and I had first met on a winter morning that felt like years ago now.

Mrs. Lynch was already helping Jude out of the car when Jim and I rolled into the driveway at Cooper's cottage.

"Straight to bed with you," Mrs. Lynch commanded.

Jude didn't argue.

I waited while Jude got settled— Mrs. Lynch fussing with pillows, Jim making sure the fridge was stocked.

I looked at Jim, and he knew exactly what I wanted.

"Go on then." He smiled. "I'll stay with her while you go stretch your legs. You've earned it."

I was out the door before he'd finished speaking.

* * *

Freedom.

The word sang through me as I hit the trail at a dead run, muscles that had been cooped up for nearly two months finally, gloriously moving.

Two months of watching Jude move slowly, taking cautious short walks around suburban Adelaide streets. Two months of sitting still when every instinct screamed to do something, anything.

The river trail opened up before me and I ran flat out, revelling in the familiar smells— eucalyptus and wet earth and all the particular scents that meant *home*. I raced at top speed past the stringybark grove where I'd wanted to show her the blooms. We'd missed them, of course, stuck in Adelaide through most of spring.

But there would be other springs. Other blooms. I had to believe that.

The forest loop called, and I answered, plunging into the green shadows with abundant joy, my face split in a grin from ear to ear. Everything had changed while we were gone. Late spring had turned the whole bush into a celebration— wattles blazing yellow, early-season orchids hiding in the undergrowth.

Forest life continuing, regardless of outside dramas.

The trail wound upward and I pushed harder, feeling my lungs work, my heart pound.

This was exactly what I'd needed. The burn of exertion, the freedom of movement, the absolute relief of being somewhere familiar, somewhere without restraint.

At the ridge overlook, I stopped. The Thompson place spread out below, abandoned and beautiful as always. Jude's rented cottage was somewhat visible from here too—Jim's truck still in the drive. He was no doubt dozing in the porch swing while Jude slept.

A patch of native violets growing near the trail caught my eye— tiny purple blooms that Jude would love, their delicate petals the exact colour of twilight. I committed the location to memory. If she was strong enough in the next week or two, I'd bring her here before they faded.

The sun was getting lower as I made my way back to Cooper's cottage. Jim was gone.

I approached the porch noiselessly. Jude's bedroom window was dark— still sleeping, then.

I sat on the porch step for a while. There, in case she woke.

I'd planned to sleep in the carriage house out back, but the night was pleasant enough to sleep out. I dragged a blanket up onto the porch swing and stretched out, staring up at the half-full moon.

Home. We were home.

And tomorrow, or the next day, or whenever she was ready, I'd be here. Ready to walk whatever trails she could manage. Ready to show her all the spring things she'd missed. Ready to help her find her way back to the life she'd been fighting so hard to keep.

But tonight, I just lay there in the familiar darkness, listening to the sounds of an evening at home— bats chittering in their alien voices, the distant rush of the river, and the wind in the gum trees.

Chapter 34

Jude

The pre-dawn darkness felt different here. Subtler somehow than the Adelaide nights, with their ambient city glow and unfamiliar sounds.

I woke naturally for the first time in weeks— no medication alarm, no Anne or Jim or Andy knocking to ask if I needed anything. Just the darkness of my own bedroom in my own cottage.

My body protested as I pushed myself upright, muscles stiff from yesterday's long drive and weeks of limited movement. The exhaustion had settled in and stayed— would probably stay for months according to Dr. Chen. But I was glad to be home.

The bedside clock read 5:07 AM. Early, even for me. I'd slept enough these past weeks to last a lifetime. What I needed now was air. Space. The familiar sounds of The Ridge waking up.

I shuffled to the kitchen, moving carefully in the dim light. I filled the kettle and slid my favourite mug from the cupboard. Small things, ordinary things, that felt almost precious after so long away.

While the water boiled, I caught sight of myself in the darkened window's reflection— gaunt, pallid, the scar a visible reminder of what I'd been through. The incision had healed cleanly, a pale crescent half-hidden by uneven regrowth. I looked away.

The tea was too hot. I carried it outside, wrapping my robe tighter against the spring morning chill.

John was on the porch swing, exactly where I'd thought he'd be. He looked up as I opened the door, his expression neutral but questioning, in that subtle way he had. Checking to see if I was okay, if I needed anything, without making it obvious.

"Morning, John." I settled onto the swing beside him. "Sleep okay out here?"

He shifted slightly, making room for me, and we sat in companionable silence.

A small pile of mail sat stacked on the side table— two months of unopened life. I'd deal with it another day. Right now, all I wanted was this: the creak of the swing, the warmth of the tea seeping through the mug into my cold hands, and John's solid presence beside me.

The first kookaburras started up in the distance, their morning hysterics echoing across the hills. I'd missed that sound. I hadn't realised how much, until this moment.

Light was starting to emerge through the trees— the peculiar quality of spring dawn, rosy and full of promise. The new leaves on the gum trees caught it, turning the whole garden into something luminous.

"Oh, I missed this," I murmured to John. "The Adelaide house was lovely, Diana was incredibly generous, but... this is what I've been waiting for."

We sat there as the world slowly lightened around us. The tea cooled in my hands.

The porch swing moved steadily, the birds sang, the light grew stronger through the spring leaves, and John sat beside me as The Ridge woke up around us.

"Thank you, John," I said after a while. "For everything. For being there through all of it."

He looked at me, a simple acknowledgment of having survived something terrible together.

The sun crested the horizon properly now, spilling colour across the hills.

A new day.

* * *

Andy found me on the porch just after lunch, eyes closed but awake, sunlight filtering through the leaves overhead. I was wrapped in a light jumper, more for comfort than warmth, a pitcher of iced tea beside me. He hesitated in the driveway like he wasn't sure whether to interrupt.

"Hey," he called out to me.

"Hey. You made it up."

"Yeah. Thought I should say goodbye properly." He shifted his weight, hands in his pockets. "I'm heading back to California on Monday."

Monday. I'd known he'd be heading back, of course. Had counted on it. Still, the news landed heavier than expected.

"Well," I said lightly, offering him a glass of tea. "California will be missing you."

He smiled, but it didn't quite stick. He glanced around the porch—the swing, the hard-back wooden chair pulled up to the little table cluttered with my laptop and an array of notebooks and pens.

"You're looking stronger. Even just since the other day, it's... noticeable."

"I feel stronger," I admitted. "Still tired. But it's different now. More solid."

"I wanted to ask you something. And I want you to think about it before rushing to answer."

That made me look at him properly.

"Okay."

He took a breath. "If you wanted me to stay longer— work remotely a bit more— I could. I mean, I'd make it work. I just... wanted to ask."

The question hung there, unhurried and open. For a split second, I saw it— Andy staying. Andy driving me to follow-ups, sharing dinners, fitting himself into the empty spaces of my days. The weight of that settled in my chest.

And surprised me.

"No." The word came out sharper than I'd intended. Then, gentler, "No. Andy— this is your dream job. You came back when you didn't have to. You helped me through the worst of it. That matters. But now you should go back."

He studied my face, like he was searching for something underneath the words.

"You're sure?"

"Yes." I meant it. Mostly. "I'm okay. And I need to do this next bit on my own. At home. With my own routine. With Jim and Anne and John hovering like anxious satellites."

That earned a small laugh.

"Alright," he relented. "I just wanted to offer."

I was surprised— not just by the question, but by how much it mattered that he'd asked, by the faint echo of something I didn't quite have a name for.

"Thank you. For everything. For helping."

"I'll be back, on and off. When things are more settled with work."

"I know."

He didn't hug me. Just squeezed my shoulder lightly, like he knew better than to ask for more.

After he left, I sat there for a long time, staring at the patch of sunlight on the ground, unsettled by the strange mix of relief and something that felt uncomfortably like loss.

Chapter 35

John

Andy was halfway through a coffee at Jim's when Pilar arrived.

A wash of chemically-spiced floral perfume cut through the smell of coffee. Her skirt was tight enough to turn walking into a performance. She swept her long, straight blonde hair over one shoulder as she slid onto the stool beside Andy. She looked like she'd already rehearsed this scene in her head and was committed to seeing it through.

Andy didn't lean in. Didn't mirror her smile. He stayed exactly where he was, shoulders relaxed, hands wrapped around his mug like an anchor.

"Andy." She reached out to touch his hand like it was the most natural thing in the world. "I saw your car out front. I heard you were back from overseas."

"Yep. Heading back to Cali on Monday," he offered politely.

"How exciting. I'd love to hear all about it." She tilted her head, the beginning of a strange mating dance. "You should let me take you to dinner tonight. Something proper. A send-off."

He smiled, friendly but closed. "That's kind of you, but I'm having dinner with Mum—"

"Lunch tomorrow then?" she pressed. "Or breakfast on Monday before you go? There's a lovely place over in Hahndorf."

"I appreciate the offer. But no. I'm just up to visit Jude and help Mum with some stuff before I fly back." He set his empty cup down, slid it away.

Pilar laughed lightly, like she hadn't expected a *no*. "Surely you could fit in a lunch date."

Andy's tone didn't change, but something firm settled into it. "Maybe another time."

Jim pretended to be rearranging the biscuit tin, his face set very straight as he eavesdropped. I watched, amused, as Pilar recalibrated in real time.

"Well," she relented, standing and swinging her hair around. "Can't blame a girl for trying."

"No," Andy agreed. "You can't."

She smiled— tight, unreadable— and left without another word.

Andy finished his coffee, thanked Jim, and headed out a few minutes later.

I had the distinct feeling the drama wasn't over.

* * *

Andy flew back to California that Monday, and the days passed, turned into weeks and began to arrange themselves into a pattern again. I've always trusted patterns.

I slept at Jude's, either in the carriage house or out on the porch. I always woke before the light, long before Jude stirred. I'd stretch out the stiffness from sleep, head down the track to the river, and slip into the water just as the sky began to pale.

Spring-fed and sharp, the river still held winter in its bones, and the cold hit like a shock every time— clean and bracing. I loved that first moment of resistance, the way my breath caught before I could force myself forward. Stroke after stroke, pulling upstream, muscles burning as the current pressed back. The river never gave anything freely. You earned every metre.

I swam hard now. Every morning. Let the ache settle into my shoulders and legs, let the water scrape the sleep and the fear and the waiting clean out of me. When I finally turned and let the current take me, floating back toward the bridge, the sun would be just up— gilded threads sliding through the trees, stitching diamonds onto the surface of the water.

I came out dripping and alive, shaking the water off and heading back to the cottage with a straightforward satisfaction that only comes from having *used* your body properly. Truly, it's the best way to start the day.

Jude would still be asleep then. Or just waking.

She still slept a lot. Not the heavy, drugged sleep of her early recovery, but something closer to natural exhaustion— healing work being done beneath the surface. I learned the sounds of it. The slow, even rhythm of her breathing through the open window. The way she shifted when daylight sprang through the half-open curtain.

By mid-morning, she'd be up. Wrapped in a jumper, hair pulled back, books spread out across the kitchen table or the porch. She worked in short blocks now, no longer fighting her limits, just moving along the edges of them.

And every afternoon, when the daylight lessened, we walked. At first it was just to the corner. Then to the stand of silver wattles near the bend in the road, their yellow blooms blazing like small suns against the blue. Jude would stop there every time, tilting her face up, eyes closed, inhaling their scent.

"I missed this," she murmured, her face almost ethereal as the sunlight dappled across it.

The Adelaide Hills were showing off now— pink heath spilled across the slopes, low and stubborn, bees wove drunken paths between the blossoms. Blue wrens flashed like dropped fragments of sky, darting through the undergrowth. Magpies trilled and chirruped from fence posts, their songs complex and looping, as if they were practising variations just to see what else was possible. The air smelled of damp earth and eucalyptus sap warming in the sun.

Each day we walked a little further. Past the old stone wall where lizards liked to sun themselves. Down the narrow track where the grass grew long and the seed heads brushed against our legs as we walked. Along the riverbank, where the water ran fast and loud, swollen still with the spring runoff, talking to itself over rocks and fallen branches.

She fatigued faster than she liked to admit. I could always tell before she said anything— the way her steps shortened, the faint tightening around her eyes. We'd stop then. Sit on a log or a flat rock. Let the river do the talking.

"I'm getting better, John," she marvelled. Not as a reassurance. As an observation.

And she was. It showed in the small things. The steadiness of her stride. The way she no longer flinched from patches of bright light. The return of animation when she talked— about tannins and soil profiles and microclimates, her hands moving as she explained, as if shaping the ideas in the air between us.

I listened. Always. I liked being the one she explained things to. Liked the way her face lit when something clicked, when a concept landed cleanly. Teaching steadied her. Gave her somewhere to stand.

Spring deepened around us— and the weekly Tuesday check-ups loomed under everything, like a shadow.

The orchard trees along Wyuna Drive burst into white and pale pink, petals drifting down like confetti after a celebration no one had bothered to clean up. Insects hummed and clicked and whirred, busy with the important work of continuing things. The days stretched longer, warmer. The nights smelled of cut grass and honeysuckle.

Life felt... kind.

Not perfect. Never that. But peaceful.

In the evenings, Jude studied while I lay nearby, half-dozing, aware of the scratch of her pen, the muted tap of the keyboard. Sometimes she'd read aloud— definitions, tasting notes— testing herself. Sometimes she'd stop and just sit.

Those were my favourite moments. Nothing demanded. Nothing breaking.

Three weeks slipped past like that. Slowly. Graciously.

I believed that we'd earned this halcyon stretch of calm. That the worst of it had loosened its grip. That healing, real healing, might be something you could feel unfolding day by day, like spring itself.

If I was paying attention, there were signs even then. Small ones. Easy to miss if you wanted to.

The way my shoulders ached a little longer after the swim. The way Jude sometimes went very still, as if listening to something internal I couldn't hear. The way the river ran faster after rain, louder, less forgiving.

But mostly, those weeks were filled with movement and friendship and togetherness.

We walked. We watched. We waited— without knowing we were waiting at all.

And that, I would later understand, was the gift.

Because nothing makes loss sharper than having something too good to lose.

CHAPTER 36

Jude

The evening air carried that particular quality of late spring— cool enough to wear a light jacket, warm enough to shed it. My legs protested the uphill grade, muscles still rebuilding strength after weeks of enforced stillness. John walked beside me at a pace that might have been his natural rhythm or might have been precisely calibrated to match mine. With him, it was hard to tell.

"Almost there," I assured us both, more for myself than for him. The ridge trail had never felt this long before treatment. Now it stretched ahead like a small mountain, each switchback a minor victory.

John glanced at me, his expression holding this quality of attention that made me feel seen without being watched. He'd been good at this these past few weeks— being present without hovering, vigilant without making me feel like I might shatter.

We'd fallen into a pattern. Short walks turning into longer ones as my stamina slowly returned. Never pushing too hard. Never treating me like I might break.

The ridge finally opened up before us, the Thompson place spread out below in the golden light. The abandoned house looked almost beautiful at this hour, stone walls glowing amber, the ordered rows of vines holding their unofficial vigil.

I sank onto the weathered log that served as a bench, breathing harder than I wanted to admit. John took up his normal place at the rail, giving me space to recover without comment.

Below us, the vineyard stretched in neat lines. Old vines, at least for this area. Their roots would be deep by now, sunk into the red-brown soil that gave Adelaide Hills wines their edge.

"I booked my Level 3 exam. It's in six weeks. But I can defer if things don't go well with the follow-up scans."

"I was thinking," I started, then stopped. Restarted after I'd gathered my thoughts. "If it's even possible— I'd like to use the Thompson vineyard for my Master's Thesis. Prepare a restoration plan to bring it back into useful production."

I was babbling. I slowed myself down. Took a breath. "The vines are old but they're Shiraz— premium fruit if they were properly managed. And the location is perfect, the aspect, the drainage. It's just been neglected."

I'd been gesturing down at the fields below us, the woody vines catching the last light. I let my hands fall back to my sides.

The sun was sinking lower, painting the sky in shades of rose and rust. Below us, the vineyard was luminous, each vine casting its own small shadow.

"I know I'm getting ahead of myself. It's just, with Level 3 finishing soon, I still need something future-facing." I sounded almost plaintive, even to myself. "Something that isn't just *surviving*. Something that's actually building something."

We sat in comfortable silence as the sunset deepened, the vineyard below slowly fading into shadow. My legs ached from the walk, my head carried the familiar low throb that came with any exertion. But sitting here, looking down at those abandoned vines with the possibility of bringing them back to life— for the first time in weeks, the thought didn't just feel like a distraction, but more like a direction.

The first stars had appeared. "We should head back. Before it gets too dark to see the trail."

The walk down was easier than the climb up, gravity doing most of the work. John stayed close without crowding me, his presence an unspoken reassurance that if I stumbled, he'd be there.

Tuesday. Two days until the scan that would tell me if I had a future to plan for. And I had something else to do in between. Something important for my future.

* * *

Tuesday morning dawned clear and sunny. I knew today wasn't going to be easy—jamming two unpleasant tasks into the same day.

Jim was driving me down to Adelaide. Truth be told, my eyes were still sensitive to light, and the waves of exhaustion gave little warning before they washed over me. In any case, I still didn't have medical clearance to drive since the surgery, and six weeks of having my 'brain microwaved', as Jim liked to phrase it.

The road wound down through the hills in long, familiar curves, eucalyptus flashing past the passenger window in fuzzy green blurs. Jim drove one-handed, relaxed but attentive, the other resting near the gearstick like it belonged there. I'd been watching the trees, counting the gaps between them, when the thought of my first task nudged its way in—persistent enough that ignoring it felt dishonest. I sighed out loud.

"You sure you want to make this first stop?" Jim asked, giving me a sidelong glance, hands firmly gripping either side of the old leather-wrapped steering wheel.

"I'm sure," I confirmed, looking down at the envelope of papers in my hand. Closing one important door on my past, hoping that whatever lay behind the other door was good news.

It was just over an hour to Yatala Labour Prison, and as we approached the visitor parking lot, I felt a mild panic starting to creep in.

"I don't know if I can do this, Jim."

"Hey, what's that now?" Jim asked, cupping one hand behind his ear. I couldn't tell whether he legitimately hadn't heard me, or was pretending not to have heard, knowing that I would never admit that twice.

I straightened in my seat, closing my eyes briefly and visualising this onerous task already completed.

Jim pulled in and turned to me. "Do you want me to go in with you?"

"No. No, I should do this on my own."

"You could always mail the papers to Dylan. You don't need to see him face-to-face."

"I do, though. This chapter needs to close cleanly. I don't want him to feel like I was too cowardly to handle this myself."

"It's not a matter of who wins, Jude."

"I know that. I just— I need to do this, Jim. I'll be out soon. Less than an hour."

"I'll be here," Jim assured me.

I eased out of the passenger seat and onto the steaming tarmac. The day was already hot despite not yet being mid-morning— high 20's, and muggy. I walked to the guard shack, giving my name and indicating that I had an appointment to see Dylan Craig at 9 am. The guard pressed a buzzer and ushered me into a waiting area.

Deep breaths. Focus on the future. Get this over with.

* * *

The visitor room at Yatala Labour Prison was as institutional as I'd expected— fluorescent lights, beige walls, faintly stale air. I'd come early, hoping the morning sun might make it less grim. It didn't.

My fingers twisted the strap of my handbag— Dad's gift to me for my thirtieth birthday. His last.

When they brought Dylan in, the first thing that hit me was how ordinary he looked. Same haircut. Same calculated smile. Like this was just another business meeting, another deal to close.

"Looking good, Jude." He dropped into the chair opposite, gesturing at my headscarf. "New style?"

I ignored him, placing the folder on the table between us. "These are divorce papers, Dylan. You need to sign them."

He leaned back and tapped the folder, looking pleased with himself. "I figure you should hear the truth first, so we can both have what we want. I want this off my conscience. You want your freedom."

The fluorescent light buzzed overhead, a monotonous drone that matched the sudden ringing in my ears.

"I didn't mean to kill him, you know," Dylan confided, fingers drumming on the metal table. "I just wanted to shut him up. Show him he couldn't control everything. I wasn't even going that fast when I turned the wheel."

His bark of laughter was short and ugly.

"I just wanted to clip him. Make him jump. But then his head hit the kerb and—" He spread his hands, palms up. "Well. Here we are."

My throat tightened until it burned. I kept my face still— worked very hard to keep it still— while something hot and black pressed behind my eyes.

"Truth is," he went on, his familiar smirk sliding into place, "it worked out pretty good for you, right? Between the life insurance and the estate settlement, you'll be set for life. No more corporate grind."

I lifted my eyes to meet his. My hands were shaking. I held his gaze anyway.

"Hey." He tapped his temple and then pointed at me. "I'm trying to give you closure. Part of my rehabilitation. Getting honest. Owning my actions."

"Your *actions*." The words felt like glass in my mouth. "You hit my father with your car. You watched him fall. And then you drove away."

"I panicked! I was drunk—"

"You were sober enough to give a statement blaming me for your actions."

The smirk finally wavered. His face twisted in disgust as he shoved the folder back to me. Papers slid loose across the table. "Take these. I'm not signing a damn thing."

I gathered the pages neatly, my movements controlled. I slid them back into the folder, then the envelope. His façade was starting to crack. Good.

"You want to make amends? Try this: I don't forgive you. I never will. And my father's death isn't your stepping stone to redemption."

"Jude, listen. You're missing the point of—"

"No." I planted my hands on the table and leaned in. The metal table was cool under my palms. "For once in your life, *you're* going to listen."

He went still.

"You didn't just kill my father. You tried to twist his death into a story where you're the victim. Keep your amends, and whatever's weighing on your conscience."

I straightened. I could feel my pulse roaring through me. I turned to leave.

"You know," Dylan called after me in that familiar condescending tone that used to make me feel two inches tall. "I'd think about signing the papers if you'd be nice. If you acknowledge right now that without me, you wouldn't be financially set."

The crack of my palm hitting the metal table echoed through the room like a gunshot. Dylan flinched so sharply, the guard shifted his weight from the wall. For the first time, fear flickered across Dylan's face. Real fear. Not performance.

I kept my voice low, precise.

"Read, understand, and then sign the papers," I told him. "Put them back in this envelope. Give the envelope to the guard to send. It's quite simple, Dylan."

I slid the envelope across the table, right into his space. Across a boundary line.

"And then lose my address."

Dylan stared at the envelope. His hands came down on it— both of them— like he was holding it in place. He didn't open it. He didn't sign.

Walking out, I didn't look back.

Outside, the heat hit like a wall. Cicadas screeched from the trees. My whole body started shaking as the adrenaline drained away.

I climbed into Jim's truck and sat there, blank, listening to my heartbeat until it evened out. When I finally looked at Jim, he was watching me— reticent, steady.

"He didn't sign. But he will."

I caught myself nibbling on the corner of a fingernail. I tucked my hands under my legs and pushed out a firm breath.

"Otherwise it'll have to go through court. Same outcome, but it'll just take a lot longer. Either way... it's done."

Chapter 37

Jude

We were only about ten minutes from the hospital, a little bit early for my follow-up scans. I glanced across at Jim and casually asked, "Do you know who owns the Thompson place?"

Curious, not invested. At least, that was the idea.

Jim glanced over briefly, then back to the road. "Pretty sure the nephew still owns it. Pat left it to his sister, and it got passed down to her son after she died. Sad thing. Place was old Pat's pride and joy. After he died, it just got left to go to seed. Why?"

I folded my hands in my lap, considering how much to say. "I'd like to use it for a project early next year. For my Level 4 Thesis. Soil composition, vine health, develop a restoration plan— purely academic."

I added that last part quickly, as if it might reassure both of us. "It's neglected, but I think the vines are good."

Jim nodded slowly, absorbing that. "Sounds like a decent project. Useable work. Not just theory."

After a moment, he added, "I can make a few calls. See if the nephew still holds the title."

Then, without looking at me, he added, "Why don't we wait and see how things turn out today, hey? No sense biting off more than you can chew, my girl."

I watched the road unspool ahead of us, grey ribbon cutting through the green. He wasn't dismissing the idea. He wasn't promising anything either. It felt like the right balance.

"Yeah. That makes sense."

And it did. For now, it was enough to know the thought had somewhere to land— someone willing to hold it lightly, without asking me to carry more than I already was.

We drove the rest of the way in silence, the road narrowing, then widening again as the hospital loomed in front of us. Jim eased the Ram into a parking spot and cut the engine. I sat for a moment longer than necessary. When Jim asked me if I was ready, I was able to confidently lie.

"Ready." I breathed in resolve, breathed out anxiety.

* * *

The MRI performed its usual symphony of mechanical violence: clanging, buzzing, the sense that my skull was a bell someone was striking over and over. When it was done, I changed slowly, aware of the heaviness in my limbs and the slight unsteadiness in my legs. Jim waited outside, sitting with hands folded, eyes tracking the corridor like a man trying not to hover.

"All finished?" he asked.

"Hopefully they don't want an encore," I said. He chuckled and fell into step beside me, ambling slowly down the hall.

"Lunch?" Jim asked.

We had almost two hours to wait before my appointment with Dr. Chen. Lunch sounded like the best part of my day.

* * *

Dr. Chen's specialist rooms were modern— pale wood and white everywhere. The receptionist waved us straight in. That was a clue that the news wasn't great. Specialists don't usually run ahead of schedule unless there's a reason.

She stood when we entered— she must have literally been waiting for the scans to be read even as they were being conducted. Greeting us each by name, she offered for us to take the chairs.

I sat. Jim settled beside me, close enough to be a presence but not so close that I felt crowded. He has a knack for that, for giving people room even when they don't know how to ask.

She pulled up the MRI images. I'd seen enough of them now to recognise the shapes— the dark cavity where the tumour had been removed, the subtle halo of post-radiation inflammation. And an odd white speck near the surgical bed.

"There's still something there," I pointed out before she could speak. I sounded calmer than I felt.

She nodded. "A small area of enhancement. Very small. It may be residual tumour cells, or it may be tissue that didn't respond fully to the external beam radiation. It's very small, which is positive news, but given the location, we can't leave it."

I exhaled slowly through my nose, the way my meditation app always suggests. "So we're not finished."

"We're *close*," she conceded. "Gamma Knife radiosurgery was designed for this. One focused treatment, maybe two, targeted precisely to this spot. No more radiation. No chemo."

I glanced at the screen again. That tiny point looked impossibly insignificant— and yet of course it was the piece that refused to cooperate. The last guest at a party who wouldn't take the hint.

Jim shifted, his big hands resting loosely on his knees, his flannel shirt moving against my arm. "Whatever needs doing, we'll sort it."

His tone was matter-of-fact, the way he might talk about fencing or irrigation. There was comfort in that— in someone treating this as a solvable problem rather than a tragedy.

"Gamma knife. Sounds science fiction. But like Jim said, whatever needs doing." I spoke with significantly more bravado than I felt.

"I'd like to get you in within the next two or three weeks, ideally. Given where it sits, sooner is better."

The room had shrunk. Not suffocating, just compressed. Like the air itself was waiting for my reaction.

Dr. Chen outlined the head frame, the planning scan, the strange precision of it all— engineering disguised as medicine. I nodded at the right places and kept calm.

"Right. Let's do it." I sounded enthusiastic. I wasn't.

"Of course." She gave me a small, warm smile. "You've done incredibly well, Jude. Truly. This is not a setback— it's the last piece."

I didn't trust myself to respond to that, so I stood and thanked her. Jim followed me out, not saying a word until we reached the Ram.

"You alright, kiddo?" he asked finally, in that loving, gruff way of his.

I hesitated, weighing the instinct to deflect. "Ask me tomorrow," I said. "Today I'm... processing."

He accepted that, like that was a perfectly reasonable answer. And he didn't push. He just unlocked the door, waited until I'd climbed in, and started the engine.

As we pulled out of the car park, I stared down at my hands. They weren't shaking. That surprised me. Maybe this was newfound strength. Or shock. Or just the stubborn refusal to be knocked over again after making it this far.

Whatever it was, it held me up. For now.

Chapter 38

John

Some things definitely don't go as planned. Jude and Jim were heading down to the city, to do things I couldn't help with on this gloriously hot Tuesday.

I'd headed down early for my morning swim, planning to catch them before they left to wish Jude luck.

The river was perfect— clear and cold, the kind that touches every nerve in your body and makes you feel truly alive by snapping you awake from the inside out.

Ahh, the river. My river. My greatest joy.

I waded in slowly, savouring the shock of it, then pushed off and let the current carry me downstream toward the deeper pools.

This was freedom. Water sliding past, rising sun on my back. The world reduced to cool water surrounding me and the occasional dart of fish below.

I turned and swam upstream, muscles burning in that good, clean way. Feeling strong. Feeling good. I turned and let the river carry me, floating on my back, watching clouds drift lazily across the blue.

That's when my foot caught.

Not a rock. I knew every rock in this stretch.

Something that moved. Something that shifted with the current and closed around my ankle.

I kicked once, lightly, expecting it to slip free. It didn't.

I kicked harder.

The current tugged. My foot stayed where it was.

A flicker of unease stirred— sharp and immediate. I twisted to look, but the movement made everything worse. Whatever it was—

a branch, a log— lodged and waiting, rolled with my weight. My hip wrenched violently sideways as my head was dragged under.

Cold water flooded into my face. Into my nose. My mouth.

Pain. White-hot and searing.

Panic. Red and black and chaotic.

Raising my head viciously, I snorted water out through my nose as my body jack-knifed in the water. I thrashed, the river roaring in my ears now, louder than thought. I tried to pull my leg free, but the current pressed me down, twisting me, stealing my sense of direction.

Up.

Which way was up?

My hip screamed as I jerked again— a sickening, grinding sensation that told me something had gone very wrong. My chest burned. My lungs spasmed. I swallowed water and coughed, uselessly, underwater.

Not here. Not now.

Jude's face flashed through me— pale, determined, walking into places she was afraid of because she had to.

I couldn't die in my own river. I couldn't leave her to come home to this.

With a desperate, all-or-nothing wrench, I twisted again. Something gave.

The branch released me with a violent snap, and I surfaced, choking, dragging in air like it might disappear again at any second.

I half-swam, half-crawled toward the shallows, one leg refusing to work properly, my body moving on instinct alone.

I dragged myself onto the bank and lay there, chest heaving, hip throbbing with a deep, wrong kind of pain. Not a muscle pull. Something worse. Something that felt like the joint had been wrenched out of place and wouldn't ever quite settle back right.

I forced myself upright when I was ready. My left leg buckled immediately, sending a bolt of agony through my side and ripping an involuntary sound from my throat.

Not good. Dislocated, maybe. Or badly sprained. Either way, it hurt like the devil.

I limped back toward town, each step a mindful negotiation. I worked out a shuffling, sliding gait that minimised the pain, though probably looked ridiculous. By the time I reached Jim's, I was soaked with sweat and river water, jaw clenched hard enough to ache.

Mrs. Lynch was there, her handbag on the counter.

"There you are! Jim and Jude were looking for you—they've just left." She stopped, her smile faltering as she took in my awkward stance. "John, are you alright?"

I shook my head dismissively. Just a bit of a knock. *Nothing serious.*

I leaned into the counter, afraid I might fall over.

She didn't say anything at first. Just came closer, her gaze sharp now, assessing in that wise way she had.

"Let me see," she directed, not unkindly. Not optional.

I hesitated, then eased myself down at the counter, jaw clenched. She crouched in front of me, peering at my leg.

"You've cut yourself quite badly," she noted. "And that hip doesn't look right."

I gave a small shake of my head. It would ease. It always did. I just needed to lie down. Sleep it off. In my experience, sleep fixes most things.

Mrs. Lynch straightened, already moving toward the cupboard as I shuffled out to the back room and lay down on my bed. "You're not going anywhere today." She came into my room with a bottle of liniment and an ice pack. "And you're certainly not pretending this is nothing."

The sharp, medicinal smell of liniment filled the room as she poured some into her hands and rubbed them together briskly.

"This might sting," she warned.

It did. The heat bloomed almost instantly, seeping deep into the joint, loosening something tight and aching. I let out a low moan despite myself.

"There," she soothed, working the liniment into my hip and down my leg with firm, practised hands. She cleaned and bandaged the cut before laying the ice pack over my injured hip.

"You just lie down for the day. That's all. See how it feels tomorrow."

I wanted to argue. Wanted to insist I was fine. But the relief of not having to move anymore was too strong.

She pulled the blanket up over me. Tucked it in around my shoulders like she'd done a hundred times for Jude.

"You just rest," she ordered. "I'll pop back later to see you."

The pain settled into a heavy, pulsing ache as I lay there— deep and insistent, dulled by warmth and stillness. I listened as people came and went, the sounds fading in and out.

Eventually, the store dropped into the mid-morning lull. Guilt gnawed at me for needing help when Jude needed it more, but the pain was louder.

Sleep will fix it, I told myself. I had to believe that. Because the thought that this was something more— something that couldn't be rubbed away with liniment and sleep— was unthinkable.

* * *

I heard the crunch of tyres on gravel through my hazy dream. The squeak of Jim's driver's door, then a slam and then a second slam. Then Jim's voice— low, rumbly— followed by Jude's, thinner than it should have been.

They were back.

Mrs. Lynch appeared in the doorway of the back room at once, like she'd been waiting for that exact sound. She glanced at me— a quick, practised assessment— then turned and swept out front, already rearranging the world.

I stayed where I was. Stretched out on one side, leg useless, hip pulsing with that deep ache that hadn't improved despite my best efforts at denial.

I wanted to be upright. Wanted to be out there, finding out how Jude's day had gone, what Dr. Chen had said, whether she was alright. Instead, I stared at the wall and listened.

"Jude, sit," Mrs. Lynch was saying briskly. "Jim, put the kettle on."

"I'm fine, Anne," Jude protested, faint but automatic.

"I want to hear everything about today," Mrs. Lynch insisted, which told me everything I needed to know about how this was going to go.

Jude paused and then spoke again. "Where's John?"

"John injured himself today. He's in bed. In the back."

Brisk footsteps came down the short hallway. Jim appeared in the doorway, still and intent, followed by Jude, her eyes scanning the room. I realised she'd never been back here— never seen my private space.

She took everything in— the ice pack, the bandage, the fact that I was very deliberately not moving. Her mouth tightened.

"What happened?" she asked.

Mrs. Lynch answered for me. "River, I think. He arrived here soaking wet, cut and limping early this morning. He's hurt his hip quite badly."

Jude came closer, protectively, like sudden movement might make things worse. She crouched at the edge of the bed, not touching me yet, just looking.

"Oh, John," she murmured.

I shifted a fraction— immediately regretted it.

Mrs. Lynch made a sound of sharp disapproval. "Don't even think about it. You're not moving. In fact, if it were up to me, you'd be nailed to the mattress."

Jim came over and sat gingerly beside me, one hand smoothing my forehead. I blinked at him, trying hard to hold back tears. Jim didn't speak at first. Just looked, pressed his lips together. Took stock.

He glanced at Jude, then back at me. "You alright, mate?"

I closed my eyes. The lie sat heavily on my chest. I was not alright.

Jude's hand found me then, resting on my arm— warm, grounding. I could feel the faint tremor in her fingers.

"Okay then, John," she began, easing onto the bed beside me ever so gently and telling me about her day as though nothing was awry.

"We started with a stop at Yatala. And then saw Dr. Chen." She paused.

"Well. There's... a bit more work to do in there."

Gamma knife, she said. Soon.

I wanted to know more. I had a hundred questions. But the effort of staying still was already costing me more than I wanted to admit, and Jude looked like she'd poured everything she had into simply getting home.

"Alright. One thing at a time," she murmured.

Mrs. Lynch brought in a small sandwich for me and a fresh ice pack. "Let's let John rest while we have some dinner."

Jude stayed a moment longer, her hand brushing once over my forehead.

"You don't get to break yourself while I'm gone, you big silly," she whispered, dropping a light kiss on my cheek.

I let out a sound that might have been a laugh. She stood, clearly torn, then let Mrs. Lynch herd her back out front.

Jim lingered at the door. “We’ll have a proper look at that hip later. And if it’s not any better tomorrow, we get Dr. Val in to look at it. No heroics.”

I closed my eyes in agreement. When they left, the room fell into a lull again— the familiar sounds of the store drifting in faintly. The kettle. Low voices. Life continuing, stubborn and ordinary.

The pain throbbed.

Chapter 39

John

Jim didn't leave me alone that night.

He pulled an armchair up beside the bed once the store was locked up, and dragged an afghan over his legs. Mrs. Lynch hovered for a moment, issuing instructions neither of us needed, then finally allowed herself to leave, satisfied that the situation was firmly under control.

The lamp stayed on low. Just enough light to keep the room from tipping into shadows.

The pain didn't ease as the night wore on. If anything, it grew heavier— a deep, grinding presence that pulsed with its own ugly rhythm. Every time I shifted, even slightly, it flared in protest.

Around midnight, I needed the bathroom. I tried to do it noiselessly. Tried to pretend I could manage on my own. Jim was up before I'd even slid off the bed.

"Easy, now." He was already bracing me, lifting the weight from my legs, steady as a fence post. "No rush."

There was no dignity in it. Just the slow, cautious negotiation of movement— my weight leaning into him far more than I liked, his arms firm around my ribs, taking the strain without comment. By the time we made it back to the bed, I was shaking. Sweat prickled along my spine despite the cool night air.

Jim fetched the liniment again. Rubbed it in with firm, methodical care, his hands warm and sure. The smell filled the room— menthol, medicinal, oddly comforting now.

"That's it. Breathe."

He swapped the ice pack out later. Then heat. Then ice again. Like he was tending a stubborn engine that refused to cooperate. I watched him through half-closed eyes. The lines around his mouth deeper than usual. The slump in his shoulders when he thought I wasn't looking.

"Get some sleep," he said roughly.

When morning crept in— pale and tentative through the high window—Jim was still there. Chin tipped forward, arms folded, asleep in the chair beside the bed. I lay awake, listening to him softly snoring.

* * *

Dr. Val arrived mid-morning. I could smell him before I saw him—clean soap, the faint tang of antiseptic carried in from elsewhere. He had the look of a man who spent his days breaking bad news. Jim filled him in on the situation while Val crouched at the foot of the bed, listening with his whole body.

"Let's have a look then."

The examination was brief and thoroughly unpleasant. There was no drama. No sharp inhale. Just a tightening around his eyes, a pause that stretched a second too long.

"How bad is it?" Jim asked stiffly.

Val glanced at me. Met my eyes. Honest.

"Well," he said at last, straightening. "Hip's been fully dislocated. It's back in place now, but the joint's unstable and everything around it is angry. Bring him down for an X-ray today if you can. I'll know more once I see the images and get some of the swelling down."

He hesitated, then added, "For now, bedrest with bathroom breaks and gentle stretching as his only exercise."

I stilled.

"For how long?" Jim enquired.

Val didn't rush the answer. "Couple of weeks. Maybe longer. I'll prescribe some muscle relaxants, something for the pain. But I don't want him walking, or doing anything that puts load through that joint."

The words landed heavily in the room.

Val patted my shoulder once— competent, professional. "We'll get you sorted, John. But you'll need to be patient."

After he left, the silence felt louder than before. Jim stood at the window for a moment, staring out at the street like he was recalculating something important. Then he turned back to me.

"A few weeks, mate. No river swims. No trail walks."

I closed my eyes. The thought of stillness— real stillness— pressed in from all sides. Of watching from the sidelines while Jude fought her battles. Of being unable to walk beside her, to anchor her, to move when she moved.

Jim tucked a blanket around me, preparing to haul me up and into the truck to go for my first ever X-ray.

"We'll manage." His strong arms lifted me, supporting me out the door. "Same as we always do."

I wanted to believe him. But for the first time in my life in The Ridge, I wasn't sure what my place in the pattern was anymore.

And that frightened me more than the pain.

Chapter 40

Jude

I hadn't realised how much of my healing had been tied to movement until John lost his.

The back room of Jim's store had taken on a different rhythm. Slower. Dimmer. The windows were kept half-covered to spare us both the glare, and the air smelled faintly of liniment and clean cotton. John lay on his side, hip immobilised beneath layers of bandage, his body arranged strategically for necessity rather than comfort.

He hated it. He carried tension even at rest— the way his jaw tightened when footsteps passed the doorway, the way his eyes shifted whenever Jim reminded him that he wasn't allowed to get up.

"You're grounded," Jim had reprimanded him again that morning. "Doctor's orders."

John hadn't even bothered to respond. He rarely did, these days.

So I brought my books in instead. I set myself up beside the bed, nestled deep in Jim's old armchair with my notes spread across my knees. Level 3 material. Chemistry. Geology. Climate influence.

"Okay. Let's try this again."

John's eyes opened briefly. Not fully. Just enough to let me know he was there.

"Shiraz in the Adelaide Hills," I read aloud. "Cool climate expression. Tighter structure. Better acid retention than warmer regions."

I waited— out of habit more than expectation. Nothing. But his gaze stayed on me.

I kept going. Talking helped. Not performing. Just explaining. Teaching John anchored me, and helped me retain the information in my brain. Gave my thoughts somewhere orderly to land.

"Soil depth matters," I continued. "Especially with older vines. Roots go deep, but balance is everything. Too much vigour and you lose concentration. Too little and the vine just... gives up."

John's eyes slipped closed again, but his breathing stayed steady, attentive in its own way. Medication blurred the edges of him, but he was listening. I could feel it.

Every so often I stopped, watching the slow rise and fall of his chest, the stillness of a body being forced into rest when all it wanted to do was move. I understood that feeling too well.

When my head began to throb, I stopped reading and just sat there. The room hummed softly with the distant sounds of the store out front— conversation, the hiss of the espresso machine, life continuing at a manageable distance.

I leaned forward, stretching out a hand toward John. My fingers curled against his forearm.

"Waiting to heal is the worst. Worse than the pain. It's the waiting."

John sighed. It sounded like reluctant agreement.

I stopped trying to make the time useful. Stopped organising the empty space. And just sat with him inside it, letting neither of us rush our way through what couldn't be hurried.

* * *

I'd just walked into Jim's after a short solo trail walk and was making myself a tea when I heard an unfamiliar noise— movement— from the back room.

The scrape of fabric. A breath pulled too sharply. The unmistakable sound of effort.

"John?" I called, already moving.

I rounded the doorway and stopped short. He was upright. Or trying to be.

One foot on the floor, leaning against the wall, his injured hip trembling under the strain, his whole body locked in a stubborn, determined posture. He'd made it halfway across the room— toward the back door, toward wherever he thought he was going by himself. My chest seized.

"What are you doing?" The words came out sharper than I meant them to.

John froze.

"Don't—" I crossed the room in three quick steps, wrapping my arms around him, knowing my arms were too weak to take his weight, terrified to touch him the wrong way. "You're not supposed to be up."

He tried to shift his weight. Winced. A sound escaped him— low, involuntary. That did it. Fear flooded in, hot and immediate.

"Do you have any idea what happens if you make this worse? Dr. Val said surgery is still on the table if it doesn't settle. Surgery. Do you understand that?"

John looked at me, eyes dark and unfocused, confused more than defiant.

"I can't watch you go through that because you couldn't stay still for two weeks."

The silence stretched between us.

Then, slowly, carefully, he let me help him back to bed. It was cumbersome, and painful, but we got there. He lowered himself back down. Every movement deliberate.

I sat back on my heels once he was settled, heart racing, guilt and relief tangling together until I couldn't tell them apart.

"I'm sorry," I muttered. "I didn't mean to yell."

I leaned forward and rested my forehead briefly against his shoulder.

"I know you're not trying to be difficult. You're trying to be yourself."

That was the worst part. I helped him get comfortable, rearranging pillows, checking the bandage with hands that still trembled. When I was sure he wasn't going to move again, I dragged my chair back beside the bed and sat down heavily.

"Alright." I picked up my notes, forcing myself to be calm. "Where were we?"

No answer.

"Old vines," I continued. "They survive because they've learned when not to push."

I glanced at him, then down at my own hands before I spoke again.

"Sometimes the smartest thing you can do is nothing at all."

He stayed still this time.

And so did I.

Chapter 41

Jude

I'd read the brochure in detail. I'd watched the explainer videos Dr. Chen's office had sent. I'd even Googled 'Gamma Knife success rates' at three in the morning, which isn't recommended for anyone who doesn't enjoy spiralling into statistics at an hour when their brains are least equipped for nuance.

None of that prepared me for my first sight of the head frame.

It sat on a stainless-steel tray like some medieval instrument— four pins that would be drilled into my skull, a rigid halo, the promise of precision built on immobility. I felt Jim's presence behind me, solid, the way he always was. Stoic. Brave. Nothing about medical machinery seemed to intimidate him. I wished I had even half that steadiness, and I was grateful that they'd allowed him to be in the prep room with me.

The nurse smiled as she worked, like she understood all of this— the fear, the bravado, the ridiculous urge to joke about the situation to hide my fear.

"Ready, Jude?"

No. Not even a bit.

"Sure."

They led me to a reclining chair and explained each step again— topical anaesthetic, the pin sites, the tightening, the pressure, the temporary discomfort. I listened, tried to convince my body that we were being logical about this.

Jim stood to the side, hands in his pockets, hat tucked under one arm.

"You're doing fine," he assured me.

I wasn't doing anything yet, but somehow his faith made it easier to stay in the chair.

The numbing injections stung more than I expected. The frame tightening hurt less than I expected. But the sensation— four pressure points screwing persistently into the bones of my skull— was indescribably strange.

“Good,” the nurse encouraged. “You’re tolerating it well.”

I wasn’t sure ‘tolerating’ was quite the word. More like ‘enduring on principle’.

Once the frame was secured, they covered my head with a net and guided me toward the machine. I caught a glimpse of myself in a reflection and didn’t recognise the expression on my face. Grief, maybe. Hard to tell these days.

During the treatment planning, I lay on a table while they slid me into the machine, the frame locking in place with a click that vibrated through my jaw. The room hummed with practical efficiency— computers, murmured voices, the whirring of motors positioning things I couldn’t see.

It felt like being held in place by the world itself. The treatment finally began, the machine rotating around me with muted mechanical sounds, stopping and starting in increments so small I could barely sense the movement.

No pain.

Just the knowledge that the Gamma Knife was carving its path toward the small, stubborn speck that refused to disappear.

I focused on a point on the ceiling— a tiny grey mark in the white paint— and anchored myself to it. My thoughts slid in and out like water.

This is the last part.

You’ve gone through worse than this.

Don’t cry. Not now. Not over this.

It was over quickly. Quicker than I’d expected.

They removed the frame— the pressure released, leaving behind four angry pinpricks and a dull headache setting in behind my eyes. I sat up slowly, testing my equilibrium. Not terrible, but not good either.

The technician stepped forward to help me. “Easy.”

It wasn’t patronising. It was simply factual.

“I’m fine,” I assured him, though my legs were having a small debate about that.

He didn't argue. He just held out a hand— not to take mine, just to steady the space between us, like he was guiding a skittish horse. I let him walk beside me to the door, where he handed me off to Jim.

Eventually, I was alright to go, and Jim wordlessly walked me out to the big old Ram, waiting in the car park like a big friendly dog.

The drive home was quiet. The headache deepened into something sharp at the temples. A wave of nausea came and went. My eyes kept drifting closed despite my best efforts to stay alert.

"You let me know if you need to stop," Jim said.

"I'm not going to throw up in your truck," I muttered.

"That's not what I said."

I didn't even have the energy to laugh.

We got back to the house, Jim unlocked the door, nudged it open with his shoulder, and waited while I shuffled in. Fatigue settled over me like a weighted blanket— the kind that was supposed to calm you but only reminded you how heavy your body had become.

"Couch," he directed. "Feet up."

Normally I'd bristle at being told what to do. Today I was grateful that someone was thinking on my behalf.

He helped me lower myself onto the couch— not touching me unless necessary, always giving me space. He draped a light throw over me, then crouched down to my level.

"You need anything? Water? Tea?" he asked.

"Just tea. And maybe the curtains pulled."

"I can manage that."

Then, after a hesitation, "Proud of you, kiddo."

The word *proud* hit harder than the frame had.

Not in a painful way. In a way I didn't quite know how to handle.

"Thanks." Anything more would've been too much for me.

Jim straightened, turned off the overhead lights, closed the curtains, and let the room soften into shadow. He moved around the kitchen for a while, the sounds easy and familiar. I drifted in and out of sleep, then I heard him whisper that everything was going to be fine, and then finally the snick of the door catch as he left.

I kept my eyes closed, the ache behind them pulsing steadily. Beneath the pain, beneath the exhaustion, there was something else.

A sense of finality. A fragile hope I didn't dare name yet.

Maybe — just maybe — this was the last of it.
And for now, that was enough.

Chapter 42

Jim

Jude was asleep by the time I finished making tea. Not just light dozing after a hectic day, but the heavy kind— the sort that pulls a person under whether they're ready or not. The throw Anne had knitted for her rose and fell with each breath, her face pale against the worn cushions. I stood there a moment longer than necessary, making sure she was settled, then turned back to tidy the kitchen.

Old habits took over. Papers straightened. Appointment cards stacked. Mail sorted. Order helped. Always had.

That's when I saw the envelope.

It was half-hidden under a magazine, the corner of it peeking out just enough to catch my eye. Yatala Labour Prison stationery. Thick paper. Institutional beige. Dylan Craig's name printed neatly in the corner like it was his business letterhead.

I knew I shouldn't read it. Knew it the second I picked it up. It was none of my business, whatever poison he'd written.

But the handwriting stopped me from just straightening it and moving on. Jagged. Heavy in places, like the pen had been driven down harder out of spite than emphasis. My thumb traced one indented line before I realised what I was doing.

... more than half, for putting up with your stupid face...

... wouldn't want Daddy's little princess thinking she can just walk away with everything...

... bet you're still the same pathetic...

The words swam in front of my eyes. Beneath the letter lay the divorce papers— unsigned, of course. Even locked up, the bastard was still finding ways to keep his hooks in her.

I laid the letter down carefully. Too carefully. Everything in me wanted to put my fist through the wall, wanted to drive straight to that prison and put my fist through Dylan Craig.

Instead, I folded the letter back into the envelope, trying hard not to crush it in my fist.

Jude stirred slightly on the couch, a small sound escaping her lips.

I lowered my voice. "Just rest, darlin'. Everything's going to be fine."

I pulled the door closed behind me with exquisite care, the way you close a door when someone's sleeping. The way you move when you're afraid any sudden motion might shatter something precious.

But my hands— normally so steady, hands that had built half this town and raised a son and poured a thousand perfect cups of coffee— were shaking with rage.

Sixty-six years old, and I'd never wanted to hurt someone as badly as I wanted to hurt Dylan Craig in that moment.

I made it to the Ram before the fury really hit. Sat there gripping the steering wheel, knuckles white, vision blurring at the edges. The letter on my lap felt like it was burning through my jeans. Those words. *Stupid face. Pathetic. Daddy's little princess.*

Simon's face swam up in my memory. Simon, proud and protective of his girl. Simon, who'd died trying to save her from this monster. Simon, whose ashes were scattered somewhere in Adelaide while his daughter fought brain cancer and her waste-of-space husband tormented her from a prison cell.

I started the engine, reversed down the drive with more force than necessary. My mind was already working through logistics. Yatala Prison was just over an hour's drive. I mentally ran through what I'd say. What I'd do.

What I *wanted* to do.

The rational part of my brain— the part that ran a business and paid taxes and followed the law— was screaming at me to calm down, think this through.

But the rest of me— the part that had watched this girl waste away, had lifted her from the chair to her bed when she couldn't hold herself upright, had driven her to appointments and filled her prescriptions and tried so damn hard to be the father she'd lost— that part wasn't listening to reason.

I stopped briefly at Pokey's to ask Anne to look in on Jude, and then at the store to make a phone call. One I probably shouldn't have made. To a man who might be able to persuade Dylan to cooperate. To see things my way.

Then I was on the highway out of town, before I could second-guess my plan.

Chapter 43

Jude

A few hours had passed. I had just woken up when Jim's old Ram rumbled into the drive. I meandered towards the porch.

He sat in the cab for a long moment after killing the engine, both hands gripping the steering wheel. There was tension in his shoulders, the way his jaw was set. Something had happened. Panicked, I moved as quickly as I could to the stairs— all I could think was that something had happened to John.

Jim saw me and finally climbed out.

"Is it John?" I called out, anxious.

"No! No, John's fine. Everything's fine. You should be resting," he admonished.

He moved with purpose as he approached the stairs— not his usual ambling stride but something more determined, deliberate. A thick envelope was clutched in his right hand, looking worse for wear, one corner torn.

My whole body went still. I recognised that envelope.

Jim crossed to me and handed me the envelope with exaggerated care, like he was defusing a bomb. The movement was so controlled it made me nervous.

"I saw these papers needed signing, so I took them down to Yatala to get that taken care of. One less thing for you to worry about."

I stared at the envelope, my throat working. "Jim. How did you manage that?"

I wasn't sure I wanted to know the answer.

"Just had some sense talked into the boy." Jim's tone was flippant, but his hands told a different story. They flexed once, then curled into fists before he forced himself to relax.

I raised my eyebrows at him. My expression said *I see you, and I know you're not telling the whole truth.*

Jim caught my expression and laughed, though it came out more like a bark. "Don't worry. He's no worse for wear, just a bit shaken. Important thing is that's done."

"Oh God, Jim. What did you do?"

He pulled out a chair and sat down heavily, suddenly looking every one of his sixty-six years.

"I drove down to Yatala. Had a conversation with your waste-of-space ex-husband. Explained to him clearly that continuing to harass you from prison was not in his best interests."

I didn't know whether to be horrified or grateful, or somewhere in between.

"He signed. Called the guard, got the papers witnessed. Said to tell you he's sorry. Personally, I think he's more sorry for himself than for what he did to you."

"You shouldn't have, Jim. It's not your battle. You could get in trouble."

"Possibly." Jim's mouth quirked up at one corner. "But I doubt it."

"Well. Thank you," I said.

Jim stood, crossed to me, pulled me into a sympathetic hug that minded my healing skull. "You're family, love. You don't thank family for doing what needs doing. Anyway, your solicitor can file those papers Monday. Get it finished."

"Monday. It'll really be over." I held the envelope against my chest.

"It's *been* over," Jim confirmed. "This just makes it official."

A wave of fatigue washed over me. "I'm going to lie back down. Can you let John know I'll be by to see him in the morning?"

"You bet. Rest now, love. Anne'll bring some dinner over later. Probably enough to feed the entire town, knowing her."

"Thanks, Jim. Really."

I felt a weight lift from my shoulders. One less burden to carry.

CHAPTER 44

John

"Confession time," Jim's rumbly voice pulled me from a doze as he stepped into my dim room, bringing me some slices of cheese and sausage.

Moments like these that I knew how much Jim loved me— it was written into the small acts of kindness like provolone, mild salami and aged cheddar.

But wait, what? Confession time?

I wondered what I'd done that needed confessing, and worried that Jude might have dobbed me in for trying to walk without help.

Jim sat heavily in his armchair, a stiff measure of whiskey in his favourite glass. I stretched my neck and shoulders and looked at him, waiting to be berated.

"John, mate, I did something today that I'm not proud of. But it needed doing, so I don't regret it."

I kept watching him, my expression open.

Jim sank deeper into the chair. He looked at me, and some of that fastidious control finally slipped.

"I found a letter. In Jude's kitchen. I shouldn't have read it, but I did."

He glanced across at me, as if to gauge my reaction. I gave nothing away. My trust in Jim was paramount. If that letter needed reading, then I was glad he'd read it. I waited for more.

"It was from that dirtbag Dylan. Her ex-husband." He studied my face for understanding, and I blinked slowly to show I was following. It was my hip that was injured, not my noggin.

"I saw red. I wanted to kill him, John," he confessed, shocked by his own words.

"I called an old buddy of mine. He's in Yatala too. He's got some standing there."

I wasn't quite sure what he meant, but was reluctant to interrupt.

"He'd had a conversation with Dylan before I arrived. I didn't ask for details. Didn't want them."

Jim stopped talking, and heaved a sigh. He took a long sip of his drink, and I watched him press his lips together and swallow hard. He laid his head back against the chair and stared at the ceiling for a moment. I let him have the moment in peace.

"Sitting there in that visitors' room, John, looking at his bruised, smug face. I've never wanted to hurt someone so badly in my life."

I understood. *I know.* I told him in the only way I could.

"I told him, calmly and clearly, about how things might go for him in prison. About how quickly word spreads, and what happens to men who prey on sick women."

His hand reached out to me, gripping with more force than usual.

"He was scared, John. Underneath that smugness. Signed those papers so fast his hand shook. After everything he did— he was scared of *me*— an old shopkeeper from the Hills." Jim laughed, but there was no mirth in it.

"She can't ever know the details. Can't know exactly what happened. She's got enough to worry about without adding that."

I agreed. Some burdens were meant to be carried alone. Or shared only between friends who understood.

We sat there in the back room of Jim's store, his whiskey slowly dwindling, not saying anything. Outside, the evening sun slanted through the trees. Life in The Ridge continued its patient rhythm. And over at Cooper's cottage, I knew that Jude could finally let go of one more piece of the past that had been dragging her down.

Jim had done that for her. However he'd done it, whatever he'd implied or threatened, didn't matter.

I'd taken his confession and I'd keep his secret. That's what family did.

Chapter 45

Jude

The afternoon light slanted through Jim's front windows, catching dust motes in the air. I'd positioned myself in John's usual chair—he still wasn't using it, and the wide wooden armrests made a decent surface for balancing my textbook and notes. My eyes were still weary, but I could manage an hour or two of study now without a headache.

Diana appeared carrying a small bakery box, her face lit with that joyful energy people get when they're bursting with news.

"Jude! I brought some lamingtons from that place in Stirling."

I straightened immediately, closing my textbook. "The chocolate ones with the raspberry filling?"

"Is there any other kind worth having?" Diana settled into the chair opposite mine, opening the box with a flourish.

The scent of coconut and chocolate hit me like a salve. "You're my favourite person right now, Diana."

"I'll try not to let that go to my head." Diana's eyes crinkled with warmth. "Though I did have an ulterior motive. I wanted to see how you're doing, and I have some news."

I reached for a lamington, the squishy sponge giving slightly under my fingers.

"I'm better. Genuinely better every day. Still tired, but..." I took a bite, closing my eyes briefly at the sweetness. "Lamingtons help."

Diana selected one for herself. "I did read somewhere that Lamingtons are medicinal."

Jim emerged from the back room, spotted the bakery box, and made an appreciative sound. "Are those what I think they are?"

"Hands off," I said, pulling the box slightly closer. "These are for me and Diana."

"Hmph. Getting territorial about lamingtons." Jim shook his head with mock solemnity. "Should've warned me before I adopted you."

"Well, since I adopted YOU too, I might share." I took another bite. "Maybe."

Diana watched this exchange with obvious pleasure. "It's good to see you smiling, Jude. You've been so serious lately."

I considered her observation. Jim answered for me. "It's been a rough couple of months."

"Fair point. Speaking of which— treatment all finished?"

A heaviness settled over me. "Another MRI next Tuesday. They're ramping down the steroids now and monitoring swelling. I don't think about it too much in between. I'm feeling good though. One day at a time, right?"

"Sensible approach."

Diana leaned forward slightly.

"Okay, so are you ready for my news? It's good news, I think. Andy's company has offered him a project right here in the Adelaide Hills— six to twelve months. He'll be back next week. And can help you with anything you need help with— appointments, study sessions, whatever— he'll be around."

I took a sip of my tea, buying time to arrange my expression. "Well. That's great news for him. But I'm managing fine with studies and whatnot." I tucked the lid back down on the lamington box, needing something to do with my hands.

"Of course you are. But there's no harm in having people around who care about you."

Anne arrived carrying a foil-wrapped tray that smelled like lasagna. "Sorry I'm late! Had to finish a batch of— oh, Diana! Lovely to see you. Coming for dinner? There's plenty here."

Jim materialised at Anne's elbow to take the container, his hand brushing hers as he did. "You spoil us with your lasagna, Anne. John will be stoked to see lasagna for dinner tonight."

"Someone has to make sure you all eat properly." Anne's tone was mock-stern, but her eyes were kind as they met Jim's.

"We eat just fine."

"You eat toast for dinner when left to your own devices."

"Toast is a perfectly acceptable meal."

"Toast is not a meal, Jim James."

I caught Diana's eye and we shared a small smile. There was something comforting about their friendly bickering— the kind that came from decades of friendship slowly but obviously shifting into something more.

Diana gathered her things, checking her watch. "I should get going— I have some gardening I want to finish up before the lasagna is served." She squeezed my shoulder as she passed.

After she left, I returned to my textbook, letting Jim and Anne's muffled conversation wash over me.

The bell chimed. I glanced up. I could have sworn Pilar McKeown had been browsing in the wine section, but she had left without a word.

Then the bell chimed again almost immediately, and Pilar swept back in, phone in hand, her face glowing with barely contained excitement.

"Forgot something, Pilar?" Jim's tone was mild, but I caught a slight edge of confusion in it.

"Oh! Right. Yes, I stepped in earlier but had to step out." Pilar waved her phone vaguely. "Andy rang. The time zones are such a nuisance." She paused and then appeared to recall why she was in the store. "Oh! I need three bottles of my wine please, Jim."

She moved toward the counter, then pretended to notice me for the first time, as if she hadn't been lurking around the store for the past ten minutes. "Jude! Still studying, I see. How dedicated."

I kept my expression neutral. "Getting caught up."

"Well, don't work too hard. You need your rest." Pilar's tone was syrupy with false concern. She glanced at her phone again, the screen lit.

"Andy's been keeping me posted from California. He's moving back to The Ridge for six months, maybe more. We caught up before he left— a quick lunch in Hahndorf— and he mentioned then that it was a possibility."

She was watching me intently. I left the comment about their lunch date in Hahndorf unanswered. It was none of my business who Andy had lunch with, or who he kept in contact with.

I kept my voice even. "Diana mentioned that he was coming back. Good for him."

"Ah. Did she? That's good. I'm glad he finally told her." Pilar's smile widened, recalculating since I hadn't taken her bait. "He's been waiting to hear about it for a while."

"Fantastic." I turned a page in my textbook, even though I hadn't finished reading the previous one.

Jim appeared at the counter, three bottles of wine in hand. "These should do you, Pilar. Same as last time."

"Perfect." She paid quickly, gathering the bottles. As she turned to leave, she stopped, looking back at me with something that might have been sympathy if it hadn't felt so calculated. "Do take care of yourself, Jude. You need your strength."

She left. The silence felt heavy.

Anne spoke first, slightly amused. "Well, isn't she a breath of fresh air?"

"Not even slightly," Jim disagreed.

I stared at the page in front of me, the words about Rhône appellations blurring together. My hands wanted to shake but I wouldn't let them.

Andy keeping Pilar in the loop. Coming back. For six months or more. None of which he'd mentioned to me. I hadn't even heard from him.

But then, why would he mention any of it to me? We were only friends— barely that, really. Just people who'd been thrown together by circumstance.

The fact that he'd been so helpful during my treatment didn't entitle me to updates on his life. The fact that finding out he'd been in touch with Pilar made something twist unpleasantly in my stomach was... inconvenient.

Jim moved to set the big dinner table. "Staying for dinner, Jude?" And then, sensing my barely contained irritation, he added, "Don't let Pilar get to you."

"I'm not." I picked up my pen, made a note in the margin that I'd never remember the meaning of later. "She's just being Pilar."

"Pilar's always been good at saying things that sound nice on the surface but dig in like splinters." Anne moved to the chair Diana had vacated, settling in with her own cup of tea. "You know Andy's not... I mean, he wouldn't. Not Pilar."

"It's nothing to do with me." I cut her off. "Really. I don't care who Andy keeps in touch with."

The lie tasted like ash, but I kept my expression composed, my focus on the textbook. Anne and Jim exchanged a look I pretended not to see. I studied until the words stopped making sense, then closed the book and let my head rest against the chair back.

Chapter 46

John

Jim helped me out of bed and over to the table, which in practice meant guiding me slowly across the back room and lowering me onto the thick beanbag cushion Anne had bought for me. I hadn't argued. Pride was a luxury item these days.

The past few days, I'd been doing some stretching and short laps around the store— nothing ambitious. Just enough movement to convince myself the joint was still mine, not something I'd borrowed and needed to return in worse condition than I found it.

"Easy." Jim was as present as ever, one hand hovering near me even when I wasn't leaning on him. "No rush."

Lowering myself down was a slow negotiation. The hip complained enough to remind me it was paying attention. Watching. Waiting to see what I'd try.

Jude was already at the table, lasagna steaming in front of her. She was looking better every day. Still thin, but stronger. More present. The fragile edge had softened.

She smiled when she saw me down there on the cushion.

"Well," she teased. "Look at you down there on your beanbag. Your walking is improving."

I grunted, slightly amused, knowing how cock-eyed I must look shuffling around.

"Don't encourage him," Jim admonished, setting plates down. "He'll get ideas."

"I trust him," Jude countered easily.

I looked at her fondly. Her trust landed heavier than the pain ever had.

Dinner was delicious and ordinary in the best possible way. Lasagna, fresh bread, the clink of cutlery around the table. Family dinner.

Jim moved around with practised familiarity, but I caught him watching me out of the corner of his eye.

"You wanting to get back to bed?" he asked eventually.

I shifted slightly, immediately regretted it. The ache flared— not enough to draw attention, but enough to steal my breath for half a second before settling back into its deep, watchful throb.

"I'll help him," Jude offered, and I gratefully accepted. It was the longest I'd spent out of my bed in the past three weeks, and I was admittedly getting a bit shaky.

I heard Jim telling Diana, "Jude and I are taking John down to Dr. Val's tomorrow. Another set of X-rays. See whether any surgery is needed."

Surgery. The word lodged itself somewhere unpleasant.

"He's done everything right." Jude was confident, as if she could hear my thoughts. "Whatever happens tomorrow."

But one pesky thought kept circling— persistent, unwelcome.

Not *how bad is it?*

But instead, *what if this is as good as it gets?*

* * *

The store had gone quiet. I was back in bed. I wasn't asleep, but I was close to it— floating in that space where pain dulls and thoughts loosen.

Voices drifted faintly from the front room. Jim and Anne. Low. Careful.

"Is everything okay, love? You've been a bit off these past few days," Anne said gently.

A long pause.

Jim spoke at last. "I had to take care of something. To help Jude. Would've preferred not to. But it needed doing, and it's done."

Silence.

"Do I want to know any more?" Anne asked.

"No," he admitted quietly.

I heard the scrape of a chair. The kettle clicking off.

Anne didn't push. She never did.

"Well," she said finally, "whatever it was, don't let it eat at you."

"It won't." Jim didn't sound entirely convinced.

The murmur of their voices faded after that. I lay there staring at the ceiling, hip throbbing in slow rhythm.

Everyone carrying something.

Everyone pretending it didn't hurt.

* * *

Dr. Val's office smelled like antiseptic and old carpet and something faintly metallic underneath it all. Familiar enough to be unsettling.

Jim guided me inside with a hand at my shoulder, unhurried, like he had all the time in the world. Jude walked on my other side, close but watchful, her presence a constant, grounding warmth even when she wasn't touching me.

The X-rays hadn't taken long. Only long enough to make my hip ache from the awkward positioning, long enough to remind me how much of my world had narrowed to small, controlled movements and mindful breathing.

Dr. Val studied the images in stretched-out silence.

Jim stood with his arms folded. Jude's hand resting lightly on me. I watched Val's face instead of the screen, reading him the way you learn to read people when words start to matter too much.

Finally, he leaned back.

"Well, the good news is, we don't need surgery."

The relief hit first. Immediate. Physical. Like something unclenched inside my chest.

"But," Val continued— and there it was, that small word— "that doesn't mean you're out of the woods yet."

He turned the screen slightly so we could all see. I didn't understand the details, but I understood enough. The joint sat where it belonged, but everything around it looked exposed. The images showed a joint that had found its way back home. But the lines around it— the things meant to keep it in place— told a different story.

"You're healing. Just not in a way that gives you your old margins back."

He looked at me then. “From here on, it’s about management, not recovery.”

“What does that mean, exactly?” Jim asked.

Val didn’t rush the answer. I respected him for that.

“Not just weeks. Months of diligent management. Another course of anti-inflammatories. Strict limits on activity. Slow, gradual improvement.”

I waited.

“No running. Nothing strenuous. No sudden turns. No uneven ground. And definitely no swimming.”

The word landed harder than I expected.

No swimming.

The river rose in my mind without permission— cold and clear, the familiar pull of current, the way my body knew exactly what to do without thinking. The rhythm. The freedom. The sense of being exactly where I belonged.

No running.

The trails unfolded in my mind— long, winding ribbons through gum trees and shadow, the joy of racing through, of pushing harder just because I could. The triumph of cresting a hill without slowing.

No more freedom.

Val was still talking.

“Long term, this hip will always be vulnerable. You’ll need to take care with it for the rest of your life. Slow walks only. Flat ground. No pushing through pain. If it flares, you stop and rest.”

I moaned and hung my head. Because what else was there to do?

Jim asked about timelines. Rechecks. Warning signs. Val answered them all, calm and thorough.

“Six weeks. We’ll reimage then. If things settle, great. If they don’t— if there’s instability or worsening pain— you come straight back. No heroics.”

Jim agreed. Jude thanked him. I stayed perfectly still, head hung low, heartbroken.

It wasn’t that I disagreed. Or didn’t understand. It was just that the joy inside of me had gone very still. As if a door had closed on a room I’d spent my whole life in.

On the way out, Jim kept his hand near, steering me. Jude matched my pace without comment. Neither of them tried to fill the silence.

That was a kindness.

Outside, the air was sultry and warm. The day carried on exactly as it always had. Cars passed. People chattered. I focused on the slow, measured placement of each step. On staying upright. On doing what I was told.

And I understood— with a clarity that hurt worse than the hip ever had— that some losses don't announce themselves. They just settle in.

And you either learn to walk around the space they leave behind— or you don't.

Chapter 47

Jude

The last week before my Level 3 exam blurred into something narrow and deliberate. I woke, studied, rested. Walked. Repeated.

My world had shrunk to tidy, manageable pieces— flashcards spread across the kitchen table, tasting notes stuck to the fridge with mismatched magnets, my textbooks stacked in neat, reassuring piles like they were holding the place together by sheer force of organisation.

Healing, apparently, thrived on routine.

John and I took short walks in the late afternoons, when the sunlight had mellowed and I couldn't take any more studying. Never far. Never fast. Just slow loops through the flattest paths we could find, the same stretches of road, the same flat track by the river— close enough to hear it, not close enough to tempt fate.

At first, I'd worried the sameness would drive him mad. It didn't.

What worried me more was how little he seemed to care.

He still walked whenever I was ready. Still moved beside me. Still watched the world with that attentiveness I'd come to rely on. But his spark— his restless joy and barely contained anticipation— was gone.

He walked because I walked. Not because he wanted to.

I told myself it was temporary. Pain medication. Frustration. A natural response to being told your body would never quite be yours again. Anyone would struggle with that. But it was impossible to ignore.

John slept more than usual. Not the heavy sleep of exhaustion, but a flat, disengaged kind— like he was opting out of the day rather than resting for it. Sitting was still difficult, so when he was awake, he lay still, eyes tracking things without interest.

He ate. He complied. He followed the rules. He just wasn't... himself.

I caught him one afternoon standing on the porch, staring out toward the trail that disappeared into the trees. He didn't move when I spoke his name. Didn't startle. Just stood there, weight balanced, gaze fixed on something I couldn't see.

"Hey," I nudged gently. "You okay?"

He turned then, slowly. Looked at me. And for a split second, something raw and unguarded flickered across his face before he smoothed it away.

"You're not fooling anyone," I told him, trying for lightness and missing. "Especially not me."

He huffed a loud sigh— a sound that might have been agreement, or might have been nothing at all.

We walked later, the same measured loop as always. I talked through my exam material as we went— partly for retention, partly because silence felt too heavy these days.

"Adelaide Hills Shiraz tends toward restraint," I lectured aloud. "Less alcohol, more structure. It's about elegance rather than power."

John's eyes met mine. He was listening. Always listening.

"And balance," I added. "That's the thing they'll test me on. Not just what something *is*, but why it works. Why it holds together."

I'd stopped walking without meaning to. John took another step before realising I wasn't beside him anymore, then turned back. Waited.

"I think that's what scares me. Not the exam. Not really. It's the idea that things can be... permanently out of balance. And you don't get to fix them. You just have to adjust."

"I know I sound ridiculous," I went on. "I've had brain surgery. Radiation. Gamma Knife. And here I am, philosophising about wine theory like that's the hard part."

I smiled, thin and tired.

"But I think I get what Dr. Val meant. About management, not recovery."

John didn't move. I stepped closer and placed my hands on his shoulders, feeling the warmth there. Solid. Real.

"We don't have to be brave about this," I told him. "We don't have to pretend that everything is fine."

His only reply was to turn around and keep walking the flat track back to Jim's, my worldly revelations settling into the dust between us.

* * *

The rest of the week followed the same pattern. Study in the mornings until my eyes protested. Short naps. Lots of tea. Notes. Revision questions.

John stayed close. Always nearby. But something in him had pulled inward, like he was conserving what little energy he had left for reasons he couldn't articulate.

Andy was due back on the weekend. I tried not to think about it. Tried to keep my focus narrow and practical— just get through the exam, then we'd see. One thing at a time had become my mantra.

But late Friday afternoon, as I packed up my textbooks to head home, I saw John watching me from the doorway.

Not with his usual patience. With something like... devastation.

"Hey," I whispered. "You okay?"

He came over, settled awkwardly into the chair beside me.

I sat beside him, pulling my knees up and watching him get comfortable. For a while, we just existed there together in the dim light.

He rested his cheek on the back of the chair, looking at me. His breathing slowed, steadied, finally letting go of the effort of pretending.

I rested my chin on my knees and smiled at him.

"We'll figure this out," I promised. "Both of us. Even if life looks different than we thought it would."

Outside, the night was still. No wind. No rush of river. Just the unremarkable sound of life carrying on.

John stayed still in the chair, unmoving, grieving.

And somehow, that felt like the most honest place either of us had been in a while.

* * *

The drive to Adelaide felt easier this time. Not shorter— the hills still unravelled at their own pace— but lighter, as if my body had finally stopped bracing for impact every time we crested a bend. Jim drove one-handed, relaxed, the radio low. I watched the familiar landmarks slide past and realised, with mild surprise, that I wasn't counting the minutes.

Dr. Chen's rooms were running on time— a good sign. The nurse smiled when she called my name, her tone casual, unhurried. No urgency. No tight expressions. I took that as permission to relax.

The appointment itself was almost anticlimactic. Neurological checks. Questions about headaches, vision, balance.

"Everything seems stable," Dr. Chen confirmed, scrolling through my file with efficient confidence. "Exactly what we want to see at this stage."

I tried not to let the relief overwhelm me.

"We'll continue tapering the steroids this week," she went on. "You're on the final reduced dose now. If you tolerate that without rebound swelling, we'll discontinue completely."

The words landed decisively, like a door clicking shut behind me.

"And after that?" I asked.

"After that, we monitor. Still weekly for a couple of months, then we can start spacing things out."

Jim settled beside me, releasing a breath he probably didn't realise he'd been holding.

I thanked her, asked the sensible questions, accepted the next appointment card. By the time we walked back to the car, the city felt less sharp, less overwhelming.

Jim unlocked the Ram and paused. "Coffee?"

I smiled. "Please."

We sat outside a small café a few blocks from the hospital, the late-morning sun warm on my face. I wrapped my hands around the mug, took a sip of the coffee like it was something restorative.

"So," Jim enquired, stirring his own coffee. "Any word on the exam yet?"

"Not officially. But... I know I did well."

"Of course you did," he agreed, smiling.

I was oddly proud of myself for the first time in a very long time. "Thanks, Jim."

"Level 4 starts in February, which gives me a couple of months. But I'd like to start early. Get a headstart on my thesis."

"Speaking of which, I should have mentioned it earlier. Didn't want to jinx it. I spoke to Pat Thompson's nephew, Mike. He still holds the title to the Thompson place. Lives up in Darwin. Practical bloke. Straight shooter."

I straightened in my seat, waiting.

"I told him about you, about what you're studying. Your thesis idea— soil analysis, vine health, historical land use." Jim shrugged. "Didn't oversell it. Just told him you were serious, and a good friend."

"And?"

"And he said yes. I've got his contact details back at the store. When you pass your Level 3, you give him a call and get started on your project."

I was going to write a restoration plan for the Thompson vineyard. Century-old Shiraz vines. I couldn't even understand why this was so important to me, but it felt like a lifeline.

"He said old Pat would've liked that," Jim continued. "Thinks the place deserves to be studied again, maybe even put back into production one day."

For a moment, I couldn't speak. My chest felt too full— not with fear this time, but with pride. Pride I'd earned.

"Thank you, Jim," I managed.

Jim waved it off. "No need to thank me, I just opened the door. You're the one who'll walk through it."

As we pulled back onto the road toward The Ridge, the hills rose up to meet us, green and familiar and waiting.

For the first time in a long while, my future didn't feel like something I had to survive.

It felt like something I might be allowed to build.

Chapter 48

John

Andy came in mid-afternoon. He was on his phone, carrying on what sounded like a business call with a relaxed, friendly tone.

"Jim," he whispered, holding the phone away from his mouth. "Flat white?"

Jim looked up from the counter and gave him a thumbs-up.

Andy turned then, and saw Jude.

"Right-O, sounds like a plan. I'll connect with you in the next few days and let you know what I've come up with." Andy wrapped up his call and took a step toward Jude.

She was seated at the small table by the window, textbook open neatly in front of her, posture very straight.

"Hey," Andy said.

Jude looked up. Her expression warmed automatically, politely.

"Hey yourself," she replied. "You're back."

"Got in last Saturday. Been up and down the Hills the past few days. I was going to swing by your place and say hello."

He glanced toward me, stretched out on my cushion near the dining table.

"And John," he added. "How's the hip? Mum told me you had a bit of a slip."

I lifted my head a fraction. *Still here. Still not moving the way I was meant to.*

Andy nodded, like that told him enough.

He pulled out a chair but didn't sit immediately, waiting— giving Jude space to decide whether she wanted company.

She didn't invite him. She didn't refuse either. So he sat. Jim carried over a flat white in a mug, eyebrows raised at Jude, wordlessly asking if she needed anything.

"I'm good, thanks, Jim."

"How are you feeling?" Andy asked.

"So much better," Jude replied, and you really could see the improvement in her. "I still get tired, but that's from the radiation. Eventually, it'll fade too."

"That's good." He meant it.

There was a pause. Andy took a sip of his coffee. Jude picked up her pen, then set it down again.

"So. Seen Pilar?"

The question wasn't casual. It wasn't sharp.

It was a test.

Andy answered without drama. "I've run into her once since I've been back. Briefly. Why?"

"She's well?" Jude asked.

"As far as I know." Andy's confusion was evident. "Same Pilar as always."

I watched Jude's face. The way her eyes stayed neutral, her mouth relaxed. She accepted the answer. I could see she didn't quite believe it.

Andy shifted slightly, recalibrating.

"Mum told me you've been doing weekly check-ups. That things are tracking well."

"They are. Getting a gold star each week from the doctor. This is my last week on the steroids. And for now, no more treatments, just monitoring."

Andy smiled. "That's huge. Really great to hear, Jude." He slid a hand halfway across the table but didn't make contact. Jude looked at it and leaned back in her chair.

She inclined her head. "It feels like progress."

He glanced at the books. "And study?"

"I just passed Level Three," Jude enthused, lighting from within. "I knew I'd done well, but didn't expect a 98% on the final exam. Really happy with that. And I am really loving the material. It's so interesting."

Andy's pleasure was immediate and unguarded. "Fantastic! I never doubted you'd do well."

She looked away at that, unwilling to step into the warmth of it.

"I've registered for Level Four— it starts in February," she added. "Gives me a little breathing room."

"That's your Master's, right?"

She nodded.

Andy hesitated, then suggested, "Look, if you ever need a lift down to Adelaide for a check-up— or just want to talk— I can make my schedule work around yours."

The offer was simple. Practical. Kind. And Jude shut it down just as simply.

"Jim and Anne have it covered," she declined. "But thank you."

Not unkind. Final.

Andy absorbed that.

The line drawn cleanly. No anger in it. No opening either.

"No worries. I just want you to know the offer's there." He finished his coffee and stood.

She looked up at him. "I appreciate that."

He looked at me once more— something tired in his eyes— then over to Jim.

"Thanks for the coffee, Jim," he said, heading towards the door.

"Anytime."

Jude didn't look up again for a long moment. When she did, she turned a page she hadn't finished reading.

I lay there, watching her hold herself together with the same discipline she brought to everything now— healing, studying, surviving.

Andy had offered help. Jude had refused it.

It seemed a chasm had grown between them, wider even than before.

* * *

By the time I reached Pokey's, my hip had had enough.

Not pain, exactly— but a deep, warning ache that meant *this is as far as you go for now*. I mounted the porch and lowered myself down, letting the warmth of the wood seep into me, and closed my eyes for a minute.

Flat walk. Approved distance. No heroics.

Over the picket fence, Diana's front lawn looked velvety green in the late afternoon sun. I wasn't paying much attention until voices drifted over— familiar ones.

Andy and Diana.

They stood near the garden bed, far enough away that they didn't know I could hear them, close enough that I could— clearly.

"I can't keep trying to break through walls that just get higher," Andy was saying. "Maybe I should just forget about it. About her."

There was no anger. Just fatigue.

"Andy..."

"Every time I think I'm getting somewhere," he went on, cutting in without meaning to, "she just shuts me down."

I stayed where I was. Still. Listening.

Diana folded her arms, thinking. "She's a very independent girl. You can clearly see that. And after the tumour—"

"I know," Andy interrupted. "I know that shook everything. I'm not trying to rush her, or fix anything. I just—"

He gestured helplessly. "I don't know where I fit."

"If she thinks you see her as weak, or treat her like she's fragile—"

"That's not it, Mum. I don't think she's weak. I think she's strong. I think that's the problem."

Diana hesitated a fraction of a second. "What do you mean?"

"She's got this routine. Everything is so controlled. Safe. Maybe that's all she wants right now."

The words hung there for a moment. Eventually Diana replied.

"She's been through a lot. And when people lose control over something in their body, they cling hard to whatever certainty they can find."

"I get that, Mum. I really do. I just don't know if there'll ever be any room for me in there."

That landed. Even without knowing the whole story— the things Jude never talked about, the things she carried inside— Andy wasn't wrong. He'd hit the proverbial nail on the head.

I shifted on the porch, the movement pulling a faint protest from my hip. I welcomed it. A physical anchor.

Jude wasn't being cruel. She wasn't playing games. But she *was* holding herself inside something narrow and rigid— a life meticulously arranged so nothing could knock it sideways again.

And Andy, the poor bugger, kept offering himself up as something flexible. Optional. Easy to refuse.

For the first time, I felt an uncomfortable twinge. She *was* being hard on him. Understandably so. But still.

Diana reached out and touched her son's arm. "Give her time."

"I have been. I just don't know if it's worth trying anymore."

I looked away then, out toward the serene stretch of road leading back to Jim's store. Some truths aren't meant to be witnessed. Just understood.

When I finally pushed myself up from the bench and started the long, flat walk home, my hip still complained— but my thoughts were clear.

Jude had built walls to survive. Andy was standing at them, asking politely to be let in. And I had the uneasy feeling that neither of them could clearly see the other's perspective.

Something would have to shift. That kind of tension couldn't hold forever.

CHAPTER 49

John

A week passed, and without quite meaning to, I began to lift my head and notice things.

Jude and I still took our short walks, still moved together through days shaped by healing. The Ridge went on around us— birds singing into the morning, bees busy with their uncomplicated purpose, trees flowering as though nothing had ever been interrupted.

At some point, I stopped seeing it all as something happening beyond me, and started letting it back in. Life, it turned out, hadn't been waiting for permission to carry on.

Mrs. Lynch's Christmas baking helped. She tested batch after batch on all of us, and while my core strength and formerly trim belly were clearly losing the battle, I couldn't bring myself to object.

It was early on a check-up Tuesday, and Jim had headed down to a wine auction at Victor Harbor. Jude had arranged for Mrs. Lynch to take her to Adelaide for her appointment.

I knew something was off the moment Mrs. Lynch's ancient VW made this dramatic cough and then fell silent. She tried again. Nothing.

She'd never had car trouble in fifteen years— at least, not until 7:45 on the Tuesday morning when Jude needed to leave for her follow-up appointment.

"Oh dear!" she exclaimed, peering at the engine with unconvincing confusion. "And Jim's gone for the day..."

I watched Jude's shoulders tense. We all knew what was coming next.

"Andy!" Mrs. Lynch called, waving to where he was helping his mother arrange potted herbs on her veranda. "You're headed into Adelaide today, aren't you?"

The look Jude shot Mrs. Lynch could have withered her prized roses. I choked on my laugh.

"I can reschedule," Jude started to say, but Mrs. Lynch was already shaking her head.

"Nonsense. Andy's going anyway, aren't you, dear?"

Andy approached warily, like someone navigating a minefield. "Happy to help. I'm just dropping some paperwork at the office. No trouble to—"

"I don't need—" Jude began.

"Of course you don't *need*," Mrs. Lynch interrupted briskly. "But sometimes it's nice to have company, isn't it? Especially when my car has developed such an unfortunate and mysterious problem."

She winked at me. Not at all obvious.

The drive arrangement was negotiated like a peace treaty— Andy would return to pick Jude up at exactly 2:30 pm, not a minute before. No waiting around. No hovering. No expecting to go in with her. If she was done earlier, Jude would text when she was ready to leave. They finally agreed, and Jude slid into the passenger seat.

I watched them pull away, Andy steering while Jude stared straight ahead.

When they returned that afternoon, something had shifted. Jude's shoulders were looser, and Andy was telling a story that had her almost smiling. They pulled in in front of Pokey's, and for the first time, Jude invited someone else to join us for afternoon ice cream. Though the invitation seemed to surprise her as much as him, she didn't take it back.

I considered my options. The small table by the window was our space— had been since our first ice cream together. But I was learning that we all had to leave room for change.

Mrs. Lynch appeared with ice cream— ginger for Jude, vanilla and a crushed sugar cone for me—as always. But she'd also brought a third bowl for Andy, with two scoops that she'd chosen for him and a secret smile on her face.

* * *

That day trip to Adelaide had shifted something loose in Jude's carefully constructed walls. I noticed it in small ways over the next few days— how she lingered whenever Andy was around, the way her hand didn't immediately withdraw when their fingers brushed over dinners at Jim's.

But it was the second drive that really changed things. This time, when Mrs. Lynch's VW miraculously developed another suspicious rattle, Jude just shook her head and yelled out to Andy, who happened to be at Diana's again.

"I suppose you're conveniently headed to Adelaide today?" she asked. Andy was desperately trying to look surprised by this turn of events.

"As it happens..." he started.

"Of course you are." Jude waited a second, then added, almost casually, "Mind driving me down for my check-up?"

"Don't mind at all," Andy grinned, grabbing his keys from the table and taking the steps down two at a time.

I watched them go with a strange mix of relief and something I didn't yet have a name for.

The drive became a routine after that. Tuesdays with Andy. Jude didn't make a fuss about it. She didn't announce anything had changed. She just... adjusted. As if a door she'd kept bolted for safety had been opened a cautious inch, then another.

She still came back, still spent time with me. She still sat beside me in the evenings, talking through ideas that didn't really need an audience, or reading aloud until I dozed off. She still walked with me along the flatter paths, matching her pace to mine without comment, without impatience. Still worried— a hand on my shoulder, a glance that asked without words how I was travelling today.

But her world had widened.

Andy took her places I couldn't follow. Long lunches that stretched into afternoons. Bike rides through Hahndorf and along vineyard lanes where the road rolled easily and the air smelled like mulch and summer dust. Conversations that didn't have to pause every few steps to accommodate my injury, or restrain themselves around what I couldn't do anymore.

It wasn't lost on me that while Jude's healing pointed forward, mine circled in place.

She was expected to recover. Fully. To reclaim what had been interrupted.

I was expected to adapt.

No one said it cruelly. No one needed to. The language was different— *long-term, ongoing, management.* Words that didn't ask when I'd be finished, only how I could live with what remained.

Watching Jude step back into her life— cautiously, but with confidence growing each week— I felt the truth settle deeper than pain ever had. I wasn't moving toward an old version of myself. I had to learn how to be someone new— or throw in the towel.

And I realised something uncomfortable, sitting there one evening while she recounted a Mount Lofty hike and garden tour with subtle enthusiasm, her hands shaping the story in the air.

I had been a bridge.

Not the destination. Not the future. Just the thing that had helped her cross from isolation back into connection.

At first, the thought stung. I'd grown used to being needed— used to anchoring her, walking beside her through fear and pain and recovery. There had been purpose in that. Clarity. A role I knew how to play.

Now, as her trust in the world returned, my role was shifting. Without ceremony.

And yet— watching her laugh at something Jim was saying one afternoon, watching the way she stood taller these days, shoulders no longer curled inward, bracing for impact— I couldn't bring myself to resent it.

If anything, there was a strange pride underneath the ache.

She'd learned, the hard way, that walls keep danger out— but they also keep life from getting in. That trust doesn't have to mean surrender. That connection— real connection— didn't have to cost her everything. I'd taught her that.

As for me, I was learning a harder lesson— that purpose isn't always about being central. Sometimes it's about stepping back once you've done what you came to do. Or about knowing when to loosen your grip.

One evening, as Jude settled beside me on the porch steps after a long day out, she leaned her head lightly against my shoulder and sighed.

"John. I'm so grateful for you. You're such a special soul."

I didn't move. Didn't need to.

Because even as parts of my world shrunk— even as I learned to measure distance differently now— I could feel, with some modicum of certainty, that I hadn't been left behind.

I'd helped her remember how to walk forward.

And maybe— just maybe— that was enough.

Chapter 50

John

It was our third evening trek up to the ridge at the Thompson place. The walk strained my hip more than I'd like to admit, but each time felt a bit easier. We'd sit amongst the vines, and Jude would collect samples of soil and vines and pooled water, and take photographs of everything in preparation for her thesis. I'd stretch out long in the grass, enjoying the feel of the setting summer sun on my face.

Andy appeared at the edge of the vineyard one evening just as the sun had started its final descent to the horizon. I'll admit, I was surprised to see him. Not upset— Andy was alright, even if I still wasn't entirely sure what his intentions were toward Jude. He wandered down to where we were, clipping a tape measure into his pocket, and folding his notebook closed.

"Andy? What brings you up here?" Jude looked up from where she was kneeling by an old root system. Her hands were shaking slightly with fatigue— I'd been watching her work for the past hour, knowing she'd only be annoyed if I suggested we head down before she was finished. Her eyes were filled with purpose, that spark that had been missing during the worst of the treatment.

"Just wandering up to watch the sunset," he pointed toward the west.

I raised an eyebrow at that. The best sunset spot was another hundred metres up the ridge, at the old fence line. I kept my thoughts to myself and settled against a fencepost to watch whatever was about to unfold.

"What about you?" Andy asked. "School work?"

"Getting a head start on my thesis for next year. I'm testing the mineral content in the soil, trying to understand why these particular vines produced such extraordinary wines."

I'd heard variations of this explanation about a dozen times now— to Jim, to Mrs. Lynch, to herself when she thought no one was listening. Each time, her voice got a little more certain. Like she was convincing herself as much as anyone else.

"Well, the vines themselves are extraordinary, so it's no wonder, really," Andy said, kneeling beside her to examine a gnarled trunk.

I watched him run his hand along the bark, and something in the gesture made me pay closer attention. That wasn't the casual touch of someone just making conversation. It was the same way Jim handled his rare vintage bottles— with reverence and respect.

"Original rootstock," Andy continued. "South Australia's phylloxera-free."

Jude raised an eyebrow. "Yes, I know."

"Quarantine's a big part of why it's stayed that way. It's how we can keep producing vines on their own roots— vines that would've been replanted somewhere else. And these..." He traced the twisted wood with his fingers. "Given the location and age of this place, they could be some of the earliest plantings in the Hills."

Jude laughed nervously, and I knew she was about to launch into an explanation. "I'm hoping that it's about more than age and vine health, or that blows apart my whole hypothesis." She pushed her hair back, leaving a smudge of dirt on her forehead she didn't notice. "The geology here is unique— ironstone, gravel, loamy sand. I'm looking at how elevation, soil composition, and runoff shaped what Thompson was getting out of these vines."

She trailed off, mentally tracking how much she'd just revealed. Jude had a habit of talking fast when she was excited— then realising, all at once, she'd said too much.

"Seems pretty intense for a thesis." Andy picked up her methodology notes. Even from where I sat, I could see how detailed they were— pages covered in her precise handwriting, diagrams, charts, notes in the margins.

"I know." Jude labelled another soil sample, her hands steadier now that she was absorbed in the work. "I get pretty excited about soil chemistry. It's kind of my thing." She gestured at the scattered papers covered in chemical formulas that might as well have been ancient Greek to me.

Andy and I both knew that, but we kept mum. The girl could talk for hours about mineral content and pH levels and something called cation exchange that I'd stopped trying to understand.

"And yet, you left your career as a soil scientist." Andy teased.

Jude shrugged. "Every day was the same as the next, working in the lab. Simple contaminant tests, reported results. No context, no bigger picture. Just another link in an endless chain."

Andy's head tilted, like he'd heard something important in those words.

"That's how people lose decades of their lives, isn't it?" Jude mused, and now she was talking to herself more than to Andy, staring out at the old vines silhouetted against the sunset. "Repeating steps in the proverbial chain. Never testing new theories. Not even trying anymore. Just living by rote, day after day, same thing by same thing. Time passes. And then—"

I felt something tighten in my chest. This was the Jude who'd stared death in the face and come out the other side changed.

"Before you know it, life's gone," she finished.

The three of us sat there in the growing dusk, the old vines casting long shadows across the ground. A currawong's descending whistle drifted down from somewhere up the hill.

"Vine philosophy?" Andy suggested, lightening the dark moment, and there was something easy and accepting there that made me like him a bit more.

"Something like that." Jude gathered her samples, organising them with the precision I'd come to recognise as her way of regaining control when emotions threatened to overwhelm her. "Maybe that's why I'm going overboard with this project. It feels good to think again. To really think."

I stretched and got to my feet, shaking the dust from my coat. Jude started packing up her equipment, finally acknowledging her exhaustion.

Andy stood too, still holding those methodology notes. "Mind if I come by to look at these one day? I'd be interested to see your findings."

"Sure." I caught the slight hesitation, but only because I knew her so well. She was protective of her study, and I could understand why. None of us really knew what Andy's work here entailed.

We made our way down the hill— Jude and I both moving slower than we once did. Andy walking beside her, I trailed behind. I couldn't shake the feeling that there was more happening here than soil samples and sunset watching.

Both of them were being secretive about why they were really here. But eventually, the truth had a way of working itself out.

I just hoped when it did, it wouldn't break whatever fragile thing was growing between them.

* * *

It was the second week of December— and summer had roared in like a lion. I was sitting directly under the fan at Jim's, statue-still, feeling the cool breeze down the back of my neck.

Andy was leaning against the counter, phone to his ear, posture loose in that way that suggested he wasn't negotiating anything urgent— just talking through ideas with someone who understood his shorthand.

"Yeah," he confirmed. "Barossa first. Maybe swing down through the McLaren Vale vineyards that you want me to look at if I've got enough time."

I raised my face to the fan, eyes half-lidded, enjoying the way the breeze wicked the sweat from my forehead and cheeks almost before it had formed. Jim had a stupid rule about running the air conditioning— he refused to turn it on before Christmas Day.

"I'll spend three days," Andy went on. "Nothing formal. Just tasting, wandering, seeing if anything sticks. Get a report to you early next week."

Pilar had been in the shop for a while by then. Too long, really, for someone who'd probably just come in to get wine. She stood a few metres away, hidden by the shelves just enough that she could plausibly deny listening.

Except she *was* listening. Each time Andy spoke, she typed something into her phone, then she'd lift her head and wait for the next bit of information.

"Couple of small cellar doors I haven't been to in years," Andy was saying. "No, no. Mate, I don't mind at all— be good to get out of town for a bit. Yeah, I can leave Friday morning."

Pilar angled herself closer. Not obvious.

Andy wrapped up the call soon after, murmuring goodbyes and slipping the phone into his pocket. He turned toward the counter, oblivious.

Pilar didn't wait, but nor did she approach.

I stayed still, watching the door swing closed behind her. Whatever she'd just overheard, she was already putting it to use in that crafty little brain of hers.

A few minutes passed.

Then Jude came in through the back door, probably assuming I'd be lying down in bed after a somewhat long morning walk. Her hair was pulled back loosely, her movements unguarded, a short sundress showing off her lightly tanned legs. She looked lovely and breezy, without making a show of it.

Andy turned when he saw her, his expression lifting.

"Oh— hey. Perfect timing."

Jude hesitated. "For what?"

"I just got a request in from the boss. I need to go do a bit of winery wandering this weekend. Barossa, maybe McLaren Vale. Nothing serious. Thought I'd see if you wanted to come along."

He said it simply. No build-up. No glance toward the door. No awareness at all of the woman who'd just left with stars in her eyes and a plan forming.

Jude considered him for a moment.

"Where would we stay?" she asked.

"Wherever's convenient. Separate rooms, obviously."

Her eyes lit— I wasn't sure if it was the idea of seeing lots of wineries, or the idea of a weekend spent with Andy. "Then yes. I'd really like that."

Andy smiled, clearly pleased. "Great. I'll sort the details. Pick you up around 10 on Friday?"

Jude nodded, leaning against the counter to wait for Jim.

I mused on what would happen next. Pilar had overheard everything— except the part that mattered.

Chapter 51

Jude

Friday morning. The forecast for the weekend was beautiful summer weather. I walked over to Jim's to join John for a walk and pick up a few things for the winery road trip with Andy.

Pilar was at the long cooler when I came in.

"Oh, Jude! Maybe you can help me?" Pilar chirped, waving me over. "Do you know anything about cheese?"

I slowed, an expression that showed I was thinking hard about cheese on my face. She stood straight, pushing a wicker basket lined with gingham toward me for inspection. It was brimming with curated things— artisan crackers, olives in glass jars, dark chocolate wrapped in paper. A weekend basket. A statement basket.

"Hi, Pilar. That's quite the haul."

She glanced down at the basket with false modesty. "Just picking up a few things for the weekend. I need some cheeses. What do you suggest? What would Andy like?"

"Oh?" I tilted my head. "You're buying cheese for Andy?"

Her eyes lowered— just a fraction. Then she recovered.

"Taking a little trip away." She waved one manicured hand vaguely. "Wine country. You know. Tastings, long lunches, scenic drives."

I smiled. Interested. Neutral. "Sounds lovely. Where are you headed?"

"Barossa, mostly," she said smoothly. "Though Andy mentioned McLaren Vale as well. Depends how the mood strikes."

Andy mentioned?

Something twigged in my recent memory. I recognised this feeling. The implication that she and Andy had had lunch before he left for

California. The keeping in contact while he was away. Implied, not explicitly stated. Pilar was trying to gaslight me.

I leaned my hip against the table. "Sounds fabulous. You must be looking forward to it."

"Oh, I am," Pilar agreed, warming to the topic now. "Andy's been talking about the wineries in those regions for ages. Three days, two nights."

I let her continue.

"Andy knows all the best places," she went on. "The smaller cellar doors. The ones you don't just stumble across."

Jim appeared behind the counter, saying nothing. John had emerged from the back, and I could see he was ready to go for a walk.

"And where will you stay?"

"Oh— probably somewhere central. I don't think it's been decided yet."

Of course it hadn't.

The bell chimed. We all turned. Andy walked in.

He took in the basket first, then Pilar, then me— his expression puzzled as if the pieces didn't quite fit together.

"Hey there. What's up?"

Pilar turned to him too quickly. "Oh! There you are. I was just telling Jude about the little weekend getaway."

Silence. It wasn't dramatic. It didn't need to be.

I met Andy's eyes and smiled.

"Pilar's been filling me in on your weekend trip."

Andy frowned slightly. "My—?"

"The wineries," Pilar pressed in quickly. "Barossa, possibly McLaren Vale—"

Andy looked from her to me. I watched Pilar's colour drain in real time.

"Right," he said, drawing out the word as he approached the counter and accepted a flat white from Jim.

"Have I walked into the Twilight Zone?" he muttered to Jim, sotto voce.

"Oh!" I snapped my fingers to show that I'd just clued in as I turned back to Pilar. "Pilar, you must be talking about *my* weekend trip with Andy. Our getaway to Barossa and McLaren Vale."

Pilar laughed— a brittle, confused sound. "No, I— I must've misunderstood."

I straightened then, not unkindly, not sharp.

"No," I told her. "You didn't *misunderstand*. You *assumed*. And you were trying to get under my skin."

Andy shifted his weight, uncomfortable. "Pilar, I don't know what your caper is, but it has to stop, okay? I don't want to be cruel, but I need to be clear. You were my mother's real estate agent. For one day. That's it. We're not dating. We've never dated. We're not going to. Okay?"

He didn't even say they were friends. He didn't soften it. He didn't apologise. But he wasn't rude either. He let Pilar preserve whatever dignity remained.

Pilar gathered herself, her mask slipping but not entirely gone.

"Well," she announced stiffly, "I suppose wires get crossed."

"Sometimes," I agreed.

She dropped the basket onto the cooler, manicured fingers outstretched as though she'd just handled something distasteful. Her eyes darted once— sharply— back to Andy.

"Enjoy your trip," she spat, and swept out without waiting for a reply.

The bell chimed. The shop settled.

Andy exhaled. "I'm sorry about that."

"It's fine." And it was.

Jim cleared his throat. "Jude, want a coffee? Tea?"

I shook my head. "No, thanks, Jim. I'm just here to meet John for a walk.

I caught John's eye and found a cross between amusement and approval in his eyes.

For the first time in a long while, I hadn't bent to keep the peace. And the world, it turned out, kept spinning.

* * *

The Barossa shimmered in shades of green when we arrived— vines marching in disciplined rows across the low hills. I was always amazed how orderly vineyards looked from a distance. Controlled. Intentional. As if nature had agreed to behave.

Andy drove with one hand loose on the wheel, sunglasses pushed back in his hair.

"I promise this isn't a sneaky holiday disguised as a work trip," he said lightly. "I truly do have work reasons for all of our stops."

"And what's our intention? What are we looking for, from a work point of view?"

"Nothing formal. Just... curious. Gathering intel."

"Intel about what?" I asked.

"Potential."

The word sat between us.

We spent the afternoon wandering through a cellar door that smelled of oak and sun-warmed stone. I listened as Andy asked questions that sounded casual but weren't— about yields, distribution channels, long-term contracts.

Later, walking between rows of old Grenache vines, I crouched to scoop a handful of soil. It crumbled easily, red-brown and fine.

Andy watched me. "You can't help yourself but touch the dirt, can you?"

I brushed dust from my palms. "There's quite a different drainage profile here compared to the Hills. Less fractured rock. More uniform."

He tilted his head, genuinely interested. "Can you tell me why that matters?"

I was starting to feel like I was being quizzed. "Well, I guess it depends what you're trying to grow."

He studied the ground then, as if seeing it differently.

At dinner that night— a small pub with ceiling fans and chalkboard menus— he told me outright what his mission was.

"The Reed Group's looking to expand. Strategic vineyard acquisitions. Consistent large-scale blends for international distribution.

"Giving Reed a wide swath of control," I added.

His smile thinned just slightly. "You make it sound sinister."

"I don't mean it that way." I traced the rim of my glass. "Just... wondering, I guess."

He waited.

"I mean, you've always spoken about sustainable agriculture like it's your passion. But this sounds more like consolidation. Scale.

Efficiency. Not about caring for the vines. Sometimes those don't sit easily together."

The words surprised even me. I hadn't meant to say them aloud, to sound like I was criticising his job.

Andy didn't bristle. He leaned back, considering.

"That's fair," he admitted. "And you're right— this part of the job is a bit out of my scope. But I wanted to be back here in SA. Sometimes you have to jump into an available role rather than pursuing your passion. In any case, I do believe in the project, if that's what you're wondering. Scale is what keeps some smaller vineyards alive. Capital means better irrigation, better soil management, fewer desperate harvests."

He didn't come across as defensive. Just honest. I hadn't expected that answer.

The next morning, we walked the small vineyard properties he'd mentioned. He took notes. Measured rows. Asked about rootstock and water rights. At one point, he paused beside a struggling block.

"See how uneven the canopy is?" he pointed out. "They're compensating above ground for something they're not addressing below."

I stepped closer, scanning the soil line.

"I think the subsoil might be compacted," I said after a moment. "If the roots can't push down, they'll spread shallow. Makes them vulnerable. You'd have to fix that first."

He blinked at me.

"That's... exactly what I was thinking."

I smiled faintly. "No, it isn't. You were thinking irrigation."

A beat.

He laughed, unguarded. "Okay. Maybe you're right."

We stood there longer than necessary, both of us looking at dirt.

"You were wasted in a lab," he said finally.

"I'm not going back to a lab."

"No," he agreed. "You're not."

There was something different in the way he said it. Recognition, possibly respect.

Early that afternoon we drove through McLaren Vale. Windows down. Music low. Heat pressing in from every side.

We didn't talk about Reed Group again. We talked about wine. And bad university lecturers. And travel. And John.

At a lookout high above a vineyard, I rested my elbows on the railing and let the wind lift my hair.

"What are you thinking right now," he asked quietly beside me.

"I'm not thinking anything."

"Good. Because the only thing you should be thinking of is lunch."

His hand brushed mine on the railing. Not deliberate. Not accidental either.

I didn't pull away, not right away. But eventually I pushed back from the railing.

"Lunch it is."

When we drove back to The Ridge on Sunday evening, I wasn't exhausted the way I'd expected to be. And when Andy parked outside my little cottage and turned off the engine, he didn't make a speech.

"Thanks for coming," he said simply.

"Thanks for inviting me."

That felt like enough.

Chapter 52

Jude

The whole town— and a few visiting tourists— had shown up for Jim's Christmas party.

By the time I arrived, dusk was already claiming the edges of Jim's side yard, the sky holding that deep summer blue that comes just before night properly settles in.

Fairy lights glowed overhead in elegant sweeps, their warmth reflected in glasses and eyes alike. White linen covered the long tables ready for food, silver tinsel wove through the backs of the Adirondack chairs. A towering Christmas tree stood proud near the old stone wall, lit and decorated in a way that felt both extravagant and somehow perfectly Jim: tasteful, generous, meticulous.

Waiters in black tie moved through the crowd with practised ease, offering sparkling wine. Somewhere near the fig tree, a string quartet played instrumental versions of Christmas carols— unobtrusive, almost incidental, part of the atmosphere.

"Jim doesn't do things by halves, does he?" Diana accepted a glass of bubbly from a passing waiter.

"But since when does Jim do *this*?" I asked, taking in the scene again. "I thought this was just going to be Christmas drinks."

Andy smiled. "Define 'just'."

John was unusually alert beside me, posture straight, eyes tracking the crowd with what I could only describe as contained anticipation. Every time I looked at him, I had an odd sense that he knew something I didn't.

"Have you seen Jim?" I asked. "Or Anne? She isn't here either."

"You're right," Diana noticed. "How odd. I hope everything is alright."

Barbara Tate drifted past clutching a napkin and beaming. “This is the nicest party I’ve been to this year,” she announced, apropos of nothing.

Laughter rippled through the group, and the conversation seemed to rise in volume.

Then— without warning— the music rose to a crescendo and then stopped, and all the lights dimmed.

Conversations stalled. Murmurs rippled across the yard.

“What’s happening?”

“Is this part of it?”

“Did Jim say anything to you?”

A small stage near the tree— which I could have sworn hadn’t been there ten minutes earlier— caught the soft glow of a spotlight. Jim stepped forward, looking impossibly calm in a dark suit that fit him like he’d been saving it for exactly this moment.

A collective intake of breath moved through the crowd.

“Good evening,” Jim announced, his voice carrying easily. “And welcome to our family Christmas.”

A ripple of smiles circled through the yard. Nods. Familiar warmth.

“But tonight,” he continued, pausing just long enough to set every nerve humming, “is not just a Christmas party. John? Where are you?”

John moved then— stepping forward, climbing the small steps to stand beside Jim. I stared, awestruck. They both looked so handsome.

Jim smiled broadly, his whole face shining.

“Tonight,” he said, “you are all wedding guests.”

The reaction was immediate and glorious.

Gasps. Laughter. A hand flying to a mouth. Someone actually squealed. The murmurs sharpened.

“Is this a joke?”

“Wait— what?”

“Whose wedding?” someone called out loud.

Jim waited. Let it breathe.

“And I am very proud,” Jim continued, steady despite the chaos blooming in front of him, “to introduce you to my bride— Anne Lynch.”

The first cello note of *Canon in D* swelled into the evening air, rich and unmistakable. The other strings followed, layering warmth and inevitability into the moment as Anne stepped into view from behind the tree, radiant and entirely herself.

The yard erupted.

Diana clutched my arm. "I *knew* something was going on," she whispered fiercely. "But not this."

Barbara Tate was openly crying. The Petersons were hugging anyone within reach. Someone popped a cork with reckless enthusiasm.

Anne reached Jim, took his hands, and the crowd settled into silence. For a brief, magical moment, the world seemed to revolve entirely around the two of them.

Then the celebrant stepped forward, conducting the ceremony while the entire town looked on.

When Jim and Anne embraced for the first time as husband and wife, the music rose. The lights brightened again. Laughter and cheers spilled into the space.

The yard erupted into movement— congratulations, embraces, dancing under the fairy lights, wine flowing freely, a discreet van out front ready to ferry anyone home who needed it.

"How did you keep this secret?" I demanded later, cornering Jim with a champagne flute I didn't remember acquiring.

He just chuckled.

I turned on John. "You *knew*."

He wore that infuriatingly serene expression— the one that said everything without saying a word.

"You didn't even tell me!" I scolded, half-laughing now. "I thought we were friends."

His eyes crinkled. The smile deepened. He'd never give away his best mate's secrets.

I shook my head, helplessly fond of both of them.

Around us, the night hummed with joy, the newlyweds dancing beneath the lights as if they'd been waiting years— not just to be together, but for the right moment to be revealed.

And when they were, the world made room.

Chapter 53

John

Christmas Eve dawned sunny and humid. I'd been staying out at Jude's since Jim and Mrs. Lynch's wedding— well, she'd be Mrs. James now, I suppose, but she'll always be Mrs. Lynch to me.

The day's heat was already fierce when Andy's car turned into Jude's drive. He'd gone all out— tinsel shimmering in the sun, and two kayaks strapped on top of his car. One was dressed with ribbons that were wilting slightly. The other looked like a well-worn old friend.

"What in the world?" Jude stepped onto the porch, an iced tea forgotten in her hand. A bead of condensation rolled down the glass and dripped onto the floor.

"Merry Christmas!" Andy called, climbing out. His Santa hat looked decidedly optimistic in the December heat. "I thought about waiting for tomorrow, but..."

"But patience isn't your strong suit," Jude finished for him. She was already moving down the steps, drawn to the ribboned kayak. Her hand reached out to touch the smooth hull, and something in my chest tightened. The river could be dangerous. I knew its moods better than most.

"Andy..." she started.

"Before you say anything," he cut in quickly, "I've been kayaking since I was twelve. And I got you a life jacket. And I know the perfect spot to start— the calm stretch past Miller's Bend."

I agreed with that location as a good spot to learn, but was still a bit wary of Jude kayaking.

She thought for a moment, fingers tracing the kayak's edge. "This is too much, Andy."

"It's actually not enough," he replied matter-of-factly. "But it's a start."

I shifted uneasily. There was something about the way he said it—like he knew exactly what this meant to her. Like he understood that this wasn't just about kayaks or Christmas or even the river. It was about her physical ability returning. Her future. About trust. About believing in more tomorrows.

A cicada started up its summer song in the nearby gum tree. Jude wiped a bead of sweat from her forehead. "Can we go try it out today? It's perfectly still, a nice day for being on the water."

"I was hoping you'd say that."

Jude waved goodbye to me, hopped into Andy's car, and they drove away.

I heaved myself up off the top step and headed down the river trail. I knew a short-cut to Miller's Bend, and a spot where I could watch without being seen.

By the time I got there, my hip was singing and my whole leg felt numb, overused. I stretched out in the long grass, rolling back and forth over that hip joint to ease some of the tension.

I took up my position as sentinel in the shade of a river gum, trying to quell the anxiety rising in my chest.

The morning light danced on the water as Andy adjusted Jude's life jacket.

"Remember," I could hear Andy say, demonstrating the proper grip on the paddle for a second time, "the river might look calm, but it's got its own mind. Never come out here alone."

Jude agreed, but she had a gleam in her eyes— that spark of independence that both drew me to her and terrified me.

Andy steadied her kayak as she climbed in, his hands sure and confident. Too soon, they were both gliding away from the bank, Jude's movements awkward at first, then smoothing out as she found her rhythm.

The sound of her joy carried across the water. She'd tied her hair back, but strands had already escaped in the morning breeze, catching the sunlight like copper wire. Andy paddled beside her, close enough to help if needed, far enough to let her feel the freedom of moving through the water on her own.

I followed down the slope of the bank, moving through the morning shadows. Watching. The way I always had. The way I always would.

"Look!" she called out suddenly, and for a moment I thought she'd spotted me. But she was pointing to her wake, the way it sparkled in the sun. "It's like I'm drawing with light!"

Her choice of words reminded me of some of our first walks together, before her diagnosis, long before my injury. How she drew comparisons between human life and nature— comparisons which were unlikely, but which made total sense.

Andy's answering smile was amused. Understanding. And I unclenched, just a little. He saw it too— the magic of watching Jude rediscover joy, one small moment at a time.

They practised for over an hour— Andy teaching her how to turn, how to backpaddle, how to read the water's surface for hints of what lay beneath. His instructions carried clearly across the river, patient and competent.

"See those ripples there? Means there's something under the surface. And watch how the current bends around that point— it's stronger than it looks."

Jude absorbed it all, her focus complete. I recognised that look from watching her study— the same intense concentration she gave to understanding tannins and terroir. But pure delight was there too. Every successful turn, every smooth glide brought joy to her eyes.

"Ready to head back?" Andy called finally.

"One more minute," she answered, and I watched her just sit there, letting the kayak drift in a calm patch. Her face turned up to the morning sun, eyes closed, drinking in the moment. The peace in her expression made my throat tight.

As they headed back toward the car, I took one last look at the river. The surface was glass-smooth, betraying nothing of the currents beneath. Like everything else that looked peaceful from a distance, it had teeth.

I knew that better than most.

I waited until they were out of sight before I turned away and began the slow climb back up the embankment. The path was steeper here. Uneven. All the things I'd been warned against.

I took it cautiously, testing each step, placing my weight where the ground felt most solid. My hip throbbed dully, a reminder I'd already pushed it too far today.

Halfway up, my foot slipped. Not enough to send me tumbling, but enough to hurt.

The rock shifted under me, my leg shot sideways, and pain ripped through my hip with a sharp, breath-stealing jolt that set me on fire from the inside out.

Bloody hell. A moan tore out of me before I could stop it.

I froze, heart hammering, waiting for the pain to settle. It didn't.

The joint felt all wrong again— hot and unstable. When I tried to straighten, my leg buckled and I dropped heavily, breath coming in short, furious bursts.

Stupid. Stupid, stupid, stupid.

I stayed there for a moment, face pressed against the dirt, cicadas shrilling overhead as if mocking me. The world carried on, uncaring.

Eventually, I forced myself up. Every movement was the same series of steps— grit teeth, shift weight, curse, repeat. By the time I reached the top, sweat was running down my sides and my legs were shaking with the effort of holding me upright.

I didn't look back toward the river. I didn't want the sight of it tangled up with this— with pain, and failure, and the sharp reminder that I no longer belonged to that part of my life.

The walk back to Jude's was slow. Painful. Private.

By the time I reached the porch, my breath was ragged and my whole body felt ruined, but I straightened anyway. Set my face into something that looked normal.

No one needed to know. No one was home to see me arrive anyways.

Jude and Andy arrived an hour later, sun-flushed and smiling, excitement still buzzing as she told me about how steady the kayak felt, how alive the river was, how she couldn't wait to go again.

I listened. I told myself the pain would ease. Inside, something had shifted again.

Another small betrayal by my body. And this time, I carried it alone.

Chapter 54

Jude

The mid-summer evening had brought the usual crowd to Pokey's front porch. I watched from my table near the steps as John finished his bowl of vanilla. I was waiting for Anne to be finished bustling around inside before I shared my news. Eventually she came out, settling heavily into the chair beside me.

"Dad's solicitor called today. Everything's settled. The estate. The life insurance." I looked down at my hands. "The divorce."

A weight lifted from my chest as I said that last one. I paused before continuing. "And I've made a decision."

Anne waited. I caught John's eye— he was sitting tall, looking nervously apprehensive. I couldn't bear to keep them in suspense any longer.

"I could go anywhere now. Start fresh somewhere completely new."

"You could," Anne agreed mildly, rearranging already-neat sugar packets and serviettes on the table.

"But then I think about Jim's coffee. John in his chair by the wood stove. About friendships. About belonging somewhere. Really belonging." I stopped to gather my thoughts. For once, Anne stayed quiet.

"Dad loved it here. All these little vineyards. The history. The way everyone just comes together, but also know when you need space. Or when you don't."

"I have a friend down in Mount Barker. Shawna Wilder," Anne jumped in. "She has real estate listings all over the Hills. Even one locally. The Carter place, up past Peterson's. Nice stone house. Good bones. Needs some love. Want to see it? Maybe a few others?"

If my mind hadn't been fully decided before, it was now, seeing the eager happiness on both Anne and John's faces. I started to laugh.

"Yes, Anne. I'd love to go see some houses with you." I knew she'd be pleased to be included.

Anne reached across and folded both John and me into a group hug. I could smell lilac and lavender, a scent that was perfectly Anne James.

She smiled as she held me by the shoulders and studied my face.

"My, dear. I do believe you've stopped running away and started walking forward."

Chapter 55

John

Shawna Wilder had taken Jude and Mrs. Lynch to see three other houses before we could get a viewing of the Carter place. I'd gone along for the ride, of course, although I wouldn't dare offer an opinion. All three homes had been nice, with manageable yards. All within a half-hour drive of The Ridge. None of them felt right for Jude. But other than not being close enough to The Ridge, I couldn't put my finger on what, exactly, was missing.

On a fine Thursday morning, Jude and I had walked down to the Carter place, meeting Mrs. Lynch and Shawna Wilder there.

"We saved the best for last. This is all the original stonework," Shawna Wilder was saying as we approached the front entry. Jude trailed her hand along the lavender hedge.

"The roses still bloom every November," Mrs. Lynch added.

Inside, we moved from room to room slowly, taking in the well-worn floorboards, the kitchen's bay window, the reading nook that caught the morning sun. It was the kind of cottage one would expect to find in a storybook. Exactly what Jude thought she wanted.

"It is lovely," Jude observed, but something in her voice made me do a double-take.

She stood in the kitchen doorway, one hand resting on the door frame. The morning breeze carried the scent of jasmine through the open window, and somewhere a crow called. But instead of examining the room, her gaze had gone distant, seeing something else entirely.

"You know, I thought I'd be looking for a hiding place. Something like the Cooper cottage, only mine," Jude continued, moving to touch the old copper kettle that hung by the stove. "Somewhere to... live my life alone, I suppose."

She gestured at the room around us. "This would be perfect for that."

"I feel like there's a 'but' coming," Mrs. Lynch prompted.

Jude paused, as though unsure of what to say next. I moved closer. Mrs. Lynch waited, arranging herself against the kitchen counter, watching Jude with those knowing eyes that had seen so many of The Ridge's stories unfold. Shawna Wilder looked on, confused.

"I'm not that person anymore. I don't want to hide. I want... I want dinner parties with too many people crowded around a long table. Space to maybe have a family someday. Maybe I want some land, a few rows of vines to experiment with."

She laughed suddenly, the sound echoing in the small kitchen. "God, when did that happen?"

The morning light caught the tears in her eyes, but her smile was real— it made her whole face light up as the last of her walls crumbled away.

"Well." Mrs. Lynch's eyes were suspiciously bright, "I suppose we'd better start looking at properties with a bit more scope then."

Shawna Wilder cut in with ideas, as real estate agents are prone to do. "You know, not all the old logging families went into wine when the timber trade died. Some of those properties are available, although not here in The Ridge."

Jude took one last look at the cosy kitchen, thanked Shawna Wilder, and then we left.

As we walked back toward town, Jude's steps were lighter, more purposeful. Like she'd set down a weight she'd been carrying. Or maybe picked up a new dream instead.

Chapter 56

Jude

The late afternoon sun had started its descent when I arrived at the Thompson place. Jim's truck was already there, his familiar outline near the porch, gazing out over the valley. I joined him at the house, letting the peace of the view wash over me. Below us, the old vines stretched in neat rows, neglected but still standing.

"Anne tell you the estate is all settled?" I asked.

Jim just nodded, kept looking out over the valley.

The sun touched the horizon, and suddenly I couldn't hold it in anymore. "I want to buy this place, Jim."

He turned to look at me then, those keen eyes missing nothing.

"The vines need work, but they're still good stock. And the house..." I gestured at the old stone walls behind us. "Dad would have loved it. All that history, just waiting to be restored. I could start small, just a few vintages. Build something real."

"Thompson's old cellar would still be solid," Jim mused. "Had excellent temperature control, I recall."

Jim smiled slightly. "Ol' Pat always said these slopes had perfect aspect for grapes. He reckoned it was the morning sun."

I touched the post, weathered wood warm under my fingers. "I know it's a huge undertaking. Especially with everything else..." I gestured vaguely at my head.

"Some things are worth undertaking."

Then he added, "What about Andy?"

I felt my cheeks warm. "Andy? I'm not. I mean, we're not... I'd be doing this on my own, Jim."

"Some things need time." Jim straightened, brushed off his hands. "Like good wine."

"The thing is," I continued, watching the sun paint the landscape gold, "I've been working on the restoration plan for these vines. And I think I can do it. It's all I can think about. Small batches. The house renovated. A tasting room built near the cellars. The folks over at Shadow's Reserve would help me get started, I know it. My own small vineyard, this unique terroir, the Thompson history... it's exactly what I'm looking for."

Tears sprang into my eyes, unwanted and untimely. I didn't want to appear weak or emotional about this. I wanted Jim to understand how much I'd thought this through. How important it was to me.

Jim's eyes crinkled. "Thinking big, Jude?"

"Maybe. Thinking of my future. And my family legacy." I took a deep breath. "Dad taught me that wine wasn't just about the grapes. It was about stories. About place and time and..." I gestured at the view below us. "This place has stories. The logging days, the transition to wines, all of it. And now..."

"Now it needs a new chapter," Jim finished.

"Yes." I turned to face him fully. "Am I crazy? Thinking I could take this on by myself?"

"Crazy?" He considered this. "Maybe. But by yourself? No. You've got all of us, Jude. We're all pulling for you. You know that right? You'll have all the support you need."

The sun was almost gone now, the first stars appearing above us. In town, lights were starting to come on.

"Your father would have loved this," Jim assured me, sliding his arm around and pulling me into his side. "Not just the wine part. The courage part."

* * *

The store was in that late-morning lull when the tourists had drifted off and the locals had all they needed. Jim placed a sign on the counter—*Back in Five or Ten*— and ushered me into his office, closing the door behind us.

I opened my laptop on the desk, pages of listings pulled up— stone and timber houses, producing vineyards, former grazing blocks, tired hobby properties scattered across the Hills. Comparables, I guess you'd call them, but nothing really compared.

"You've done your homework." Jim glanced at the screen. "This is solid."

I knew that. My numbers made sense. The offer I'd settled on was fair— maybe even generous— given the location and condition of the place. The vines were neglected. The house needed work. Others might see it as a risk. I could only see it as my future.

Jim picked up the phone and put it on speaker. It rang twice.

"Mike Thompson," came the voice on the other end— older, clipped, but not unkind.

"Mike, it's Jim James. How are you?"

"Can't complain. What's happening with you, Jim?"

Jim leaned back in his chair. "Remember that girl we spoke about a few weeks back? The one studying the vines up at Pat's place?"

"Ah. Yes. The soil girl. The restoration plan."

"That's the one. She's interested in making you an offer on the property."

Another pause— longer this time.

"Well, I'll be damned. Funny timing. No one's been interested in that place in over a decade, and now I've had two offers in a week."

My stomach dropped. I flopped backwards in the chair, raising my eyes to the ceiling.

Jim's eyebrows lifted slightly, but his voice stayed even. "Have you?"

"Sure have. Came out of nowhere."

I slid a piece of paper across the desk to Jim, my hand steady despite the rush in my ears. He glanced down, then back up at me, one eyebrow arching just a fraction.

"That's a serious offer," he muttered discreetly, placing one hand over the phone. He looked hard at me, making sure I knew what I was doing.

It was justifiable. It still left wiggle room.

Jim cleared his throat. "Mike, she's offering—" He read out the figure.

Silence crackled over the line.

Finally, Mike replied. "That's a fair price. More than fair, honestly." A beat. "But the other offer's higher."

My chest tightened.

"If your friend wants to sharpen her pencil," Mike continued, "I'd be happy to consider it."

I leaned forward and rested my forehead on the desk, eyes closed. For one ridiculous moment, I considered pretending I hadn't heard that response. My pen hovered over the notepad. I scribbled a new number— higher, tighter, uncomfortable— and slid it back across to Jim without lifting my head.

Jim looked at it. His mouth pressed into a thin line and he started to shake his head.

"Hang on, Mike. She's giving me something else here. Just one second."

He held the phone away and mouthed at me, "Have you gone mad?"

I gestured for him to make the offer. He read out the new figure.

Another pause.

"I appreciate that. But I'll be straight with you— the other buyer's still higher."

The room seemed to shrink around me. I shook my head once, barely perceptible. Jim caught it.

"Alright. Let me have a chat with her, Mike. I'll call you back shortly."

"Fair enough. I'll wait to hear from you before I get back to the other buyer."

The line went dead. For a moment, neither of us spoke.

Then Jim leaned forward, folding his hands. "Alright. Let's talk."

I lifted my head, blinking hard. Tears threatened to spill. "I can't go any higher. Not without risking everything."

"Then you don't. Not yet."

I swallowed. "He's going to sell it to the other buyer."

"Maybe. Maybe not."

I looked at him. "They're offering more."

"They're offering *money*," he corrected. "That's not always the same thing."

I let out a shaky breath. "I thought... I really thought this was it."

Jim's gaze softened. "This is the part where it gets hard, Jude. Where wanting something means you have to sit with the possibility of not getting it."

I let the weight of it settle in.

"Finish your tea," he added as he left the office. "It's not over yet."

I wrapped my hands around the mug, the warmth grounding me.

Outside the office door, the shop hummed back into life.

Inside, my future hovered— uncertain, unfinished, and suddenly very real.

Chapter 57

Jude

By the next morning, I'd reworked the numbers three times and drawn up a rough set of plans.

I spread my notes across the kitchen table— purchase price, contingency buffers, staged renovations. Roof first. Plumbing. Cellar reinforcement. Then a modest tasting room. A partnership with other local wineries to use the tasting room. Nothing flashy. Nothing borrowed from someone else's dream.

I wrote timelines in the margins. Two years. Five. Ten. I didn't let myself imagine beyond that.

When I was finished, I folded the pages neatly and walked down into town, past the bakery and the post office, to the bank branch.

The loan officer was kind. That almost made it worse.

She listened. She flicked through my documents with interest that felt genuine. She asked smart questions. She even smiled when I explained the restoration plan.

Then she leaned back in her chair and folded her hands.

"Jude, I can see how much thought you've put into this."

I waited.

"The issue isn't the property," she continued. "It's risk."

I already knew.

"If you use all of your savings as a deposit, you'll have no buffer. And without current income— well."

I stared at the edge of her desk, the grain of the wood suddenly fascinating.

She slid the pages back to me. "I'm sorry. At this stage, we can't approve any lending."

There it was. Clean. Final.

I thanked her, then walked back out into the heat, papers tucked under my arm, the world continuing exactly as it always did. By the time I reached Jim's, I'd smoothed myself out again. Shoulders back. Chin up. One foot in front of the other.

Pilar was at the counter, sunglasses perched on her head, lips pursed as Jim rang up her wine. She turned when she heard me.

Her gaze flicked over me— quick, assessing, faintly contemptuous.

"Well. Look what the cat dragged in. God, Jude, you look so *fragile*."

Jim shot her a warning look, but she waved it off.

I met her eyes. Held them. Then I smiled and stepped past her.

No heat. No defence. No energy wasted. No room in my day for that kind of madness.

She blustered, offended by my lack of reaction, and swept out of the store in a cloud of perfume and indignation.

Jim watched her go, then turned back to me. "You alright?"

I nodded once. "I went to the bank. I was hoping they'd approve a mortgage. But they declined. They won't lend me anything."

He didn't rush to fill the silence. Didn't pretend it was fine.

"Alright," he relented, putting the sign on the counter and motioning toward the office. "Talk me through it."

I followed him back, the papers warm in my hands.

* * *

Jim closed the office door behind us and leaned back against it, arms folded. I handed him the paperwork without ceremony.

"They won't lend. Not without income. Not if I use all my savings as the deposit."

He skimmed the first page, then the second, jaw tightening just a fraction. When he finished, he set the papers down.

"Well. That's unfortunate."

It wasn't pity. It wasn't dismissal either. Just fact.

"I can still increase the offer a bit. I just can't go any higher *and* do renovations, or restore the vines. And I don't even know if I can increase it high enough to beat the other offer. And what if they counter, go even higher?"

Jim studied me for a long moment.

"How much help do you need?" he asked.

I blinked. "I'm not—"

"I know," he cut in. "I'm asking."

"I could back part of it," he went on. "Not the whole thing. Enough to make the numbers work until you're producing. Until you're solid, back on your feet."

My throat closed.

"You don't have to—"

"I know. But I want to. I believe in your plan. And I'm not the bank. I'm not going to punish you for having a bad year."

I looked down at the desk. "Jim..."

He shrugged, like this was the most obvious thing in the world. "I've backed worse ideas than this. And none of them had your smarts behind them."

That afternoon, we reworked the figures. Purchase price. Revised deposit. Conservative renovation staging. A plan that didn't pretend money grew on vines.

I printed it all and slid the pages into a folder. Neat, sensible and professional. I was proud of the plan.

Jim stared at it. Then he pushed it back toward me.

"Nope," he said.

My stomach dropped. "What?"

"This won't win it. This just tells Mike you've done your homework. Which is good. But it's not enough."

I bristled. "It's solid. It's realistic—"

"And it's bloodless. Mike doesn't need another tidy proposal. He's got one of those already. One with a higher dollar value."

He leaned forward, eyes intent. "What did you say to me up at the vineyard?"

I opened my mouth. Closed it.

"You talked about your dad," he continued. "About legacy. About restoring something instead of flipping it. About stories and time and patience. You made me *see* it. You didn't just sell it to me. You let me *stand in it*."

I stared at the folder.

"You really want this place? Then don't send him a bunch of spreadsheets. Send him *you*."

He reached for the phone. When Mike Thompson answered, Jim didn't waste time.

"Mike, she's got a sound plan, and a good offer. And I'm ready to back her. But before you decide anything, I think you should meet her."

There was a pause. Then Mike's reply came through, curious but guarded.

"I'm heading down to South Australia next week anyway. Could meet Wednesday afternoon."

Jim looked at me, eyebrow raised.

"How about at the vineyard?"

"Yeah, we can get up there. How's 4 pm?"

Jim smiled. "We'll see you there."

When he hung up, he slid the folder back to me.

"Now. Go prepare the offer. Not just with numbers."

I grabbed the folder, pulse racing.

"Present it so he can see what you see," Jim added. "Because if he does—"

He didn't finish the sentence. He didn't need to.

Wednesday's presentation was suddenly everything.

Chapter 58

John

We went up to the Thompson place in the late afternoon, when the heat had lessened just enough to make the climb tolerable. Jude carried her folder tucked under one arm, pages dog-eared from revisions, her mouth moving occasionally as she rehearsed lines under her breath. I kept pace beside her, or close enough that she didn't notice when I lagged, the ground uneven beneath my feet.

My hip had been angry all day, a grinding ache that crept outward, tightening my thigh, my lower back. The kind of pain that didn't flare so much as *settle in*, like it intended to stay. But I didn't complain.

The vineyard was peaceful as always. Rows of old vines stood in loose formation, leaves catching the low sun, their shadows long and skeletal against the dirt. Jude stopped near the same gnarled section she always did— her anchor point— and turned to face me.

"Okay," she exhaled. "Tell me if this sounds insane."

I lowered myself gently into the grass, arranging my body so the slope took some of my weight. She smiled and launched in.

Talking in detail about the vines. About the soil profiles she'd mapped. About elevation and drainage and why these particular slopes produced grapes with tension instead of weight. She spoke about restoration in stages— not rushing, not forcing yields— about honouring what was already here instead of bulldozing it into something trendier. No notes— all knowledge. Her hands moved as she spoke, sketching invisible rows, tracing lines only she could see.

"This isn't about turning it into something flashy. It's about stewardship. About patience. About letting it be what it already is— just cared for."

She stopped, watching my face. "Too much?"

I indicated that she should go on. She inhaled slowly, then went again. Sharpened it. Refined a phrase. Tried a different opening. Each pass made her sound more sure, more grounded— less like someone asking permission and more like someone laying claim.

I loved watching her like this. Unarmoured. Alive.

By the third run-through, a hot, insistent throb had crept up my side every time I shifted, every time I tried to straighten. I tried to stay still.

"Again?" she asked, excited.

I stretched, but stayed put while she ran through it for the fourth time.

When we finally headed back down, the light was nearly gone. I took the descent with cautious, measured steps, testing each one before committing to it. I focused on breathing. On keeping my gait smooth. On not letting my body tell the truth before I was ready to hear it myself. By the time we reached Jim's, my leg was stiff and uncooperative. I masked it with stillness, settling onto the porch with more care than usual.

Jude watched me for a moment, brow creasing.

"I don't think you're okay," she said.

Inside, she found Jim.

"I think I might have overdone the walks. John's hip seems like it's in rough shape again. Do you have an ice pack? Or that anti-inflammatory rub?"

Jim was already moving. "I'll grab it."

I stared out at the yard, the evening humming with crickets ticking and the distant lowing of cattle, and kept my expression neutral.

They thought this was the old injury talking. They didn't know I'd slipped again. They didn't know something had shifted.

And I wasn't ready— not yet— to let anyone know that the ground beneath me was less solid than it had been before.

* * *

Some nights I still slept out on the porch at Jude's, stretched long on the swing with the sounds of the night critters and the smell of warm timber rising up through the dark. Those nights felt easiest.

Honest. The sky overhead, the world doing what it always did, nothing expected of me.

Other nights, the mozzies were relentless, or the air too still and heavy to bear, and I'd go inside instead— back to the narrow bed in the carriage house, the one I'd slept in when Jude first came home from the long weeks of radiation. Back when everything was fragile and sharp-edged and terrifying, and my only job had been to stay close.

The bed still held the shape of those weeks.

I lay there now, listening to the building settle around me. Jude had gone to bed hours earlier, exhausted in that deep, earned way that came with healing done properly.

I stared up at the ceiling, letting memory drift where it wanted.

Back then, I'd slept lightly. Always half-awake. Tuned to every shift, every small sound that might mean pain, or fear, or the return of something we'd fought so hard to push back. I'd learned the rhythm of her nights the way you learn a tide— when she turned, when she stilled, when she woke and lay there thinking.

Those nights, I'd known exactly who I was. I was the constant. The steady thing. The presence that didn't flinch.

Now, the world had rearranged itself.

Jim and Anne were married— properly, joyfully, with the whole town bearing witness. Their house was full in a way it hadn't been before, movement and shared glances that didn't need explaining. I was welcome there, of course. Always would be.

But welcome isn't the same as *essential.*

At Jim's, I'd started to feel like a pause in the room. A helping hand offered when needed. A kind word, but never a request to do anything useful.

No one had pushed me out.

Life simply... flowed around me.

At Jude's, it was steadier. More familiar. And yet even here, I could feel the subtle shift. The way her days now stretched beyond me— Adelaide drives, vineyard walks, a future unfolding that didn't need my constant presence to hold it together.

She still walked with me, still sat beside me and leaned against my shoulder some evenings like nothing had changed. But something *had* changed.

I was no longer the axis. That realisation didn't come with bitterness. Just an aching clarity.

I thought about the first nights I'd slept out here. How she'd curled inward then, as if trying to make herself smaller, safer. How I'd lain awake, convinced that if I watched closely enough, nothing bad could happen to her.

I'd believed that vigilance was love. Maybe it was, once. Now, love looked different.

Now it looked like letting her go down the road without me. Like listening to her come home flushed and happy with stories that didn't include my footsteps beside hers. Like smiling and meaning it.

The bed creaked as I shifted my weight. I pushed through the pain, slow and controlled, the way Jude had taught me.

Management, not recovery. Funny how that applied to more than injured joints.

I thought about purpose— how folks talk about it like it's something you choose and keep forever. As if it doesn't change shape without asking. As if it doesn't sometimes slip silently out of your hands when you're not looking.

For a while, my purpose had been clear— help tear down her walls. Be her friend. Get her through.

I'd done that. She was here. Laughing again. Planning. Wanting things.

Outside, a breeze finally stirred, carrying the scent of eucalyptus and dry grass through the open window. Somewhere nearby, a night bird called— a single, questioning note— then silence.

I wondered, briefly, what came next for someone like me.

Tomorrow, Jude would want to walk up to the Thompson place again. To tell me more about the vines and her plans that stretched well beyond the present moment. I'd listen, like always. I'd encourage her. I'd mean it.

There was time to work out where I fit now, I told myself.

I closed my eyes, letting the darkness settle, and let the night move on without me.

Chapter 59

Jude

Tuesday evening settled placidly over The Ridge, the kind of evening that made you forget how hot the day had been. The air finally moved. Somewhere down the road, someone hollered. A screen door banged shut and then opened again. John slept through it all, stretched out on the porch swing.

I sat at the small table by the window with my notebook open, pages covered in crossed-out figures and half-sentences. Numbers blurred into words, words into ideas. Mike Thompson. Wednesday afternoon. The vineyard. Jim there for support. I tapped my pen against the margin, once. Twice.

And then— uninvited, inconvenient— Andy crossed my mind.

He'd be good in front of Mike Thompson. Calm. Informed. Someone who spoke the language of land and long-term thinking. Someone who could lend weight without trying to take over.

The thought unsettled me. I stared at my phone for a long moment, hovering. This wasn't really about needing his help. It was about whether I *wanted* him there.

I picked up my phone, already knowing the answer would complicate things, and dialled anyway.

He answered on the third ring.

"Hey." He sounded tired but warm. "Sorry— I'm in between things. What's up?"

"No, that's okay. Haven't heard from you in a bit."

A pause. Then a rueful breath. "Yeah. Sorry about that. I've been in Victoria— meetings, site visits, the usual chaos. It's been full-on."

"That's alright. How are things?"

"Busy, but good. Promising. Things are happening with acquisitions. How about you? How're you feeling?"

"Good. Really good, actually. Had my final weekly check-up today, now we move to monthly. Dr. Chen is really happy with my progress."

"That's great news. Listen, are you around this weekend? I'm planning to head up to Mum's. We could catch up."

"I was actually wondering if you'd be around tomorrow afternoon."

"Tomorrow?" He thought for a second. "No— I can't get away tomorrow, I'll be tied up in Adelaide for the next couple of days. Why?"

"Oh." I smiled faintly, even though he couldn't see it. "No reason. Just thought I'd ask."

Another pause. "Everything okay?"

"Yes," I stated, more firmly than before. "Everything's fine."

"Alright, I'll see you on the weekend then?"

"Sure. That'd be nice."

We said goodbye, the call ending without ceremony.

I set the phone down. John was watching me. I smiled at him and we listened to the tick of the wall clock, the evening settling deeper around the house.

Just as well, I thought. If Andy'd been here, he might've had opinions. Might've asked questions. Might've tried to reshape the plan.

And this was one thing I couldn't afford to dilute. This was mine, no matter how it turned out.

I closed the notebook, squared the pages, and stacked them neatly.

Tomorrow, I'd stand in front of Mike Thompson with nothing but my vision and my nerve. No buffers. No intermediaries.

Better this way. This was mine.

* * *

The light was already changing by the time Mike Thompson arrived.

Late afternoon at the vineyard had a way of mellowing everything— the rows of old vines casting long shadows, the air cooling just enough to remind you that heat didn't get the final say. Jim stood a few paces back, hands folded loosely, giving me space but not distance. I could feel him there, steady as a post sunk deep into the ground.

Mike stepped out of the car slowly. He was older than I'd expected. Weathered, in that way people get when they've spent long years in the Australian sun. A woman— his wife, I assumed— came around the other side, sunglasses pushed up into her hair, eyes already taking everything in.

"Afternoon." Mike and his wife— Claudia— extended their hands first to me, then to Jim. They were friendly. Curious. Not unkind.

"Thank you for coming." My voice didn't shake. That alone felt like a small miracle. "I know you've had a lot of interest suddenly."

Mike gave a short, wry smile. "After more than ten years of no interest, yeah. Funny how that happens."

We walked together toward the vines. I hadn't planned to start talking yet— not formally— but the words were already there, pressing forward, like they'd been waiting for permission.

"I want to be upfront," I began, stopping near one of the oldest rows. "I don't have a glossy brochure. I don't have investors lined up. What I do have is a plan— and a reason."

Mike folded his arms. He nodded once. "Alright. I'm listening."

And suddenly, I was on.

I moved closer to the vine, resting my hand lovingly against the gnarled trunk. I didn't need notes. I didn't need rehearsed lines.

"These vines are original rootstock. That alone makes them rare. But rarity isn't the point."

I turned to him then, fully.

"The point is that they're still alive. Still producing. Despite neglect. Despite time. Despite the industry moving on and forgetting them."

Claudia glanced down the row, her expression shifting— a new perspective.

"The Adelaide Hills didn't become wine country by accident," I continued. "This land— this slope, this elevation, this soil— it tells you what it wants to grow, if you're willing to listen. The geology and the drainage here— that's what forces the roots to work. To go deep. To be strong."

I took a breath. Steadier now.

"I've spent months studying this site. Not just academically— physically. Walking it. Sitting with it. Taking samples. Learning where the frost settles, where the morning sun hits first, where the vines struggle and where they thrive."

I gestured toward the lower rows. "I don't want to rip this place up and make it something fashionable. I want to restore it. Prune back responsibly. Rebuild the soil health. Keep the yields small and the quality high, creating thoughtful vintages."

Jim shifted slightly behind me. I didn't look at him, but I felt the warmth of his pride like a hand at my back.

"This place already has a story," I went on. "Logging. Then wine. Generations of work layered into the land. I'm not interested in erasing that. I want to add to the legacy of the Thompson Vineyard."

Mike tilted his head. "You'd keep the name?" he asked thoughtfully.

That was my opening. I didn't hesitate.

"The name stays," I confirmed. "Thompson Vineyard."

The words landed between us, solid and sure. I swallowed, emotion tightening my throat, but I didn't let it slow me.

"My father taught me that wine is an act of faith. You plant knowing you may never drink the best of it yourself. You work for the future, not the applause."

Mike stared thoughtfully out across the row of old vines.

"I don't know what the other potential buyer has planned. But I know what I have planned. I want this to remain a living vineyard. A place people come to taste something honest. Wines with integrity. Wines from this land. To understand where the wine came from."

I gestured toward the old stone building. "The cellar stays. The bones are good. A small but classy tasting room. No spectacle. No shortcuts."

I looked him squarely in the eye.

"I don't want to own this place just to say I own it. I want to *belong* to it. To earn it. To carry it forward."

Silence followed. Mike exhaled slowly. His wife slipped her arm through his, murmured something too quiet to hear. He nodded once, almost to himself.

"Well," he said at last, "that's... quite a vision."

"This is what I'm offering." I handed him a folder. "It's the absolute best I can do."

We walked back toward the cars together. The sun dipped lower, gilding the vines in bronze light. At the door, Mike turned.

"We're meeting in Adelaide tomorrow with the other offer. I'll hear their proposal, then I'll be in touch."

He hesitated, then added, "Thank you for showing me what this place looks like through your eyes."

When they drove away, the vineyard fell silent again.

I stood there, heart hammering, suddenly empty and full all at once.

Jim came up beside me.

"Well, if passion counted for everything, you'd have won already."

I laughed— breathless, disbelieving. "Was it too much?"

He shook his head proudly. "No, Jude. That was exactly enough."

I looked back out over the vines, the shadows stretching long and patient.

Whatever happened next, I'd given my best pitch.

And that mattered.

Chapter 60

Jude

John and I were halfway along the flat forest loop when my phone rang.

I almost ignored it. The afternoon light was grey, the air cooler than it had been all week, and John was moving well enough that I didn't want to break the rhythm. But when I glanced at the screen and saw Jim's name, something stopped me in my tracks.

"Hey, Jim." I stopped under a jacaranda just starting to shed purple blooms onto the footpath.

"Jude, any chance you can come into the store?" Jim asked. "Now, if you can."

I looked at John. He'd stopped, patient, eyes on me as if he knew this was one of those moments.

"Yeah, we'll be there in ten."

We hurried back as quick as John's hip would allow— despite the urgency in Jim's voice, there was no way I was leaving John behind.

The shop felt emptier than usual. John limped out to the back room. Jim didn't say anything— just gave me a look and pointed toward his office.

I stopped short when I saw them.

Mike Thompson stood as I entered, Claudia beside him. No vineyard. No sunset. Just Jim's small office, sunlight slanting through the window, dust motes suspended in the air.

"Jude," Mike greeted. "Hope you don't mind us dropping in."

"Of course not," I managed. My pulse was suddenly everywhere. "I— hello."

His wife smiled. Warm. Open. The kind of smile that steadies you rather than tests you.

"We thought it was better to tell you our decision in person. No phones. No back and forth."

Jim closed the door behind me. He didn't sit. Neither did I.

Mike cleared his throat.

"We've had time to think. And to talk. About what you said. About what you want to do with the place."

His wife reached for his hand. He let her.

"The other buyer is still offering more money," he continued. "They're very keen. Seems they have endless funds."

I already knew what he was going to say. No matter how high I could go, the other buyer could go higher. I felt my heart sink.

"But." The word settled like a stone finding its place. "We didn't get the sense that they wanted the vineyard."

I must have looked confused, because he explained further.

"They're wanting to buy the land. The vines. Not the legacy."

Silence followed. Everything teetered.

"Our concern is that the offer you've presented us here," he said, flapping the folder that contained my plan, my offer and my future, "is going to be a bit of a stretch for you."

My breath caught. I didn't let it show. I waited.

"So, after some thought, we're prepared to accept your second offer. The one Jim presented on the phone to me last week." He stated the number— the one which allowed just enough breathing room.

It was my middle offer and meant I wouldn't need to borrow from Jim.

"There's one condition," Claudia reminded him.

Here it is, I thought. The catch.

"You mentioned you'd keep the Thompson name. We'd like that included in the offer," Mike requested. "Just a simple clause. Protects the name. Protects the history. Thompson Vineyard. On the gate. On the bottles."

I felt something bloom in my chest so fast it almost hurt.

"Yes," I replied immediately. No hesitation. No calculation. "I wanted to do that anyway. Absolutely yes! This is really... amazing."

Claudia smiled wider then. Relieved.

"Good," she said. "That really mattered to us."

Jim glanced at me, eyebrows lifting slightly. *You okay?*

I nodded. More than okay.

"What do we do next?" I asked.

"Here are my solicitor's details." Mike slid a paper across the desk, much the same as I had slid the offer across to Jim. "Have your solicitor draw up the offer to purchase, and send it through. I assume the offered price includes everything as is. And the name. How long do you need to close?"

Just like that.

"Thirty days? I don't need an inspection—I know it's an old property. I know what work is needed."

Mike stood, offering his hand. "Well then. Looks like we have a deal, and the vineyard's got a future."

When they left, the office felt suddenly too small to hold what I was feeling.

I leaned back against the door, one hand pressed to my chest, laughing and crying at the same time.

Jim didn't say anything for a moment. Then he stepped forward and pulled me into a hug that was all humble strength and pride.

"You did it."

"No," I corrected. "*We* did it."

And for the first time since long before I'd arrived in The Ridge, the future felt like it had finally turned toward me.

Chapter 61

John

Jude suggested we take the long way up the ridge. It was late on Thursday afternoon and our earlier walk had been cut short, but I'd been grateful for the extra afternoon rest.

We didn't take the steep track— we'd learned that lesson the hard way— but instead took the flatter path that curved its way through the shade of the gums, rising slowly until the vineyard came into view. My hip protested, low and insistent, but I didn't care. Some walks were worth the ache.

She was restless beside me. Not anxious— excited. I could feel it in the way her steps quickened and slowed. We reached the edge of the Thompson vines just as the sun tipped toward the horizon. I took up my usual place, forearms leaning on the rail, my hip grateful to have the burden of weight off it.

The rows stretched out below us, old and uneven and stubbornly alive, the land waiting for the cooler days to come. Jude stopped, turned to me, and laughed— an almost disbelieving sound.

"I bought a place, John."

I tilted my head, waiting.

"I made an offer on the best place," she clarified, eyes bright. I wondered when she'd gone to see a place without me.

"They accepted my offer today. There's still paperwork, and solicitors, and all that stuff to sort— but the hard part's done."

She pressed her hands to her face, then dropped them again, grinning like she couldn't quite contain herself.

"John. I bought this. I bought this vineyard."

For a moment, I couldn't move.

Something inside me— something old and instinctive— went utterly still. She was still talking, words tumbling over one another now. Plans. Timelines. I barely heard her. My gaze had drifted past her shoulder, down the slope, to the low stone house nestled at the edge of the rows. To the porch where I'd sat as a youngster, all gangly legs stretched out on the rough wooden planks.

I pushed off from the rail and began the slow walk down. The ground felt different under my feet. Familiar. Known. Each step carried weight— not just of my body, but of memory. Of summers and shade and the glory of youth I hadn't realised I'd been carrying with me all this time.

When I reached the porch, I lowered myself gingerly on the top step and sat. I was holding back emotions I didn't even know I could have, let alone contain.

My porch. The wood was warm beneath me. The air smelled like vine leaves and evening.

Jude reached me then, still smiling, vibrating with joy. She sat beside me without hesitation, leaning into my shoulder, her head fitting there like it always had.

"This is it. This is home now. Well, in thirty-one days from now."

I didn't answer. I couldn't.

Her happiness was a living thing beside me, alive and undeniable. And layered beneath it was something else— a profound rightness that settled into my bones.

She had chosen this place. And nothing could have made me happier.

"I can't wait to tell Andy," she went on, almost to herself. "He'll be back tomorrow. I don't even know how I'm going to say it without babbling."

The sun slipped fully behind the hills then, the sky deepening into that rich, endless blue that always comes before night. The vines darkened into silhouettes. Somewhere, a bird called, then stilled.

Jude stayed pressed to my side, head on my shoulder, content, dreaming forward.

And I sat on my porch— reclaimed, remembered— holding the weight of the moment as closely as I could.

For the first time in a long while, nothing felt temporary. Nothing felt borrowed.

This place had found its way to her. And somehow— impossibly—back to me.

Chapter 62

Jude

Andy stormed into Jim's on a call, the bell slamming against its frame behind him as he flung the door open. He had the phone pressed hard to his ear, jaw tight, colour high in his cheeks. He strode straight past the counter, one hand slicing the air as if whoever was on the other end could see him.

"No— that's exactly my point," he snapped. "You don't just lose something like this because some idiot decides to play vineyard hobbyist at the eleventh hour. I don't know what the hell they were thinking."

Jim looked up from the till, eyebrows lifting. John stirred from where he was sitting near the back, alert.

Andy turned, still talking. "No— it's been weeks for me, months for the company. *Months* of due diligence. Tests, blending trials, board sign-off—" He laughed once, sharp and humourless. "And then this."

We were all still, waiting like a tableau.

"Yeah. We may be able to change their minds. I'll work on them."

He ended the call abruptly and shoved his phone into his pocket, dragging a hand through his hair. Only then did he seem to really see us.

"Sorry." He sounded stressed. "Didn't mean to bring that in here."

Jim folded his arms. "Rough day?"

"You could say that." Andy leaned back against the counter. "Possibly the worst one I've had in a while."

I hesitated, then ventured, "What happened?"

He looked at me properly then, some of the heat draining from his face.

"A critical property deal fell over. One we thought was locked. One we'd built an entire strategy around. I could lose my job over this."

"Oh no," I sympathised. Having just been through my own small ordeal with a property offer, I knew how he'd be feeling.

Andy exhaled hard. "I still can't quite believe it. We had them on the hook, and then they just backed out. And it's not even the money," he continued, pacing again now. "Apparently our offer was higher, but they liked the other guy's *plan*," he spat, making air quotes around the word 'plan'.

A wave of cold washed over me. It wasn't possible, but it was the only answer.

"Andy, which vineyard was it?" I was trying but failing to sound casual.

"Thompson Vineyard. Some asshole swooped in. Out of nowhere."

"Oh Jesus," I whispered faintly. "That's—" I started, then stopped. I waited a beat.

"Andy, I'm the asshole," I admitted.

Andy frowned. "What?"

I pressed one hand flat against the counter, the other against my cheek. Jim was frozen in place, waiting for me to respond.

"I'm the 'asshole vineyard hobbyist'."

He stared at me, disbelieving.

"What are you talking about, Jude?"

"I made the competing offer. On the Thompson Vineyard. They accepted it yesterday."

The colour drained from his face.

"You're not serious."

"I am."

He dragged a hand down his face. "But you knew we were looking at it. You saw how much effort went into pulling all of these winery deals together?"

"No, I *didn't* know you were looking at it. How could I have known? You'd never even *mentioned* you were looking at the Thompson place. Barossa, yes. McLaren Vale, yes. Why would The Reed Group even be interested in such a small winery?"

"Isn't it obvious, Jude? The vines. You know how special they are. You've studied them yourself. Thompson wasn't the only site, obviously, but it was our keystone. The vines were critical to our blend plans— to what we'd already modelled and pitched to head office. Without them, we need to go back to the drawing board."

He went still. The vibe between us had changed— competitive now rather than cooperative.

"Why are you looking at me like that?" I asked.

Jim shifted behind the counter but didn't intervene. He knew better. This wasn't his moment to steer.

"Jude," he said, decisively. "You should withdraw your offer."

"What?" I stepped backwards. "That's not even funny, Andy."

"I'm not joking. You don't understand, Jude— this wasn't just a site. This was my first major strategy call. *My* pitch."

My eyes narrowed, the silence absolute.

"Andy, I have my own plans for the Thompson Vineyard. I made my own pitch to the owner, and so did you. I won, fair and square. You want to throw more money at them, but I want to carry on their legacy."

"You're—Jude, stop." He shook his head once, sharp. "You're talking about buying a vineyard. That's just ridiculous."

That was the truth that sat between us now, solid and immovable.

His face went through it in stages— disbelief, calculation, understanding. When it landed, it landed hard.

"You."

"Yes."

"You're the one who beat us."

I nodded.

He laughed then, stunned.

"You've got to be kidding me."

"I wish I were."

"You just torpedoed months of my work."

"I didn't know you were the other buyer. I didn't even know there was one until I made my first offer."

He stared at me, searching for something— guilt, maybe. Weakness. A retreat.

I didn't give him one, but I did offer an apology.

"Look, I am sorry that the deal didn't go as planned for you." I truly meant it, but that didn't mean I was willing to capitulate. "I'm especially sorry if this costs you your job. Honestly."

His jaw tightened.

"But I am not sorry that I won."

Jim's eyes flicked to me— pride, sharp and unmistakable.

Andy finally relented, deflating as he sagged against the counter. "You didn't do anything wrong." I knew how hard it would have been for him to say it.

"It was just—" He gestured vaguely. "Really bad timing."

"I'm still glad I won," I admitted. "I hope you can understand that. And I hope you can forgive me."

"I do. That doesn't mean it doesn't hurt."

"I know."

He picked up his phone, glanced at it, then let his hand fall.

"I need to make some calls. Figure out what this means on my end."

"Of course."

He paused at the door.

"For what it's worth," he said without turning back, "if anyone else was going to buy that place... I'm glad it was you."

I stood there for a long moment, heart pounding, hands shaking. Jim came around the counter and rested a hand on my shoulder.

"You didn't know. You told him honestly. That's all you can do."

John looked up at me, stalwart and silent.

I was willing to stand by my choices. No matter what Andy thought.

* * *

For a long moment after Andy left, the shop felt strange. Not empty exactly—Jim's store was never truly empty, even late in the afternoons. The fridge motors still hummed. A fly buzzed against the windowpane. Somewhere on the counter, the kettle clicked as it cooled. But the air had changed shape, like a room after someone slams a door and you can still feel the vibration in the walls.

My hands were shaking from the rush of adrenaline. From holding myself upright while pieces fell. Jim's hand stayed on my shoulder—firm, grounding. He didn't squeeze. Didn't pat. He just held the contact like a reminder that I was still here and still standing.

"You okay?" he asked.

"I'm okay," I half-lied.

John pushed himself up from where he'd been sitting. His eyes stayed on me, calm and supportive, as if he was offering me an unspoken choice: *Breathe. Or break. Either is allowed.*

"I truly didn't know." The words came out hoarse.

"We know," Jim replied.

"It really hurt Andy. But I still— I'm still so happy I did it."

Jim's gaze didn't move. "Yes."

The simplicity of that struck me. No lecture. No correction. No moral bookkeeping. Just the uncomplicated truth: I'd won something I wanted, and someone I cared about had lost.

That was the price.

I stayed very still, trying to get my heartbeat back under control. "He looked at me like I'd— like I'd stolen something."

Jim leaned on the counter, eyes narrowing in thought. "He looked at you like someone who just lost a battle. Which he did."

I almost flinched.

"And," Jim added with a smirk, "he also looked at you like someone he didn't expect to beat him."

"That's not exactly flattering, Jim."

"It's not an insult either. It's just... new."

I stared down at my hands. They'd left faint crescent marks in my palms from where I'd dug my nails in while I spoke to Andy. I flexed my fingers, as if I could shake the scene loose.

"What if he can't forgive me?" I asked, and hated how small it sounded.

Jim didn't answer immediately. He glanced toward John, who had come closer, sitting near me at the counter.

"He might need time. And you'll need to let him have it. Same as you." A pause. "But don't start rewriting your own story to make his pain feel smaller."

I blinked at him.

"You didn't do this to spite him," Jim continued. "You did it because you want this for yourself. For your future. You can feel sorry for him without shrinking your victory."

My throat tightened again, but this time the tears didn't feel like weakness. They felt like the body's way of releasing the pressure valve before something burst.

I changed tack. Not even Andy could take all my joy. "Well, tonight was supposed to be a celebration, but I suspect we'll be one short. Shall we celebrate anyway with wine on the porch?"

John followed me out without hesitation, while Jim uncorked a bottle of wine. We sat on the top step, against our favourite leaning post. I leaned into John for longer than usual, taking what comfort I could without asking for it.

Outside, the afternoon light had shifted, the heat easing as if the day itself was finally exhaling.

For a while, we stayed like that. Me staring out at the empty street. Him watching the world with that strange, patient attention of his, as if he understood things I hadn't learned yet.

Jim and Anne came out to join us, a platter of cheese and biscuits to share along with the wine.

I thought about the vineyard— about the Thompson name on the gate, the old stone house waiting, the rows of vines that were still alive despite neglect. I thought about Andy, storming in like the future had been snatched out of his hands.

And I thought about myself, standing my ground with my hands shaking.

You can do the right thing and still hurt people.

You can win and still bleed.

I rearranged myself, leaning back against the porch post.

"Okay," I whispered, not to anyone in particular. "Okay. We keep going."

And somewhere deep inside me— beneath fear, beneath regret, beneath the ache of it— I felt something else hold.

Resolve.

Chapter 63

John

The pain didn't wake me so much as *drag me from sleep*.

One moment I was drifting— half-aware of the morning air, the faint suggestion of dawn— and the next there was nothing but fire. White-hot, breath-stealing, wrong in a way I'd never known before.

This wasn't the familiar grind of my hip. This wasn't ache or warning or even injury.

This was failure.

My body folded without permission. Legs gone. Sound ripped out of me before I could stop it— a raw, animal sound, unrecognisable, tearing its way up from somewhere deep and panicked.

I tried to stand. I couldn't.

The world tilted violently and I forced myself outside, dragging my leg behind me like a sack of firewood. I went down hard on the driveway, gravel biting into my side. Every nerve screamed. My chest heaved, but the air wouldn't settle. Wouldn't come right.

Something was very, very wrong.

I heard it then, a high-pitched keening wail. It was coming from me.

And then I heard her— "John, are you out here?" She sounded sharp, panicked.

The porch light flicked, I heard her bare feet slap across the porch, the sharp intake of breath as the gravel registered.

She must have thought, at first, that the noise was coming from somewhere else. I could hear it in the way she hesitated, in the way her voice stayed cautious.

Then she saw me.

"Oh God— John— John!"

Her voice broke clean in two.

She dropped beside me, hands touching me everywhere at once—my shoulders, my chest, my face— trying to make sense of a body that wasn't obeying any of the rules we'd learned together.

"It's okay," she kept saying, though nothing about this was okay. "It's okay, I've got you, I've got you."

I wanted to tell her it wasn't.

I wanted to tell her to call Jim.

I wanted to tell her not to try to lift me.

I couldn't tell her any of it.

The pain surged again, stronger this time, stealing what little control I had left. I tried to pull myself together— tried to be the steady one, the way I always had— but this was bigger than will.

She tried to lift me. I felt her realise that there was no way she could.

"I'm sorry," she whispered, panic blooming. "I'm sorry, I can't—"

She fumbled for her phone with shaking hands.

"Jim," she sobbed when he answered. "Something's wrong. John—he's screaming in pain, I can't lift him, I don't know what to do—"

She listened, answered Jim's questions, even as her tears dropped onto me.

"Jim's coming," she told me, like that solved everything. "He's on his way."

The world narrowed. Sound distorted. The sky above me was bleaching toward morning, the edges of the gum trees blurring as if they were underwater.

I didn't understand this pain.

It was worse than anything before— not just in strength, but in *meaning*. My body was unravelling, piece by piece, and I couldn't stop it.

Jim's truck skidded into the drive like an answered prayer. He was out then, already kneeling, already assessing.

"Mount Barker," he announced. "Dr. Val's closed. We go now."

They moved me together— careful, efficient, urgent. I hated how helpless I was. Hated that Jude was crying so hard she couldn't catch her breath.

The ride there was chaos and terror.

Jim drove too fast. Swerved. One hand on the wheel, the other reaching for me again and again as if he could anchor me to the world by touch alone.

"I'm here," Jude kept saying. "I'm here, John. You're okay. You'll be okay."

I wanted to tell her I was trying. I swam out of consciousness.

The clinic doors flew open. Hands appeared. Voices overlapped. A stretcher rolled toward us.

They lifted me ever-so-gently. The relief was immediate— and fleeting.

The nurse looked between Jim and Jude. "We'll need some details."

Jude was barely holding herself together.

"He needs us," she pleaded. "Please— can we do that later?"

"You go," Jim offered. "I'll take care of it."

Jude didn't hesitate. She climbed up onto the stretcher beside me, arms wrapping around my chest like she could shield me from whatever came next.

The nurse asked, "I just need some information about John. Let's start with age and from here it looks like he's—"

I heard Jim's gruff voice cut in, "John's an Irish Red Setter. Probably sixteen, maybe seventeen."

Jude buried her face in my ruff of red fur then and shattered completely.

"Please, John," she sobbed. "Please don't leave me. I can't do this without you. I need you."

My heart— what was left of it— ached for her.

But I knew. I had known, in some deep inner place, for a while now.

I pulled what strength I had left into my heavy paw and lifted it, just enough. Laid it tenderly against her head, the way I always had when she had her headaches.

Her hair was warm. She smelled like home.

I looked into her eyes one last time— those grey eyes dark with tears, fierce and loving and alive— and let myself rest there.

She would be okay.

Not now. Not today. But eventually.

I had taught her how to love without fear. How to walk forward. How to belong.

That was enough.
I let go.

Chapter 64

Jude

The sunsets belong to me now. Standing at the rail where John used to stand on his powerful hind legs and lean, forepaws crossed, I understand what he saw in this view— soon to be my view— the way the light catches the old stones, turning them to living gold, the abandoned vines below still reaching for the sky like desperate hands, just as they did that first evening when I stumbled upon him here.

I thought I saw him today— a flash of red fur streaking across the field. One day, I know, that will happen less often, as fresher memories crowd in upon the ones that came before. But for now, I find myself watching the world the way he did— noticing the small kindnesses, letting moments breathe, soaking up the way the town wraps itself around its own.

I realise more than ever how the wheels of life keep turning, even after we're gone. Anne still bakes scones to place on Jim's counter every morning. Jim still stacks wood by his stove each night, though now he does it himself— no faithful Irish Setter leaving neat piles by back doors all over town. The Ridge moves in its familiar rhythms, but finally I see the poetry in it, the way John always did.

Sometimes, in the gloaming of evening, when the kookaburras are chuckling their way into sunset, I swear he's still beside me— that unwavering presence that taught me how to believe in others, how to stand still long enough to let life find me.

I hold tight onto the rail where his paws used to rest, tears pricking my eyes. I will always remember how he'd stand here for long stretches of time, watching over his town.

None of us knew that he was dying— that his last swim would cost him everything. Dr. Val said we couldn't have known, nothing we could have done in time. That John was exceptionally old for his breed, that it was bound to happen sooner or later. I try to believe that.

The river took him from us, but I still feel him in every corner of The Ridge. I half-expect to hear the click of his nails on Jim's wooden floor, to see him waiting at our bench for a morning walk.

I know it isn't just hard on me—Jim is equally shattered.

But John left us something better than memories. He left us the knowledge that love doesn't always look the way you expect it to. Sometimes it looks like a big red dog watching sunsets, guarding hearts, teaching broken people how to trust again.

"Thought I might find you up here."

Andy's voice is soft behind me, respectful of my reverie. He knows what this spot, what these sunsets, mean to me.

Thinking about John?" he asks, seeing the tears in my eyes as he comes to stand beside me at the rail. "We all miss that poor fellow. Though I doubt any of us knew him quite like you did."

The sun touches the horizon, rendering the valley shades of amber and rose. Below us, the old vines cast long shadows across ground that once yielded some of the Ridge's finest vintages, and hopefully one day soon would do so again.

Dad would have *loved* this view. John *did* love this view.

"Is this where you'll scatter his ashes?"

"Yes. But not until it's officially mine. Then it'll be John's forever."

"You know," he offers tentatively, "I might know a thing or two about vineyards."

"You might, at that," I say, a small laugh escaping me through my tears.

"Look, Jude, I am really sorry for how I reacted that day. You know."

I knew. I turn to look at him fully then, this man who has waited so patiently on the edges of my grief. Who put his career on hold to help me through the toughest fight of my life, even though God knows I never showed him any encouragement. Who understood why I needed to walk alone for a while after John died, even though he worried.

"Yeah," I say, almost stunned by the realisation, and the acceptance. "I know."

The stars start to appear, one by one. Below us, the old house seems to gather the last light to itself, stones glowing like embers. A currawong calls from somewhere near the river, and for just a moment, I swear I can see John leaning up against the rail beside me in the fading twilight.

"Come on," Andy says, understanding in his eyes. "I'll walk you home."

But I linger a moment longer, looking out across the vines.

"Goodbye, old friend," I whisper to the twilight, squeezing the rail one last time. Then I turn toward home, toward whatever comes next.

Epilogue

Jim

The sun moved along the ridge of the Thompson place—Jude and Andy's place now—the way it had done for a hundred years. The way it would for a hundred more, if we were lucky.

The late spring air held that particular crispness that made me think of John. Evening was his favourite, that perfect hour when the sun painted everything in shades of hope.

Inside, we were all pretending to be busy. Andy sat at the dining table, supposedly working on vineyard plans, but I'd watched him stare at the same page for twenty minutes. I was fussing in the kitchen. Anne had claimed the window seat, her folded hands absently twisting a napkin. Diana kept rearranging the flowers on the mantel.

Jude had left early in the morning for her one-year scan and follow-up with Dr. Chen, insisting that she go alone. We all tried to smile and say encouraging things and act normal and not think about what it would mean if the cancer had come back.

Now here we all were, waiting.

The sound of gravel crunching under tyres brought every head up. Through the window, I watched as Jude's little ute moved slowly up the drive, taking the curves with unusual care. Or maybe that was just my imagination, reading meaning into every small thing.

"I can't read her face," Andy said, half-rising from his chair, one hand braced on the table.

The engine cut. Car door opened. Closed. A pause that felt like an eternity. Another door opened— the back door. Closed.

Anne's fingers tightened around mine.

When Jude appeared around the hedge, she was cradling something against her chest. Something small and red and wiggly.

"Oh," Anne breathed beside me, and I felt sixty-seven years of holding things together threaten to crack wide open.

Jude placed the puppy on the porch steps. An Irish Setter puppy. Enormous paws, ears too big for its head, and fur the colour of autumn leaves.

The exact colour of John's coat.

Andy was out the door first, because of course he was. Young love had faster reflexes than old hearts. He stood on the porch, just looking at Jude, at the puppy, at both of them together, and I watched his face do something complicated.

The rest of us tumbled out after him.

"Is this John Junior?" Diana asked, holding the puppy close and nuzzling his head.

"No. This is Ned," Jude responded, her voice catching.

"Ned?" Andy asked as he took the puppy from his mother, cradling it in his arms. "That's an unusual name for a puppy."

"It's actually an acronym. N.E.D." She stood back from us all, smiling. Her smile was so real it hurt to look at. "It stands for 'No Evidence of Disease'."

The sound Andy made was more sob than laugh, and then he had his arms around both of them—Jude and the puppy and all the hope that little bundle of red fur represented.

Anne and Diana descended next, draping Jude in hugs, questions tumbling over each other.

The puppy— Ned— took all this excitement in stride, his tail whipping back and forth, wandering, waiting for another embrace.

I hung back, letting the women fuss over Jude, Andy hover over the puppy, and Ned squirm with delight at all the attention.

My eyes drifted to the vineyard stretching out behind them, those old vines John had gazed at from his spot up on the ridge.

A year ago, this place had been abandoned. Dying, really, just like Jude had been dying. Just like John had been dying, though none of us knew it yet. Now, one healed, one gone.

Now, the vines had been pruned and tended, new buds starting to form with the season. The old house was undergoing transformation—a tasting room combined with a learning centre, a beautiful kitchen

Jude had designed for the restaurant that would open shortly before Christmas.

Pat Thompson's dream, finally realised.

And Jude was here, alive, healthy— holding a puppy that romped with the same irrepressible joy John had brought to every morning walk, every sunset watch, every peaceful moment by the fire.

"Jim?" Anne called. They were all looking at me. "Are you coming to meet Ned?"

I crossed the porch and knelt— knees protesting— and I opened my arms, saying roughly, "Come here to me, Ned."

Ned immediately launched himself at me, snuggling his face into my neck and thrashing his tail like a champ.

"Easy there," I steadied him with both hands. He was so impossibly small and fragile and alive.

He looked up at me with eyes that would darken to amber as he grew, and something in my chest— something that had been clenched tight since the morning we'd lost John— finally loosened.

"Hello, Ned," I said roughly, tears coursing down my cheeks as I ran my rough hand over his soft fur. "Welcome home."

Behind us, the sun was setting. Not at the old fence line where John used to stand, but here, at this home that Jude and Andy had built from broken pieces.

Anne slipped her hand into mine again as we stood, the two of us watching Jude and Andy try to corral an overexcited puppy.

"John would have loved this," Anne whispered.

"He *does* love this," I corrected, surprising myself with the certainty in my heart.

Because maybe death wasn't really an ending. Maybe it was just a different kind of being. I'd never know for sure, but I liked to believe.

The puppy tripped over his own feet and tumbled into Jude's lap, making her laugh— that real laugh, the one we'd once been afraid we'd never hear again. Andy helped her up, his arm around her shoulders, and they stood there together looking out at the vineyard they'd saved, at the dream they were building, at the future that had seemed impossible a year ago.

Ned lifted his small head and howled— a puppy's attempt, more comical than anything. But in it, I heard an echo of all the times John had called across the hills, greeting the morning and celebrating the sunset.

--The End--

Author's Note

Thank you for reading *John*. I hope you enjoyed reading it as much as I enjoyed writing it.

I started writing *John* in 2020. It wasn't the first novel I began and then set aside, and I doubt I am the first author with a drawer full of unfinished manuscripts waiting for the right time to emerge.

Anyway, life did what life does, I lost the threads of the story, and poor John wound up on a USB stick. Other things— including other writing projects— took priority. *John* waited patiently— which, in hindsight, feels fitting— because there was something missing from the story.

Then last October, I was diagnosed with not one but two brain tumours (because why stop at one?)

For a brief moment, I considered shelving the manuscript yet again. Instead, while researching my own diagnosis and treatment options, I realised I'd stumbled onto the missing piece of Jude's story. Sorry, Jude.

Writing her diagnosis alongside my own was strange, confronting, occasionally darkly funny, and unexpectedly clarifying— although her diagnosis and treatment journey do differ significantly from mine. In a way I wouldn't ordinarily have chosen, the book and I have been travelling that particular road together.

A small request: If you are talking about John to others— or reviewing or recommending it (hopefully!)— please don't give away his secret.

Also, Kookaburra Ridge— "The Ridge"— is fictional. Entirely invented. If it resembles somewhere real, that's either coincidence or proof that small towns everywhere share the same charm.

One final note: Australian spelling and conventions have been used throughout. If you spot anything questionable, feel free to blame my lingering North American 'muscle memory'.

With enormous love to Donna— my biggest supporter, best friend, and only sister. I'd be lost without you (and sorry— not sorry :) I chose a different cover).

—J.A. Hoskins

About the Author

J.A. Hoskins is a Canadian-born Australian author, happily anchored on Queensland's Sunshine Coast.

Before stepping forward with her own stories, she spent years writing in other voices— across engineering, technical writing, and ghostwritten works. Those experiences, along with a life shaped across two hemispheres, now inform her fiction, which explores resilience, reinvention, and the deeply human ways we wander through life.

When she isn't writing, she loves hiking, renovations and handywork, cooking for friends, and treating chocolate as the legitimate food group it truly is.

She is the author of *Writer-in-Residence* and *John*, and is currently working on her third novel, *The Loreto Ladies' Luncheon.*

Books by J.A. Hoskins

Writer-in-Residence
John
The Loreto Ladies' Luncheon (anticipated October 2026)

www.ingramcontent.com/pod-product-compliance
Lightning Source LLC
LaVergne TN
LVHW020042110826
845155LV00029B/593

* 9 7 8 1 9 2 3 5 9 5 0 7 1 *